I0671200

HELLBENDER

By Ethan Bradenbaugh

Illustrations by Ethan Bradenbaugh
Copy Edited by Chris Evans
Proofread by Stephanie Taylor
Cover art by Patigonart
First Edition
ISBN 979-8-9886263-1-2

Resting Place

July 5th 2096 – East Tennessee

It was a small white church both in size and attendance, most weeks only two dozen or so filled the seats, this week almost half sat dead in the pews. Silence fell still the crimson mist descending through the air. As fast as it had come, the last echo from the hot barrel fled the scene through the rafters. At its passing one tiny bell rang forth, the ping of an empty cartridge bouncing up from the polished boards. It spun off beneath the padded rows coming to rest in a growing pool of warm blood. The fading breath of a dying woman wheezed faint ripples across its surface. Beside her another lay dead. Punctured in and out, blood seeped from his flesh staining the floor red.

The sobering weight of this dense atmosphere was as palpable as the taste of iron on the tongues of those still trembling in place. Their eyes danced here and there, leaping from fallen brothers and sisters to those they hoped would not be next. It all happened in seconds; the sermon hadn't even begun. Most were still coming into their regular seats before the shooting began. By this time the pastor was beginning his morning greeting. Now he was splayed out across the steps below the pulpit wide eyed and without a breath in his body.

The peace once felt on better days had passed on and in its place a sickness had entered from outside. A man stood in the center row of the sanctuary. In his right hand a black pistol and in his left a pamphlet he'd been greeted with at the door. It fell from his fingers as he reached for a second magazine. Dying shrieks of terror erupted as a second load of popping booms rang out like claps of thunder. The hymns of a murderer conducted by the angle of his outstretched arm. Lead rounds concussed the air drilling through men and women scrambling for cover. Wood splintered and flesh burst crimson geysers as he unloaded into the terrified people.

This deranged onslaught was brought to a sudden halt as a second shooter rose up and fired desperately at the first. An old woman stood at aim with her dead husband's sidearm and fired from behind her pew. The man turned at the call of this popping attempt to halt the devastation he had planned. A round struck his shoulder but in the heat of his rage he fired twice striking her midsection. She dropped instantly; overcome by dead weight she smacked her head onto the lip of the pew before lying flat in the growing pool of blood.

With one round left the shooter knew his mission was coming to an end. He'd made it clear that any attempt of defiance would not be tolerated. Though he was low on ammo he had to prolong his reign of terror. Beneath the draining corpse of a man, he saw the trembling head of a small girl. Reaching out he snatched her up and pressed the hot barrel against her head. Tears streamed down her reddened face as she begged for her dad to stand and save her, but he only lay dead without any hint of life.

Seconds later the whaling of distant sirens approached. The crucial moment had arrived. The clamped brow of the shooter scanned the room. Most of the men had been slaughtered; the others were left dying while their women screamed in panic. Just as planned; when the police enter, they will be met with an explosive surprise under his coat. Who was left to stop him? The old woman dying on the floor gazed into her dead husband's face for the last time, half of it was gone. As the blood pumped out the open holes in her stomach and the light faded from her eyes, the weight of her body began to lighten as one last sight caught her gaze. Glancing out from beneath the pews something odd trance-fixed her grim view from all other things.

A single leg of another man stood at the back of the shooter. Someone was standing behind him. Has someone come to save us? She hoped, and before she could see who, the pain and the fear began to fade. The light of the surrounding world began to darken but a growing sense of peace grew in its place.

With heavy breath the shooter's head jumped back and forth keeping track of all those left alive as they shielded their tearing eyes, making sure no others tried stopping him. Even the small girl under his arm was kept firmly restrained. Then just as the police arrived outside, he spun around at the sound of their shutting patrol doors. But instead of a rush of armed officers his widened eyes were met by something else.

Standing before him was one man. As if appearing from thin air he stood suspiciously close without making a single sound as to how he got there. His short hair was gray like that of the elderly, but he had the appearance of a younger man in his twenty's. His body was completely naked, and his pale skin was shredded to the bone with deep gashes and torn flesh. Blood spilled from his lower left leg; it was severed and was nowhere in sight. A sudden chill of dread fell upon the shooter at the sight of this man's face. It was slashed in crisscrossing gashes. He was missing his right eye where a stream of blood and tears spilled out. In panic the shooter searched for an explanation as to how he had appeared so suddenly? Why does he look this way? And why was he just standing there staring?

There was a bang on the door. The cops were breaking in, and the shooter jumped at the sound. Snapping out of the hesitation set in by the abrupt presence of this man the shooter remembered his mission and raised his gun. The young girl screamed and another bang shook the doors. The naked man remained still as the shaking barrel nearly pressed against the blood dripping from his forehead. Sweat ran down the shooters' face as tears streamed from the girls' eyes. Bang! Bang! The door split open and just as the police came barging in one final bang cried out before all fell silent.

HELLBENDER- Part 1

Chapter 1- Impendent Dispatch

July 24th 2096

My eyes snapped open, heart pounding, sweat dripping from my brow. Just like the night before, it was the same nightmare haunting my sleep. Rolling over in bed I gazed at the clock - 5:21 AM. Right on time, as this was the usual hour I awoke from the screams each morning. Getting out of bed, I stood and wandered over to the bathroom hoping a cold shower would remove these thoughts from my head as well as the fear from my heart. But as the water dripped down my face, all that came to mind was the blood that did the same in my dream. I don't care how; I just needed to be free of this torture.

Slipping on a pair of shorts I walked over to my bedroom window. It was night, but the light of a new dawn would soon arrive. I made my way down to the kitchen, a long trek considering the large expanse of my hillside mansion, courtesy of my deceased parents. Week three of their absence and I'm still getting used to the reality of them not being here when I open the door. So strange living in a house you're only used to visiting. Though it feels lonely now, at least the view is still nice, the sight of which finally bringing ease to my troubled mind.

That is, until the ever-growing development site of a new neighborhood adjacent to my house caught my eye. A once beautiful, untouched mountain range was now being overtaken by the residents of expanding cities. Even here behind the walls of my home the faint sound of construction work could be heard. I shook my head at it all. Turning away my stomach groaned on my way to the fridge; opening the door I peered inside.

"Oh, yeah," I muttered at empty shelves.

The only content was a note I had written for myself that read 'Buy food'. Sighing as I recalled writing it the night before, guess it was time I switched to plan B and catch today's breakfast. Getting dressed I zipped up my camo jacket and grabbed the octagon barrel .22 lever action next to my bed. It's only been a few days, and already, I can't wait to get out of the house. Heading down to my front door I passed by a small wooden table where my Bible sat beside a lamp. Reaching for the doorknob my hand fell still as I glanced over at it; dust was coating the leather cover. I should have been there. Slowly my gaze drifted away, and I stepped through the door coming into the cool morning air.

I always loved the woods in the early light, the yellow rays of the sun shining down through the trees and onto the glistening dew. The outdoors always felt refreshing and never failed to bring a smile to my face. Leaning back against an oak tree I sat on a flat rock between the roots, just taking in the music of the birds singing around me.

But their songs weren't enough to deflect from the recollection of my nightmare.

In it there was no escape. There was nowhere to hide. There was only the feeling, this was the way my world ends. All around me, the tortured voice of billions cried out in unison. And I, drenched in blood, fear, and guilt, reached out into the hopeless darkness, finding no comfort to extinguish my unfathomable despair. Nothing remained but the warm taste of blood and the endless rattle of chains.

My eyes clamped shut as my heart began to race, the drumming in my chest grew louder. This must have been what my parents felt as they laid dyeing in church. I should have been there; I should have gone with them. My nose scrunched as my jaw tightened. There was no escape from this guilt. How was I any better than the man who killed them? In a flash of desperation, I rested the rifle between my legs as the screaming circled me. I had to-no, I needed to be free of it. Placing the barrel in my mouth my body trembled as I reached for the trigger. A tear ran down my shaking face as I took in my last breath.

If this was how it ends, I'm glad it ended out here. Please... God..? Pressing on the trigger I prepared for the big leap. There was a click, and the moment I thought to be my last somehow continued on into the next. My eyes shot open. How am I still here? Pulling the barrel from my mouth I scrambled to eject the round. It fell into my hand, and my heart skipped a beat. There was a dent in the back of the cartridge's primer. A dud. Before I could even process what had just happened, a new scream cried out from above. I sprang back against the bark, startled by the sudden chatter of a squirrel. It gazed down at me. Slowly the suicidal delusion fled my mind between the rapid huffs of fading despair. It didn't seem frightened of me, but still, I was embarrassed to know I was seen in such a low state.

"God forgive me." I uttered as the weight of my mistake sank in.

Snapping out of it, I raised my rifle, cycled in a fresh round and took the shot. Food at last.

After cleaning my plate back home, it was time to get the mail and move on with my day. Hoping to find something to distract me from my shame, I grabbed the keys to my 2027 pickup and set out. Some would call it strange that I own a vehicle requiring keys to be started, but I didn't mind, I had grown up on antiques my whole life. Walking out the door and stepping across the yard I unlocked my truck and hopped inside. Pulling out of the driveway and riding down the gravel road I could see the distant mountains come into view. This was one of my favorite sights and it was why I'd never moved out of Tennessee.

Though, after spending most of my childhood here isolated from society maybe it was time to quit my job and move away. Somewhere I can defend those in need and prevent the terror that fell upon my family from reaching others like them. Surely that's why God spared me. A sigh of relief left my lips, now with a goal in mind a refreshing sense of peace came over me. It was the feeling that my life was finally going somewhere.

Coming up to the end of the gravel drive where the paved road began, sat my mailbox. I pulled up next to it leaving the truck running in the shade. Stepping out I saw my last name on the side of the mailbox starting to get covered in rust. Inside I grasped what I assumed to be the dreaded influx of funeral bills for my parents, most of which I couldn't afford. But surprisingly something else was there instead. Just a single envelope. It was black and stamped in red ink at the upper right-hand corner. Shutting my eyes, I exhaled with grief after reading the name Skymont Air Force Base Tennessee. Whatever was inside couldn't be good news. Reaching into my back pocket I grabbed my pocket knife. Cutting through the envelope I slid out a note:

Master Sergeant Jim Phillips

You are hereby ordered back to base for an urgent and mandatory assembly. Your leave has been canceled. An F-23 Super Hawk will pick you up at your property at 1100 hours on the 27th of July. Pack everything required for a five-month return to base. Do not concern yourself with remaining funeral expenses, all of which have been paid for in full, courtesy of General Abner.

I crinkled the letter in my tightening grip as my head dropped. This had to be a joke…

Chapter 2- New Surroundings

3 days later

It wasn't a joke and the confusion it brought was beyond frustrating. The thought of leaving the military was so peaceful and even exciting. Thinking of a life away from base felt so good. I just wish God would tell me what He wanted me to do, because despite what felt right to me, I had to go.

After packing I zipped up my blue windbreaker over my Class B Air Force uniform before shutting off the power to my house. What could be so important about some assembly that the general would cancel my leave and pay for my parents' funeral expenses? I couldn't discern one reason from the other. None of them made sense, I just hoped for more time away from the base, too many bad memories there. What's done is done and there was no changing it now.

Soon it came time for me to depart from my home, and already, the batting rotor blades of the incoming Super Hawk drew near. Pulling open the door, the aircraft descended over my lawn. Stepping forward I prepared to leave but then stopped. Turning, I gazed back inside. My eyes once again fell upon that small table where my Bible sat. Maybe God was saying it was time for a change, just not the one that made sense to me and trusting Him was the first step. So, I couldn't leave again without His word. Reaching over I whipped off the dust and slid it into a side pocket on my bag. After a deep breath I walked out the door and locked it behind me as the Super Hawk touched down in my front yard, whipping around the grass beneath it. The downwash was strong. I held down my hat, careful not to lose it. A man stepped out of the passenger door and approached me reaching out for my bags. I gave them up as we entered the open back door.

"You look worried," he said as we strapped into the seats. "Fret not; we'll get you to base on time."

"I'm not worried. Just a little confused. Why do they need me back so soon?" I asked.

He grinned. "It's not my place to say, sir, you're not the only soldier getting called in. Just sit back and enjoy the trip. No one else is getting a VIP ride there."

VIP? That's new. Just then the engines kicked up and the Super Hawk took off. My house fell further into the distance, eventually disappearing behind the mountain peaks. It wasn't a long trip to base, just fifteen minutes or so by air. Witch made my "VIP" pick up all the stranger, usually I'd just drive there. As we arrived, we looped around waiting for permission to land on the busy tarmac. I peeked out the window, glancing at the familiar buildings I had come to dread the sight of. We had just shown up and already it felt too soon. The pilot brought us down and landed on the elevated docking pad attached to the side of the main terminal. As the aircraft came to rest and the back door opened, I unbuckled and rose from my seat. The man next to me handed me my bags. I came to the edge of the door and took a deep breath as I made my first step back onto the base. This better be worth it.

The man followed behind, he and I approached the stairs leading inside. Once at the top, the doors slid open, and I was hit with a familiar smell I had come to appreciate living without. I couldn't help but assume that before the day was done this wouldn't be the only unsettling thing I'd run into.

"How does it feel to be back?"

I took a deep breath and glanced around at hundreds of people grabbing luggage as they came and went. Some were overweight, others had piercings and luminescent hair while even more wore rainbow hijabs and pride pins.

"Same as it did when I left."

By this, he could tell I didn't want to be here, and after looking down with a grin, he stepped forward.

"Not for long, be on time to the assembly tomorrow and you'll see what I mean."

I turned to him. "What's all this really about?"

A smirk stretched his lips as he began walking backward.

"Just don't be late." he said exiting out the doors.

Squinting at his lack of information I headed inside toward the front desk. After checking in with the women sitting there, I was about to leave and head for my old barracks, but before I could, she stopped me.

"I was told to give you this once you arrived, sir."

She grabbed a small, folded piece of paper and a key card from under her desk and handed it to me; it had my name printed on it.

"This is the room number for your new barracks and your new squad." she stated.

"New squad?" I questioned.

"Shh... just go. I have other people to check in."

I tilted my head at her and turned away thinking how bizarre this all was. What did she mean by new squad and new barracks? What was wrong with my old barracks? But now that I think about it, they were a little musty, certainly, that must be the reason it would be replaced. I pondered these things as I made my way to the exit door, but before

I passed through it, I stopped at the call of my name. The unexpected voice drew in my ear, not because I assumed to be ignored by everyone here, but because I recognized who it belonged to. A voice I was certain I would never hear again. Spinning around I was abruptly reunited with my long-lost friend.

"Jim!"

My bags hit the ground almost as fast as my jaw.

"Wes?" I blurted out, still not processing what my eyes were seeing, so much so that I ran up and hugged the big man. Just as I did, he lifted me off my feet with ease and reminded me how strong he was. Nearly crushing me I began to laugh and cried for him to put me down. People around us began to stare, but so what. I was just happy to see my best friend again.

"I don't understand. How are you here? You went to prison. I saw them take you away. It's been, what? Two years," I questioned.

"Shh… I'll tell you everything, but first, let's find somewhere a little less public to talk," Wes suggested.

"Yeah sure, where?" I asked.

Wes held up a folded piece of paper and a key card.

"Our new barracks."

The biggest smile grew on my face and together we immediately headed there. Maybe returning to base wouldn't be that bad after all. As we entered the building which housed our new room, I noticed something odd. It was different. Sniffing the air, I eyed Wes.

"It smells weird," he uttered.

"I was thinking the same thing." Fresh paint.

We proceeded down the corridor seeing everything more or less as we remembered it, that is until we made it to the exit door. Or at least what I remembered to be an exit door. Now standing in its place was an open archway leading to an all-new branch of the building. Wes and I rushed in, eager to see the new addition. We followed the room numbers eventually coming to ours - Room 2117.

Once there, I again noticed something strange; the door to our room was different from all the rest. It was much nicer than the others and etched into a metal plaque above it read the letters S.O.A.S.

Chapter 3- First Impressions

I pulled out my key card and held it in front of the digital screen on the door. Immediately, it lit up green, and I heard a beep as the door unlocked. Slowly, I pushed open the door, not quite sure what to expect. My eyes lit up as we stepped inside, not only at how big the room was, but how nice and elegant it appeared. There was a main room with six well-dressed beds lined up against the wall in between four windows with potted flowers on the sill. Across from that was a bar-like kitchen with stools placed around granite countertops. The next room was visible through a large archway where a couch sat in front of a massive wall screen TV, along with a pool table and a bookshelf. I shot Wes a grin.

"There must be some kind of mistake. Nobody gets rooms this nice." Wes carried the same astonished look on his face.

"You ain't lying. I don't get it either."

He stepped over to one of the beds. As he examined it, he said,

"Looks like we're not the first ones here."

Someone else's bags were on one of the beds next to Wes.

"Who do you think is in our new squad?"

I thought for a moment, coming to no decent conclusion.

"Hold on." I said. "Let's just forget about how weird this all is. Tell me how you're here and not in prison right now?"

Glancing away, Wes took a deep breath and after a short pause, he leaned back with a grin.

"Ya know that restaurant we used to eat at every Friday night?"

"Yeah," I said.

"Why don't we talk there? Just in case any new squad members show up here and interrupt." he suggested.

I shrugged my shoulders.

"Alright, as long as I get some answers soon."

Wes nodded, and we dropped our bags, leaving the room. Once out of the building we proceeded to the restaurant.

"So, Wes, how are the wife and kids?"

The muscles in his jaw tightened as he clenched his teeth.

"They're doing good," he affirmed, but sounded a little uneasy.

I'd known Wes long enough to tell this wasn't true, but it was probably too early to prod for details. Maybe after he explains himself it would be a better time to ask. Not long after, we arrived at the diner. Wes and I stepped inside, happy to see our usual booth was available. We sat down and there was a brief uncomfortable silence before he finally spoke.

"Well, where should I begin?"

Scrolling casually through the touchscreen menu on the glass tabletop I looked up at him.

"Start from when you got dragged away for being accused of murder."

He chuckled at the thought.

"Well, in case you were wondering, I didn't do it."

Staring Wes in the eye I stated,

"Not in the two years you've been gone did I ever even consider the possibility that you did. And I still don't...

but um, if you're about to tell me you did do it, I swear I won't tell."

Wes laughed.

"No, Jim, it's true, I *am* innocent. What happened was I was on patrol in an Armenian town with our old squad. Thomas and I went to scout out this abandoned factory, searching for any intel we could find on the insurgents around that area. However, a few minutes into the search we were called back to our Humvee over the radio. I returned to the truck and when Thomas didn't show up, I assumed he broke protocol, as usual, and started back without me."

"But when I got to our squad I asked if anyone had seen him. No one did, so we stormed the building searching everywhere for him, and guess what we found? Thomas, dead on the floor with my knife stuck in his throat. I don't even remember bringing my knife with me that day. How it ended up in Thomas's neck, I will *never* know, but it was mine. That, and the fact I was supposedly the only one in the building with him around the time of his death made it easy for the court to pronounce me guilty. That's when you saw me get dragged away and taken to prison."

Leaning back in my seat I took a deep breath, perplexed by his story.

"So, you got any explanations?" Wes asked.

I wasn't quite sure what to say and as I sat there thinking a woman sitting in the booth next to us announced over her shoulder,

"He killed himself."

She stared at us like it was the simplest answer and we were both idiots for not thinking it sooner.

"What?" Wes said.

"What if he killed himself?" she asked.

22

Wes frowned.

"Um, I don't think I was asking you, sweetheart."

She shrugged her shoulders.

"Sure, okay. Sorry I interrupted your super-secret conversation in a public restaurant."

"What makes you think he killed himself?" I asked.

She cleared her throat and shifted in her seat to face us.

"Well, I don't think he actually killed himself. I'm just wondering if you've considered it as a possibility?"

"Yes, I did," Wes replied, adding, "that's one of the first things I thought when I was standing over his dead body." He tilted his head, narrowing his eyes.

"I'm sorry. Who are you?"

"Katrina."

"I'm Jim, and this is Wes. He just got out of prison," I divulged.

"I heard," Katrina said, nodding.

"So, now what are you doing back at base, Wes?"

He raised his brows at me.

"I'm still trying to figure that part out."

"Why are you here?" I asked Katrina.

"Oh, I work here," she noted as she pointed around the restaurant. Wes called her bluff.

"Where's your uniform?"

"I'm on my break," she added, her lips twisting to hold back a smile. At that I realized she was lying.

"How convenient. So, Katrina, would you care to join us, so you don't have to spend your break eating alone?" I asked.

"Um, but Jim,' Wes interrupted. "I was telling you a "secret story", and if I remember correctly, you're dating

Joi so why are you calling over this random chick to eat with you?"

Katrina's eyes widened.

"Well, that's because Joi and I broke up about a year ago, and I'm still trying to figure that out."

Wes leaned back with an opening jaw. This was not how I was planning on telling him that.

"Oh, well now I have to join you, this is getting spicy." Katrina said.

She quickly took a seat next to me. I smiled at her even though I didn't feel like smiling at the time. I was still a little broken up about the whole Joi thing.

"So, aren't ya gonna tell me what happened?" Katrina prodded. "Maybe I can help you get back together with old- what's her name?"

"Her name's Joi, but shockingly she never really brought me any," I admitted.

"Well, duh, that's cause she's a woman, Jim. It's our job to drive men crazy," Katrina said. I laughed.

"Well, this girl must be an expert because I'm still recovering."

"After a year, wow! She must really be something for you to still be crying over her," Katrina stated. I glared at her.

"I never said I was crying over it."

She rolled her eyes and leaned over.

"You didn't have to. Look, there's plenty of ladies out there. I'm sure you'll find one who will want a big-ol slice of Jim."

"Wow, thanks for the therapy session. I think I'm all better." I rolled my eyes.

"Glad I could help. Next visit is gonna cost ya." she asserted.

Katrina peered down at her watch, taking a deep breath.

"Well, it looks like my break is over. I'll see you guys later."

She got up and headed toward the door, but before reaching it, she spun around and threw us a quick wave goodbye. We waved back as she left the restaurant.

Wes snapped to me. "I knew she didn't work here."

Through the window, I watched her walk away.

"Guess not."

Wes stared at me as I eyed Katrina.

"Oh no, Jim. You better cut that out right now."

"What are you talking about?"

"That look you have on your naive little face. That's the same stupid look you gave Joi when you first met her," Wes said.

"Well, I have to get over her somehow, right?"

Wes shook his head.

"You better be careful. You don't have the best track record with the ladies." I grinned.

"Yeah, well. At least I've never been to jail."

"You've never been funny either." he added.

Just then a waitress arrived bringing us our food, and I remembered why we used to eat here so often. Despite the food looking about as appealing as roadkill it tasted like a block of gold. As we enjoyed our meal, Wes spoke up with a mouth full of food.

"So can I tell you how I escaped from prison now?"

"What do you mean you escaped?"

"I'm kidding." he smiled. "What actually happened was, three days ago I was paid a visit in prison by men from here at the base. Except they were wearing strange uniforms with the letters S.O.A.S on them. The same letters above our new barracks, whatever they mean. Anyway, they came to me with a deal to join their new program or stay in my cell for the rest of my life. So here I am."

"And how do these people have the means or the authority to do all this for you?" I asked. Wes shook his head.

"I have no idea."

As we sat finishing our food, Wes and I watched the TV mounted on the wall as the BNC (Biased News Chanel as we called it) AI news lady made an announcement. It was about the recent attacks on an American embassy led by Adon Mocalla Bol. 57 dead, some of which were children. Adon was a terrorist above all the rest, an Armenian psycho with one blind eye, known as Oddball for short. He was famous for strapping injured children with bombs to be taken in by hospitals in order to bring the whole building down. His followers spread far and wide, taking advantage of the sympathy of others.

Wes frowned at the sight of his picture on the screen. His lowered brows clamped tightly over his eyes and as much as I despised Oddball, Wes seemed to have a deep hatred for the man in a way I couldn't explain. After we finished our food, I suggested that we go back to our barracks and see if there was anything we could find out about why we had been called back.

I opened the door and stepped inside to see Wes and I were not alone this time. Across from us we could hear the steady pattering of the shower running in the bathroom. Wes and I noticed more bags on some of the beds. He and I stepped over to the pool table near the bathroom door. I picked up the eight ball.

"Play ya till he comes out."

"Or she," Wes suggested.

"Whatever, just as long as they got answers, I'll listen," I said.

Wes nodded and picked up two cues from the rack on the wall, handing me one as he stepped over.

"You shoot first."

About halfway through our game, the mystery person still hadn't appeared. I like hot showers as much as the next guy, but this was getting ridiculous.

"Is he ever coming out of there?" I asked Wes as he took his next shot.

"You better do something quick, Jim, or he's gonna use up all the hot water in the base," Wes joked.

"I don't really want to disturb a man while he's in the shower."

"And what makes you think it's a man? Girls take longer in the shower than guys do, and I'm married, so I should know. And let's say it is a girl, maybe you'll get lucky and finally lose your virginity," Wes mocked.

"Ha ha, so funny."

"Hey, I'm just saying, last time I saw you, you still had your V-card. Don't tell me you and Joi broke up because of the sex."

"We broke up because…"

Just then the shower shut off and the bathroom door opened. Wes and I turned to see a man wearing nothing but a white towel around his waist as he stepped out, squinting his eyes as he examined us.

"Hello," he said.

There was an extremely awkward silence before Wes spoke up.

"Sup."

The man stepped forward. "You guys in the middle of a game?"

"Yeah, Wes was just losing," I announced.

"That's a lie, Jim. God heard that."

The man grinned as he walked over to a bed with luggage on it.

"I play the winner."

"You're on," Wes said.

I peered at our roommate. "So, what brings you here, Mr...?"

"Adam Mason. I got a letter in the mail saying I needed to attend some assembly, and I'm guessing you two are here for the same reason."

I nodded and introduced us.

"So, any idea what this assembly is about?" I asked.

Adam shrugged. "No idea, I probably know about as much as you guys do, sorry."

Wes leaned on the pool table.

"Well, Adam, I'm curious. What makes you so special that you get to join us in this oddly elegant room?"

"Must be my good looks."

"Nah, that's not it," I dismissed. "What do you do?"

Adam pulled up his pants under his towel.

"I'm an Air Jumper."

My eyes widened.

"Wow, you're the only part of the army I like."

The Air Jumpers were a division of the Army who executed their mission with jetpacks.

"Yeah, I get that a lot. It's honestly the main reason I joined. I wanted to fly in something other than an airplane."

Just then Wes shot his final ball into the corner pocket, winning the game. As it fell in, the holographic numbers on the rim of the table tallied the score.

"Ha. See, Jim, I told you I'd win."

"Yeah, yeah. You always do." I held up the pool cue as Adam walked over.

"You're up."

Wes and I spent the rest of the day with Adam while he told us how he came here with his brother from their home in Tampa Florida. I wasn't a fan of the place, mostly due to the people, but Adam seemed to be an alright dude. After a few more games of pool, we all went to dinner and then to bed. As daylight approached, I awoke from my first night in my new room and sat up grateful I didn't have a single nightmare.

Chapter 4- The S.O.A.S.

Pulling off the blanket I rubbed my eyes hearing a voice to my left.

"Morning."

I recognized who it belonged to and turned to see Katrina smirking as she laid on the bed across from mine.

"You snore," she said.

"Um, no I don't, and are you stalking me?"

She shook her head, "I'm still waiting to take your order." and bounced her eyebrows at me.

I shook my head and uttered, "You can drop the act now. I knew you didn't work there."

Just then Wes stepped out of the bathroom door drying his hair with a towel. He yawned half-dressed as he approached my bed.

"Sup, sleeping beauty!"

"Look who's here," I said, referring to Katrina. He glanced at her then at me.

"Oh, I know. I saw her when I got up."

I turned back at her.

"What are you really doing here?"

Katrina took a deep breath and answered, "I got a letter in the mail-"

"That told you to come to this base for an important assembly. And you have no idea what it's about?"

She shook her head.

"Nope. I guess we're all just going to have to find out together." she replied.

"Well, I'm tired of waiting," Wes announced.

"Where's Adam?" I asked.

"He said he was going to meet up with his brother before the assembly," Wes explained.

"Who's Adam?" Katrina asked.

"New guy."

I took note of the alarm clock next to my bed, realizing breakfast would be starting soon. Getting up I headed to the bathroom to get ready. After a quick shower, I brushed my teeth, got dressed, and left, seeing that Wes and Katrina were now ready to go.

"Hurry it up, Jim. My stomach can't wait for you all morning," Wes asserted.

"I'm coming."

As we approached the cafeteria, the noise erupting from inside was far louder than the usual army regulars the less than stellar cafeteria breakfast attracted. As we entered through the doorway, my assumption was proven correct. Hundreds of men and women were eating at the extensive tables instead of the several dozen or so that usually occupied each row. To my surprise most looked like actual fit soldiers instead of the sea of diversity I was used to.

"Wow!" Wes exclaimed as we stopped at the sight.

"Cafeteria staff must have worked through the night to get all this food ready."

"Isn't it usually this busy?" Katrina asked.

"Not even close. I don't think we'll be able to find a seat," I said.

"How about I go look while you two get the food?" Katrina suggested.

"Sounds good," agreed Wes.

"Make sure to get me the good stuff, okay?" she asserted.

I nodded but knew there wasn't any good stuff. Wes and I got in line, happy to see it was relatively short. Though, I wasn't really hungry, at least not for what was being served to us. Fruit, toast, bread, bacon, the typical breakfast one would expect, all for one exception. The eggs were unexplainably horrendous. Both taste and smell, equally gag inducing, but for some reason, the kitchen seemed to never run out. It was as if they owned their own chicken farm out back.

Wes on the other hand loved them. We used to have competitions to see who could finish a bowl of eggs first. Wes always won. As a hot scoop of it was slapped onto my tray, I frowned at their wet Jello-like texture, my stomach turning at the smell. Peeking over at Wes I winced at his growing smile as the odor enveloped his nostrils. I'll never understand his obsession with the cafeteria food. It really was one of life's great mysteries. He grabbed a plate for Katrina, and she met us as we exited the food line, saying she had found a place for us to sit along the left wall. She took us to a small booth where we sat down and ate. I was curious to see if Katrina was going to like the eggs, so I watched as she took a bite. After chewing twice and letting the taste sink in, she squinted her eyes and stretched out her throat as she forced it down.

"I thought you were getting me the good stuff?"

Wes eyed her with confusion.

"That is the good stuff."

Katrina narrowed her eyes and pointed her fork at me.

"You got me this, didn't you?"

I shook my head, trying to look innocent.

"Girl, what you making a fuss about? I got your food and made sure to only get good stuff," Wes said.

"I tried to stop him, honestly, but there was really nothing I could do," I assured with blatant sarcasm.

"I don't know what you guys are talking about. This food is restaurant quality. You're both crazy," Wes stated, then took another bite.

"Here, you can have what I got, it's the less gross stuff."

Katrina reached out to me and mouthed thank you as we exchanged trays. I shot her a nod and just when I thought that returning to base had turned out to be a good thing, I glanced to the right and made eye contact with the one who made me hate this base to begin with. Joi. Rolling her eyes as she walked past, I shut mine as my optimism faded and the dread I felt prior to my return had sunk back in. Katrina noticed my fading smile.

"What's wrong?"

I sighed as I opened my eyes and shifted in my seat. "Nothing."

But the lie didn't fool Wes, who knew me all too well. "Where is she?"

I hooked my thumb over my shoulder toward the food line. Katrina and Wes both leaned over trying to get a glimpse at her.

"Yup, I see her," Wes said.

"I don't! Which one is she?"

Katrina twisted her head trying to catch a peek. Finally, Wes stretched out his massive arm pointing straight at her.

"The blond chick in the back of the line."

Katrina's eyes widened and she gawed back at me.

"That's her? I don't get it. What's the big deal?"

"It's better if we don't talk about it," I mumbled.

"Wow, that sounds pretty bad," Katrina said and I nodded in agreement.

"We should probably get going, the assembly is about to start."

Chapter 5- The Assembly

I left with Wes and Katrina heading out of the cafeteria, not at all sad that I was no longer in the same room with Joi. The last thing I wanted was for some high school grade drama to start between us again. For now, it would probably be best if I avoided her. Just seeing her again was enough to stir up all my suppressed memories of our past. I suddenly felt a little sick. Whatever was about to be announced at the assembly had better be good. I need something new to get her out of my head.

As we approached the building, two guards opened the main doors to let us in. What we were walking into was no surprise to me and Wes, but to Katrina it came as quite a shock. As the doors swung to the sides her eyes widened as they took in the double stack balcony, lined with chairs all facing center stage where the American flag hung from the ceiling.

"I wasn't expecting it to be like this." she said turning to me.

"Neither did I the first time I stepped in." I confessed.

As the seats began to fill up from the many people coming in from the cafeteria, the three of us quickly found a place to sit, making sure we had a good view of the stage. Soon all the chairs around us were filled, the lights were dimmed, and the doors were shut.

"Guess it's too late to pee," Wes whispered.

"Do you think they'll show previews?" Katrina asked. I grinned and leaned back thinking how nice it was to be making a new friend, but with all our jokes aside it's about time we find out why we came here in the first place. As the curtains rolled back, a man stepped onto the stage.

"Good morning, men, and women of the United States military. My name is General David Abner, and I have called you all here to let you know our country, as we have come to know it, is not safe. It is my hope the soldiers in this room are the key to bringing permanent security to this nation. Today, you will witness the debut of a product almost a decade in the making. The likes of which have not been seen in our lifetimes or any before."

Finally, we're gonna get some answers.

The general paused as he stared at the crowd, the silence lasted only for a second, but to me, it seemed like forever.

"Ladies and gentlemen, without further ado, I'd like to announce our secret weapon."

Suddenly, a large screen lowered above his head and something unexpected appeared on it. Slide after slide revealed front and back images of six different but similar suits of armor.

37

38

That's it? All this fuss over some fancy body armor? Sure, they look cool and appear to offer more protection than the regular armor we wore, but this couldn't be the sole reason we were called back.

"These suits are the answer to winning the war on terror. Each one is virtually indestructible, not only due to their ingenious design, but mainly due to the lightweight super metal they're made of. The inventor is here this morning, so allow me to introduce Mr. Alan Hammond."

The general stepped back as Mr. Hammond came forward to overwhelming applause from the crowd. He was a younger man, seemingly in his mid-thirties. He wore a nice suit with shiny shoes and with each step the smirk grew on his raised head at the sound of the cheering crowd.

"This project of mine began many years ago. With the combined efforts of my team, we have invented a new super metal we call Fragmight, due to its fragmented, crystallized inner structure. It's incredibly resilient to force and heat, but because it is so difficult and expensive to make, only six beautiful works of art could be built from it. And so now, I present to you the fruition of my efforts."

As he said this the images of the suits on screen faded and a video began to play. It started with one of the suits standing alone in an empty concrete room. From the thousands of holes in the surrounding walls, I could tell this room had been through a lot, but how would the suit hold up? Suddenly, gunfire from off-screen battered the suit until the unmistakable sound of clicking triggers notified us of their empty mags.

That was cool and all, but surely the mannequin underneath the suit had to be damaged, at least in the stomach area where there was less metal. Then the suit stepped forward revealing that there was a living person inside. My eyes widened seeing how confident this man was in his product that he would risk someone's life in the test to prove it. As the man in the suit stepped closer to the frame, he undid his jacket to reveal not a single round went through nor had any of them bruised his skin.

Now I was impressed. What followed were several more short films showing the incredible durability of these suits. Each test was more impressive than the last. Especially when they demonstrated the resilience to sonic weaponry. I could hear the audience chattering the whole way through, just as astonished as I was. But as impressive as all this seemed, nothing I had seen so far was truly mind-blowing. That is until the last video played.

Standing in an open field, the man in the suit braced himself against a steel frame on the ground. The camera panned left showing a woman with glowing purple hair aiming an RPG. We all watched as she fired at the suit, clouding it in a bright flash of fire before receding into black smoke. The camera shook from the vibration of the impact and my interest peaked as the results of the blast were briefly hidden from view. Then, the breeze blew clear the smoke and revealed what only moments ago, I would have said was impossible. The man in the suit stepped forward unharmed.

The screen faded and the projector rolled up as the crowd erupted in applause. The general stepped back onto center stage.

"Now as impressive as that all was, I'm sure you're all wondering what it has to do with you. I'm here to tell you that whatever rumors about the S.O.A.S. you may have heard are indeed false. Here, now, I will tell you why you were called in."

It's about time.

"Out of all the branches of the United States military, the soldiers in this room are the best of the best. There's no denying that. And in five months, you will all be going on a highly secretive mission in order to rid the world of terrorism. Operation NEON BRAVO. Six of you will be in command of the hundreds before me, and those six will wear these suits. I will now invite them onstage."

The general pulled out a small card from his jacket pocket and read into the microphone.

"Trent Rogers, Scout sniper, Marine Recon division."

As his name was called a young man stood and walked to the stage from several rows behind us.

"Dirk Wilson, Green Berets, Army Special Forces."

A second man walked to the stage. He was much older than the first man. Halfway there the next name was called.

"Adam Mason, Air Jumper, Army Special Forces."

I quickly caught sight of Adam standing from the crowd and make his way upstage. My stomach dropped. Adam was in my new squad. Would the general be calling my name too?

"Westley Richards, EOD Unit, Air Force."

I snapped to Wes as he raised a brow at me.

"Don't get comfy," he said as he stood up and left our row.

"Guess we're next," Katrina added.

"Katrina Mires, Combat Diver, Navy Seals."

My eyes shot open.

"Failed to mention that." I uttered, stunned by her background.

"You never asked. See you up there."

"And finally, Jim Phillips, EOD Unit, Air Force."

I took a deep breath and stood, trying not to look at anyone as I exited my row. Approaching the stage, I took view of everyone who had been called staring back at me as I stepped up to stand with them. This certainly was not how I expected today to go.

Chapter 6- Work of Art

Once all together, General Abner directed us backstage where two MPs led us away while the general stayed on stage continuing with further announcements. The MPs took the six of us to a door where more MPs stood guard, we entered inside and looked around. There, before us, were a series of stations, aside each one was a person in a white coat. The man who led us to the room closed the door behind him, shutting off the sounds of the general resuming his speech.

"A doctor is waiting for each of you," he said. "Just do as they say and try to hurry, we need you back out there."

With that, he left, and the doctors called us over one by one. I went to my station.

"Remove your shirt and have a seat."

The doctor gestured to a chair next to the table with a suit on it. I did as he asked. The doctor brandished a needle gun in my direction. There was a stabbing pain followed by a burning sensation as the drugs entered my bloodstream. He gave my shoulder a quick punch to get the blood flowing.

"Master Sergeant Phillips, the substance you've just been given will raise your endurance level, prolong your stamina, and increase your tolerance to pain. This will allow you to far exceed the capabilities of the average soldier under extremely adverse conditions."

Placing a clear jar of a translucent dry powder in front of me, the doctor went on.

"Because each piece of the suit fits precisely to the measurements taken during your previous medical examinations, this dry lubricant will prevent friction from building up between the suit's endothermic inner lining and your skin. It also prevents your skin from excessively shedding its outermost layers for the duration of the usage period. Remove the remainder of your clothing and generously apply the lubricant to every exposed surface from the neck down. Once you've completed that, put on the suit's innermost layer."

Turning his back, the doctor pulled the curtain and left the examination area while I followed his instructions. I uncapped the jar and scooped out a handful. It felt like powdered graphite. After covering every inch of my body except my face and neck, I reached over to the table and picked up the first piece. The endothermic exo mesh lining. It reminded me of a typical wetsuit. The material was smooth, matte black, and covered with a honeycomb-like pattern. I had a hard time believing it could be durable as light as it was. It was seamless and slid on like a glove. He was right; it fit perfectly. I called for the doctor, and he quickly returned to check my progress.

"Now if you look on your right wrist you will see a temperature gauge."

Embedded in the material was a design that looked similar to a wristwatch, except the gauge was on the inside of my wrist not the outside. Continuing, he explained the gauge was how I regulated the internal temperature of the suit. I could make it as cold or hot as I wanted, depending on whatever conditions I might find myself in. He went on to explain that the exo mesh suit doubled my speed and strength by feeding off the energy expelled from the movement of my body. It reminded me of the alternator in my old truck.

Then, once I was ready, the doctor handed me the first section of my new armor. There were dozens of interlocking pieces of the Fragmight, all symmetrically riveted into the distinct sections of the suit. The first step of putting it all on was pretty simple.

The upper and lower leg pieces were connected to a flexible desert camo pair of synthetic fiber slacks. The rest of the suit consisted of this material and the armor wrapped around it like a hollow shell. Once I got my legs inside, I fastened it all together with the black steel clips strapped onto the sides of every section of the armor. I repeated this process with my arms and torso until finally, I had the entire thing strapped onto my body, except for the helmet.

"The visor on your helmet has been fused with a transparent layer of gold to reflect radiation and will also adjust to the surrounding temperatures to prevent condensation. Now, strap on your boots along with the helmet, step outside, and you'll be done."

I did so and followed my doctor out of my station. Peeking around the room I saw that I wasn't the first one who had finished assembling my suit. Adam and Wes had finished just before me. I walked over to join them. Their suits were different from mine.

Adam's suit was more rounded and aerodynamic. The armor was light gray over-top of a black fabric with gold lining. He also had a six-stage jet pack mounted on his back. The tiny engines ran down from his shoulders as if he had a six-pack of soda placed on either side of a parachute. This was the latest and most effective model, used only by the Air Jumpers.

Wes's suit was enormous and by far made him the most menacing-looking in the room. It was a combination of faded colors including gray, brown, and even orange.

Next out was the Green Beret, Dirk. His suit was the Assault suit. It was mainly black, with a secondary color of red uniquely placed around the armor. His suit was closest in comparison to mine, due to the similar backplate design we both shared.

Katrina's suit was the amphibious Water-to-Ground suit. It had flippers folded up to the back of her calves and a small rebreather mounted onto her back with tubes connecting it to her enclosed pressurized helmet. Her armor was a dark blue color with silver lining, along with small reddish-orange emergency inflatable pouches mounted onto her shoulder blades. She strolled over to the three of us and stood in between Wes and me.

Flipping her hair over her shoulder she shot us a look,

"Now guys, be honest. Does this make me look fat?"

We smiled, and Trent, the scout sniper, stepped out of his station.

His suit was solid black and had the most unique and distinct look out of the six of us. Littering his black armor were several thousand tiny holes about the thickness of a number two pencil lead. His suit was less jagged and more aerodynamic like Adam's suit. Before any of us could talk however, the man in the black uniform who led us here returned through the same door and faced us.

"Time's up, guys!"

He checked over to one of the doctors who gave him a thumbs up to show we were ready. The man nodded and gestured for us to follow him back through the narrow hallway. Soon, the lights from the convocation hall were shining on us again and the thunder of thousands of clapping hands erupted.

"Ladies and gentlemen!" General Abner said. "I present to you, your Special Operations Armored Soldiers!"

And to that, the assembly came to an end, and we were all informed of the S.O.A.S. true meaning. As the applause died down, the general dismissed the audience but asked the six of us to stay.

It didn't take long for the massive room to empty, and once it did, we found a seat in the first two rows as the general brought out Dr. Hammond. We shook his hand and then got a very detailed description of each of our suits. Mine in particular was very good at deflecting against large blasts and it was even light enough to swim in. He explained that our black endothermic suits were vacuum shielded making them resistant to most sonic weapons. But out of all of us, I found Trent's suit to be the most interesting. Mainly because it can grow artificial vegetation or even rock to camouflage with his surroundings. The Doctor never really explained how exactly, but he said it had something to do with yeast and microwaves. We talked with him for at least two hours, allowing us to understand the strengths and weaknesses of our suits.

As good as they were, the one area the doctor told us to protect most was the stomach. He said this was the hardest area to cover with metal so while it is still quite protected it's not as reinforced as the rest of the suit. As the conversation went on, I noticed that one question still hadn't been asked.

"Sir, is there anything you can tell us about this mission?"

"At this time, I cannot release any details about the mission, but you will all be thoroughly informed by the time you set out for it." He eyed the rest of us.

"Is there anything else you would like to ask Dr. Hammond?" Adam raised his hand, and the general rolled his eyes.

"You don't need to raise your hand."

"Are we wearing these to lunch? It's about that time?"

The doctor nodded.

"Yes, you all will be always wearing these suits around the base so your comrades will be used to the sight of them, but also by the time of the mission you'll be comfortable wearing them. Your adaptive capabilities to these suits are imperative to the success of the mission."

"Gotcha," Adam said, nodding. The General stood up.

"If that's all, you're free to go."

None of us had anything else to say so we stood up and left.

Chapter 7- Offensive Introductions

Being the last to receive my steamy glob of Indian curry I began walking over to where my new team was seated. Suddenly, my path was blocked by a figure with a hauntingly familiar face.

Joi.

My eyes widened as my heart sank. Surely, she was here to confront me after we had parted on such bad terms and with all our unresolved history, I knew I was in trouble.

"Hi Jim!" she announced in a joyful tone before flashing a smile. Not thinking straight, I blurted out in a dismissive tone.

"What?"

"Hi?" she said again. "How are you? It's been so long."

"Uhh, yeah, fine," I replied, trying to recover the conversation.

I could feel my new squad mates staring, but I did my best to ignore them.

"So... how have you been?"

Her face beamed as she slid her arm underneath mine, careful not to injure herself on the sharp metal of my suit. She spun me around and began walking beside me, away from Wes and everyone else. I went along with it, curious.

"Dang, Jim, save some for the rest of us!" Adam called out. I shot him an angry glance over my shoulder, but Joi continued to steer me away from them.

Wes snapped at Adam, "Hey shut up. That girl's got issues, don't give Jim any ideas."

"What kind of issues?" Adam asked.

"Jim used to date her."

Adam smirked. "Really? So, she's single then? I can fix her."

At that second, Dirk, the oldest of the group, stood up.

"Okay. I understand now. When all of you decide to grow up and get serious about the reason we're here and forget about all the childish drama, come find me." Dirk dismissed himself from the table.

"Wow. Great first impression, dude," declared Wes. Dirk turned as he walked away saying,

"Just being honest, and if you're the best that the United States military has to offer then I have some serious concerns for this country's future."

He spun back and continued on; Wes stood up about to go after him, but Katrina grabbed his wrist stopping him.

"Let him go, he ain't worth the effort."

"I bet his mother thought the same thing about giving birth to him," Trent mocked as Wes sat back down.

"What a jerk." Katrina said. "I mean even if that's how you feel about us, keep it to yourself."

"I sure wasn't expecting this to be how my morning was gunna go." Trent admitted as he leaned back in his seat.

I walked back toward the table with my lunch tray still full of food - cold food now and sat down next to Adam in Dirk's vacated seat. Everyone was staring at me.

"What?"

"Well, what did she say to you?" Katrina asked.

"Who?"

"Uhhh. What do you mean who? Joi!"

"We didn't really talk that much."

"Wow, you made out with her that quick." Wes uttered, sounding disappointed in me.

"No," I reassured. "I mean, she just wanted to say hi, I guess."

"Yeah, I'm sure that's all she wanted," Wes added.

"Hey, I don't know, maybe she's changed since the last time I saw her," I added.

"And how long ago was that?" Trent asked.

"About four months," I said.

Checking around I asked, "Hey, where did that older guy go?"

"Oh, that guy," Katrina expressed as she crossed her arms.

"Well, ya see, Jim, Dirk unfortunately, turned out to be kind of a jerk." Adam said.

"Why? What did he do?" I asked.

"You'll see soon enough."

As we ate, I noticed Katrina talking with Trent. I felt compelled to say something.

"Hey, Trent, where are you from?"

"Denver Colorado, I had to drive several miles out of my way to get a flight out here because they closed down the Denver airport that's closer to where I live."

"Why was it shut down?" Katrina asked.

"They opened up their "top secret" time capsule and found something "amazing" inside. But everyone knows the real reason it shut down was because of the two boys killed by the statue of the Egyptian god that fell on them, they're all just a bunch of superstitious nutjobs."

"How about you? Where are you from?" Trent asked Katrina.

"Nowhere Special Ohio." she said.

"Is that so. And what made you become a Navy Seal?" Trent questioned with a flirty smirk on his face.

"My brother." she answered in a low voice.

"Is he a Frog Man too?" Trent asked.

"Was. He died five years ago." Katrina said plainly. Trent's grin fell flat.

"I'm sorry to hear that."

"He died in an embassy bombing two days before he was supposed to come home."

I shook my head knowing who was responsible. Most people here at base had similar stories. Seeing that the table had gone silent Katrina threw up her hands.

"Anyways. I guess we should probably be going now,"

"Yeah, I can only sit down for so long." Wes announced.

He stood up and dumped the remains of his lunch into the garbage port on the wall near his seat. Trent took Katrina's lunch tray along with his own. She thanked him and they left together. I stood and went with Wes. We walked toward the exit door, but just before we entered it, I glanced over my shoulder seeing Adam approaching a man who looked exactly like him. I only saw them for a second before the doorway blocked my view as we passed through it. Other than it seeming a little strange, I didn't think too much of it at the time.

Wes and I didn't do much the rest of the day other than avoid the curious eyes of everyone at base. We didn't even see the others until late at night after Wes and I returned to our room in the new branch of the building. Once it came time for us to go to sleep, we all unbuckled our suits and stuffed them into a black footlocker underneath our beds. We had to keep on our endothermic skin-tight suits though. So, to make it appear less awkward, everyone put on shorts and a T-shirt to cover up. Dirk was the first to go to bed. The rest of us followed soon after. Except we weren't exactly sleepy. It was now 10 o'clock and when Dirk had enough of our talking, he let us know it.

"Shut up!" he yelled, sitting up in bed and glaring at us. We fell silent and gazed back at him.

"What do you think you're doing? We have a long day tomorrow and an even longer few months ahead of us. So y'all better shut your mouths and let me sleep!"

He laid back down and rolled over.

"Sorry, Mom," Wes mocked, causing everyone to laugh.

Dirk immediately leaped out of bed and walked over to Wes. Wes threw his sheets off and stood in front of Dirk. Wes towered over him.

"Don't test me." Dirk warned.

"Bring it, old man," Wes added, taunting Dirk. Jumping out of bed I threw myself between them.

"Enough. Wes, get back in bed."

Dirk just looked at me with the glare of a man who wanted to kill me, but he said nothing.

"Were all done for the night." I assured.

He just turned away and walked to his bed. I knelt next to Wes as he laid back down.

"You okay?" I asked.

"We warned you," he said.

I grinned before walking back to my bed. Pulling up the covers I fell on my side facing the bed beside me. Katrina reached out her hand.

"Good job, Jim," she whispered, and I slapped her palm. Rolling back over, we all went to sleep.

Chapter 8- It's a Learning Process

Jolting awake I gazed up at the dark ceiling. A loud noise blared in my ears. 4 AM already. Wes laid on his back groaning as he rubbed his eyes.

"Someone please kill that box."

Dirk got up first followed by the rest of us, stumbling half-awake in the dark behind him.

"Everyone up!" he ordered. "No time for showers or breakfast. We're almost late as it is."

I pulled up my slacks and tightened the uniform jacket. Once dressed, I unlocked my trunk and examined its contents. Peering at the pieces of my suit strewn in the pile I tried to recall how to reassemble it onto my body. In just a few minutes everyone was suited up and ready to go. Wes took the longest because his suit was by far the largest and most intricately designed.

"You guys finally ready? Dirk asked. "I think the terrorists might take over before you even get dressed." No one looked at him.

"Let's go," Katrina said with an exasperated voice.

Once outside, we stood quietly and waited. After five minutes, the low gurgling sound of a Humvee chariot could be heard approaching. This Humvee had an extended body that held twelve people. After it came to a stop before us, we boarded the vehicle one by one, finding a seat and strapping in. The driver shifted in his chair glancing back and forth at us.

"Good morning. My name is Sergeant Bryan Ford and each day for the next month I will escort you to every location for training. Let's get started."

Sgt. Ford whipped back around and hit the gas. On the way to our first location we passed many buildings inside the base, not quite skyscrapers but still tall. Eventually, we made it to the outer wall at the very back of the base. It was a 17-foot high 4-foot-wide concrete structure crowned with razor wire surrounding the entire base. Our Humvee came to a smooth halt and Sergeant Ford spoke up.

"Everyone out."

The back door opened. We exited the vehicle. Inspecting the view, I wondered how this could be our first location for training, there was nothing here.

"Jim," Wes asked, walking over. "What are we doing here? I don't see anything."

"I don't know," I replied.

At that moment, another Humvee pulled up next to the sergeant. Armed men in combat uniforms stepped out of the vehicle. We all turned and faced them.

They arranged themselves into what seemed to be a firing squad, aiming their rifles straight at us. My eyes widened. Had they brought us out here to be killed?

"Fire!" Sergeant Ford shouted.

A drumming barrage of speeding lead hurled toward Wes, Dirk, and Adam. The live rounds smacked against their suits but didn't punch through. The soldiers paused to reload as Katrina, Trent, and I watched in horror. Once I realized no harm had come to anyone, I let out a sigh of relief and laughed softly to myself.

"I bet that hurt," I said glancing at Trent.

Before he could say anything, the soldiers had reloaded and were aiming their guns at the three of us.

"FIRE!"

Hot lead battered our suits but as before nothing penetrated. Sergeant Ford held up his arm and shouted.

"Cease fire!"

All the soldiers stopped firing and lowered their weapons. Trent shot me a look.

"Ya know what Jim? It did!"

The sergeant approached us as we checked the condition of our suits.

"It's one thing to witness the capabilities of your suits from the comfy seats of the auditorium, it's another to be inside them and feel live rounds make impact. That should erase any doubt in your mind about the legitimacy of what you wear."

"You could have just told us! Words were invented to get messages like that across!" Adam exclaimed. Sgt. Ford chuckled.

"The enemy won't be using words. And besides, where's the fun in that?"

Afterward, Sergeant Ford led us around to one of the side gates in the concrete wall where we could see the forest leading up the mountain beside the base.

"Listen up, team! The mission you're training for is located in a mountainous region of the world, so in the case of an emergency, you all need to be efficient at climbing steep inclines. Your first objective is to traverse up the mountain!"

He pointed behind us, turning our heads to the peak.

"It's five miles up and five miles down! You have one hour… Go!"

My team set out running single file passing small streams that crossed over the trail. We went higher and higher up the mountain but remained under the canopy of the forest. As the trail went on, it soon became narrower and to the left side, there was now a steep hill. If any of us were to fall, we would surely die if we weren't wearing our suits. The suits were also perfectly adapted for running.

Huge tree roots on the path proved no problem, I noticed I didn't even feel tired. Guess the drugs they gave us during the assembly really did work as well as the exo mesh. We ran for a while longer and could see up ahead that the path veered to the right. Since I had trained on this trail before I knew exactly what was around the corner. The Shark's Fin. It was a 10-foot-tall thin rock that stuck out of the center of the trail like a shark's fin out of water.

The easiest way to get past it was to the right, but unlike my team, I went to the left. Once running beside it I glanced over to the center of the rock face seeing a carving of the initials J+J. As quick as I saw it, I turned from that memory of Joi to someone new: the girl running ahead of me. We continued up the trail for about another mile and a half, climbing over huge boulders, giant roots, and rotting trees until finally at the top of the mountain we saw it.

It was as if all time had slowed as we stepped into the golden rays of the morning sun. Peeking over the distant mountains and lighting up the endless clouds above, in a glistening array of bright yellows and oranges. As beautiful as it was, my eyes couldn't help but wander over to Katrina as the light shone through the long brown strands of her hair. I stepped up to stand beside her, but before I could, Dirk interrupted.

"Let's get moving, we're not here to sight see. We still have to get back to the base within the hour."

Katrina spun away from Dirk, rolling her eyes as she passed me. I chuckled and followed behind as we headed down. Running back was easier and faster than running up. But in doing so, we all became dirty from the red clay that coated the trail. Once we had reached the wall, Sgt. Ford led us around to the front gate. Stepping onto the tarmac, we could see to our right the same sunrise as we did from the top of the mountain. Since we had lowered in elevation, we saw it again with the same level of magnificence as it had before. Turning away from the view, I glanced over at Katrina hoping to share the sight with her, but she was already doing so with Trent.

Distracted by the sunrise, none of us noticed as Sgt. Ford snuck up from behind and blasted us with a water hose, washing off all the mud and red clay covering us. Once clean, we were allowed to leave for breakfast and then train for the rest of the day.

The next morning, I awoke once again to the most insufferable noise imaginable - the alarm clock. It quickly became the most disliked thing in the room besides Dirk. To my left, Trent walked straight over to Katrina's bed. She was still laying down under the covers in her pajamas. He gently woke her up, and they both strapped their suits on. It was good that most of us were getting along but seeing her with him brought back an old feeling of loneliness I was all too familiar with and suddenly my drowsy eyes felt a little heavier.

As the weeks wore on, things were looking good for our little team, and I was beginning to enjoy their company more and more each day, despite Dirk's relentless criticisms. But then one night after training, it came back to me, the nightmares, and this time they came with a vengeance.

The visceral slaughter of many unknown people was on full display all around me. I had no idea who they were, but in the dark, I could hear their screams. The light faded from their eyes and blood burst out to replace it. Then, one by one, they were consumed into the black, the sound of chains rattled in the distance, and I knew then I was next in line to die. But just before I did, my dream was cut short, and I awoke to the silence of my dark room. I sat up and wiped the sweat from my brow. As I glanced around to see if I'd woken anyone else, I noticed a pair of empty beds. Katrina and Trent were gone. Of course they were.

For the last two weeks they've been spending a lot of time together. The way I saw it, it was only a matter of time until they would be dating. Falling back down I tried to fall asleep, after twenty minutes had past I decided to take a walk instead.

Leaving my bed, I snuck over to the door that led to the main hallway. There I quietly twisted the knob, pushed it open, and stepped through; the hallway was dark and silent. Gently, I shut the door behind me, and the click of the lock rang like a tiny bell as it echoed down the empty hallway. I walked right and then left down the corridor, heading past a series of tall rectangular windows. The moon was more reddish than usual, almost a bright orange. The light shined through the glass onto the floor before me as I crossed over it. Its crimson glow reminded me of my dream.

Why was I having these nightmares of people dying? I want to assume it's because of the shooting at my parents' church. But it's like I'm having PTSD of an event

I was absent from. Maybe I'm just going crazy? Or is God trying to tell me something? I turned the next corner on my way back to my room unable to come up with answers, but along the way something outside caught my attention. Out of the window to my left were Trent and Katrina. They were sitting on a metal ledge just outside the bottom of the window. Like a tongue, the ledge stuck out of the building about fifteen feet and they both sat on the far edge. It was just the two of them staring out over the vast mountain range that stretched across from base.

They must have been talking all night underneath the reddish moon and the bright stars. As I watched them, they began to kiss.

I thought back to all those other moments of them together. It always stirred up a fit of old jealousy that had been my companion ever since Joi and I had parted ways. But now for the first time, there was a sort of relief. I don't know the best way to explain it, but to me, it feels like someone was telling me there's a reason for those two to be together. Smiling, I turned away and began my lonely walk back to the room, hoping to get a few hours of sleep before sunrise.

It was the start of a new month, so this meant today after breakfast we had a new training program to complete. However, before we could even think about eating, we'd have to do a five-mile run around the main landing pad. So, while everyone took turns using the bathroom to get ready, I started a new morning habit of reading my Bible. Once we were all suited up, Dirk took the lead, as usual, and rushed us out the door and onto the tarmac where the helicopters and the Super Hawks landed. The platform itself was in the shape of a rectangle at the front of the base over viewing the national forest.

We strapped our helmets on and began running. Once completed, we were on our way back to the cafeteria when a loud screeching noise accompanied by a powerful gust of wind hit us. Seconds later, the wheels of a helicopter made contact with the pad and the pilot's hatch rose. A man wearing a Hawaiian shirt, khaki pants, and a pilot's helmet sat up in his seat and flipped a switch, shutting off the blaring music he was listening to. He jumped out of the aircraft and began walking over to us.

He made straight for Adam with a 'Look how cool I am,' kind of strut. As the two met he took off his helmet. This guy looked exactly like Adam but with a slightly different haircut. He and Adam hugged and began to laugh. The rest of us were left confused.

"Haha, Adam, what are you wearing?" the man asked.

Adam laughed. "Me! What about *you*? Where's your flight suit and what on Earth are you listening to?"

"Hey, don't worry bro. Nobody's gonna notice."

"I noticed," Dirk announced, smirking with a raised brow before heading toward the cafeteria.

Adam, with his arm around the pilot, turned to face us.

"Everyone, this is Zack, my twin brother. Zack, this is Wes, Jim, Trent, and Katrina." We all shook his hand.

"So um, who's gramps?" Zack asked, addressing Dirk who was still walking away.

"That's Dirk," answered Wes.

"Yeah, can't walk past the guy without him pointing out your missteps." I added.

"Don't worry you'll get used to him," Adam assured.

"So, where's the gang off to?" Zack asked.

"Breakfast," Adam responded.

"Great! I'm starving! Let's go."

On the way into the cafeteria, Zack generously divulged to us his exaggerated adventures in the Bahamas which is where he'd been for the last four months. He told us how he was stationed there to be the personal chauffeur for a young Puerto Rican girl whose daddy was a big client for Skymont Air Force Base. He also had no restraint to inform us how he ended up in bed with her every night. In just a few sentences it was clear he was the type that couldn't help but announce every "cool" thing he'd ever done. Witch only made me disbelieve every word. His story was an obvious load of garbage, but besides his verbal imagination, I thought he was much better to hang around than Dirk. Zack at the very least was somewhat entertaining. He said he got new orders to be stationed here and be with his brothers in case the military needed a replacement pilot for the mission we're training for.

The six of us got breakfast and sat down at our booth, except Dirk who no longer sat with us. He found some Marine Recon guys to eat with. Since Dirk was gone, we now had three empty seats at our booth. Little did I know, but all three of those seats would be filled by the end of the day. Soon it came time for us to leave Zack and head to our next objective at the simulation hanger on the west side of base.

"Well, what do ya know!" Adam said. "Dirk made it here before we did. What a surprise."

As we got closer, Dirk glared at us with both arms crossed as he leaned against the hanger wall saying loudly,

"You're late!"

"I'm sure that's no surprise to you," remarked Katrina.

"Nope. You've all consistently proven to be a colossal disappointment," he professed.

"Well, guys at least we're consistent." Katrina said with a forced smile as we walked past him.

We went deeper into the steel hull of the massive hangar. Standing to our left the sergeant was in deep conversation with two other men. We couldn't hear any details about what they were saying.

"Guys," Sgt. Ford addressed, "take a seat, and I'll be with you in a minute."

We did as he said and sat down on a solitary set of bleachers that faced what seemed to be oversized shipping containers. They had black rubber hoses connected to them that led into large metal cylinders with CAUTION stamped on the sides. The containers were arranged together like a maze and there were two small cranes at each side of the metal configuration. Wes and I had never trained in this hangar before, so we had no idea what to expect.

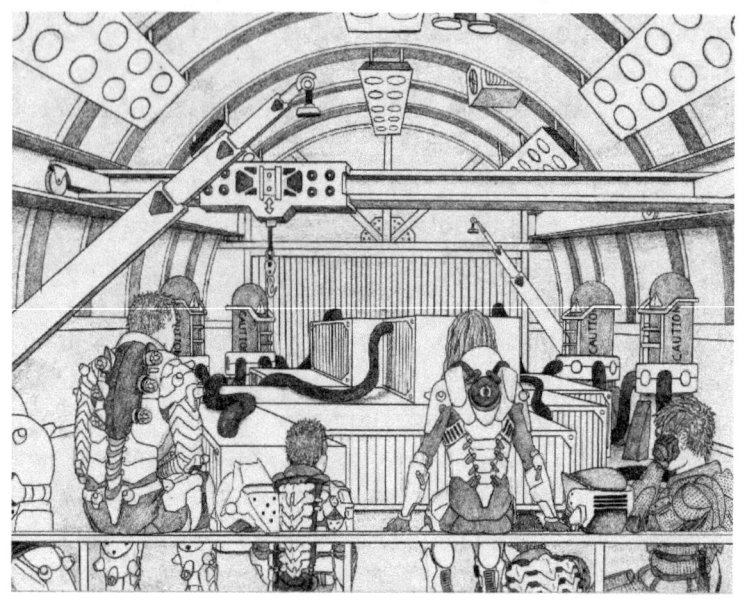

After five minutes, Sgt. Ford walked over to us.

"Alright, get up. Let's begin."

Standing from the bleachers we gathered around.

"I just finished speaking with two cadets who have agreed to contribute their skills in your new exercise for this morning."

"Well, what does that mean?" Adam asked.

"It means hand-to-hand combat," Dirk answered.

"That's right, and you'll be fighting in those metal containers." He gestured at them as he said this.

"They've been welded shut so no light can get in, when you enter, it will be pitch black and you'll need one of these." Sgt. Ford gave us each a gas mask.

"Oh, and be careful what door you open... you might find that some places may be more unpleasant than others."

"It's scary to see how excited you are about this," Katrina admitted. Sgt. Ford grinned at her.

"You should be scared, the fun is about to begin, at least for me."

Heading over to the entrance of the maze he handed Wes a tiny flashlight.

"You first. And leave your helmet behind. Also, whatever situation you may find yourself in, address it with extreme prejudice and aggression."

Wes set his helmet down, strapped on his gas mask, and opened the door. The sound of metal scraping against metal was unsettling, especially after the things Sgt. Ford implied about the new exercise. As Wes stepped in, all of us outside leaned closer together to get a peek inside the container. It was pitch black. The sergeant closed the door behind Wes, and we stood back in anticipation of what would happen.

Two minutes later the sound of breaking glass and violent banging came from inside. This continued off and on until Wes eventually burst out at the end of the maze without his gas mask on. He walked past us with one hand over his face as a nurse hurried up to him and gave Wes a bucket to throw up in. From his bloodshot eyes and runny nose, it was clear whatever was in there couldn't be good. Immediately after Wes left out of the maze, four men were sent in to drag the unconscious cadets out and onto the floor.

Sgt. Ford turned to us with a beaming face.

"Who's next?"

Trent stepped forward.

"I'll go."

He stepped up to the door, put on his gas mask, and walked through. Just like Wes, all we heard was a loud racket coming from the inside. Moments later, Trent came out of the maze falling to his knees as vomit splattered down between them.

"Guess you won't be kissing for a while," Adam mocked to Katrina.

"Shut up," she said back.

Next in line after Trent was Adam, then Katrina, and both of them exited in the same condition as Wes and Trent. When it was finally Dirk's turn to enter, I naturally got excited to see him come out of there puking his guts out. Unfortunately, Dirk exited the maze in nearly the same condition as when he entered. With the exception of having only lost his breath, and wearing a different gas mask, he seemed fine. All the staff that were watching clapped and cheered for him, this only angered me and further fueled my drive to succeed at whatever obstacle lay in the belly of the maze.

The time came for me to enter. Stepping up to the door I strapped on my gas mask and lit up my tiny flashlight. I pushed open the heavy metal door and entered into the darkness. Someone closed the door behind me, and I was now alone. I used my light to scan the room. It was different from what I had expected. There was a carpet on the floor and small tables with little potted plants. The walls had pictures on them, and even a chandelier on the ceiling. I figured the most likely reason my friends were throwing up after they left was because of the black rubber hoses connected to the containers. They must have been filled with some sort of toxic gas being pumped into each room.

70

I could see a wooden door in front of me and I slowly walked up to it. As I came close, I placed my hand on the doorknob and as quietly as I could I began turning it, but then it stopped. At first, I thought the door was stuck so I tried to gently push it open, but it wouldn't budge. The door was locked and that meant the only way for me to pass through was to kick it open. By doing so, I would be alerting anyone on the other side of my position. I didn't care, I just knew if Dirk could figure out how to do it then I could, too.

I took two steps back, raised my right knee, and thrust my boot into the door snapping the lock off the frame and throwing wooden splinters into the air. Stumbling into the room I quickly raised my small light to scan the interior for anyone or anything, but there was no one in sight. Upon quick examination, I found this room was slightly bigger and had two doors at the opposite wall. One at my twelve o'clock and another at my far left. I searched around some more and noticed a small vent underneath the ceiling bolted on the wall. So as quietly as I could I walked over to it trying my best to avoid some broken glass on the floor. I beamed my flashlight down inside, but I couldn't see anything. It just seemed to go on and on.

Removing my glove, I placed my hand in front of the vent and yes. I could feel something. Air was flowing out, and it blew much thicker around the vent. I figured this must be the toxic gas that I suspected earlier. This left me two options, push through the door to my left or the one to my far right. The closest door was to my left. I walked over to it and rattled the knob. It was locked like the first door, so I tried the one at my right, and to my surprise, it turned.

If there are people on the other side of this door when I open it, the first thing they'd do is jump me and I'd be screwed. Since the other door is locked then the designers of this maze locked it thinking the average person would go through the unlocked door. So, with all that in mind, I decided to try one last thing.

I placed my small flashlight on the ground at the base of the unlocked door facing the thin gap underneath so the light from it could be seen on the other side of the door. In the center of the room was a carpet with an unwoven edge to the left side. Seeming as though it had been undone recently, I reached down and pulled on one of the loose fibers, ripping up a long thread. After getting the length I needed, I snapped the strand from the rest of the carpet and tied one end to the ornate swirl at the end of the knob. With the opposite end of the thread in hand, I reached the locked door and leaned my head close to its surface listening for anything on the other side. Hearing nothing, I quietly pulled on the thread and rattled the knob of the unlocked door where my flashlight was, making it seem like I was trying to enter from there. I listened for about two seconds and then I heard it. It was faint, but it was a voice.

"Get ready."

I smiled.

Stepping back, I kicked open the locked door. It burst to the left and smacked a dark figure in the head who immediately fell to the ground and appeared to be unconscious. A second figure to my right rushed toward me. He latched onto my shoulders and forced me against the wall. I struggled to get him off but there wasn't enough light for me to see him clearly. Kicking off the wall with my leg I pushed him backward, tripping him over the first man

I knocked out with the door. We fell together, and I landed over top him.

His face fell into the light I placed under the door in the previous room. He was wearing a gas mask, like me. I tried to pull it off and expose him to the air, but before I could he managed to get his leg underneath my stomach as he kicked me off of him. Falling backward I landed on my back and heard the man crawling toward me very quickly. Naturally, the only thing I could think of in that second was to kick my legs at him, but that didn't stop him. As he came at me, he got a hold of my shins. Both his arms were now occupied with trying to keep my legs under control. I used this opportunity to grab his gas mask and once I had a hold of it, I pulled hard to tear it off. He let go of my legs and grabbed his mask trying to keep it on. With my legs now free I kicked off his chest with my right boot and pulled off his mask.

The gas entered his lungs and as tears blinded his eyes he fell onto my armored shins as he began to gag. I pushed him off me and stood up. The glow from my flashlight shined underneath the door. I walked over to retrieve it, but before I reached for the doorknob I noticed a small cylinder duct-taped to the door frame. It was a flash-bang with a fishing line tied around the trigger that led to the doorknob. If I had taken the easy road through the unlocked door, I would be temporarily blind and deaf. Then I surely would have been at an extreme disadvantage during the fight.

Heading back around into the previous room I got my flashlight. I pointed the light on the dark figures I had knocked out a minute ago. They were awake now but continued to lay in place to represent a dead assailant.

73

The cadets wore thick black padded combat suits that reminded me of the ones I used to wear in Tai-Kwon-Do class when I was a kid. They were also wearing a different type of gas mask than mine. Kneeling down I got a better look. It had goggles over the hard plastic visor.

I removed my gas mask to exchange with one of theirs. Picking it up I strapped it on. Not only could I breathe better, but I could now see a lot better, too. The new mask had night vision. Standing up I could see the whole room all at once. I shut my small flashlight off and put it in one of the smaller pockets on my suit. Stepping over the cadets I moved toward another wooden door with a hexagonal metal plate mounted on the wall beside it. My head tilted at the sight of it. A reverberation panel.

It had six metal rings placed one within the other where a speaker sat in the middle. These panels were a deterrent against sonic weapons, meant to reflect high pitched sound back toward the soldiers who fired them. Sonic hemorrhaging is no joke; I'd almost rather be shot than deal with that. It was interesting that one was here since I hadn't been sent in with any sonic weaponry.

Reaching down to the knob I pulled it open and made my way through to a short hallway. Located at the end of the hall was a wooden staircase. Once I had reached the top, I quietly gripped the knob and cracked open the door. With no shine of any wires, I proceeded to open it more. There was a snap and a click, and the sound of something small hit the ground. I quickly shut the door as an ear-piercing blast rocked the other side and the knob rattled under my fingers.

I couldn't hear a thing. My ears were temporarily useless as they just kept ringing. My left ear rang worse than my right. It was closer to the blast when it went off, but the good news was I could still see just fine. I opened the door and peeked inside; there was an empty hallway. Unable to even hear my own footsteps, I began the eerie walk forward. It led to an open doorway followed by stairs going down into another room. I entered this next space as quietly as I could and went down the stairs. Once at the bottom a red light just underneath the ceiling at the far end of the room shone. The light was bright enough for me to see the outline of a doorway beneath it. Must be the exit. I scanned the rest of the room before I entered. It seemed clear. Stepping forward I noticed big cabinets lined up against one wall at the end of the room.

A lamp sat on a desk with broken glass around it. I walked past the desk on my way to the doorway and placed my hand on the nob, rotating it gently in the hopes it would be unlocked. It was. Before I could open it, strong hands wrapped around my waist and yanked me sideways onto the desk. There was a cadet on top of me fumbling desperately for my gas mask. My only guess was he came out of one of the large cabinets against the wall. I got a hold of his arms and used my legs to push off the wall causing us to roll off the desk. Dropping on top of him, I lost my grasp on his right arm as we hit the ground. He took this opportunity to grab my mask and yank it off. Instantly, my eyes burned shut and my lungs stung as if filled with hot coals. The effects of the gas were taking over me; I had to get out of here fast.

I used my hands to feel where the cadet's head was. He was pulling against my grip, but it was no use. I ripped off his mask and stood above him. Holding my breath, I tried to open my eyes to find the red light above the doorway, but my searing eyes watered so bad I could barely open them. There was a red glow, I stumbled on my way to it. Groping for the knob I turned it, pushing the door open.

Fresh air enveloped me as a blinding white light blurred my vision even more. I took a step forward expecting to have support, but I placed my weight on a phantom step and fell down a foot of stairs, landing on my stomach. I started to pick myself up and then vomited. Not just once, but three times. The nurses came to assist in my recovery as well as the men inside I had fought. After I was feeling well enough to see again, Sgt. Ford told our team to take a seat once again on the bleachers.

"So, what did you learn?" After a short pause, Dirk spoke up.

"Well, sir, I didn't learn much, but I did enjoy watching the rest of you hack up last night's dinner once you got out."

"That's because you cheated," Adam claimed.

"Or it's just simply because you're not as qualified as I am," declared Dirk.

"Alright! That's enough." Sgt. Ford added. "Dirk didn't cheat; we saw the whole thing. We placed hidden cameras around every room. Dirk did everything he was supposed to. You all should learn from his example."

"Wes, what did you learn?"

"To check every doorknob before I kick through them," he replied. Sgt. Ford chuckled, then he asked everyone else the same question.

When it came time for me to answer I spoke honestly,

"I learned I shouldn't let my ego dictate my motivation."

Dirk turned his ear at me. The truth of it was that the entire time I was in the maze all I was thinking of was I had to be better than Dirk. But I wasn't better, in fact I still had a lot to learn.

"Now with all that in mind, let's run it again." Ford said.

And we did, but this time we all excelled in our ability to complete this challenge. After training, Sergeant Ford released us for lunch, so we left the hangar and walked past the Skymont Library, crossed two streets, and eventually ended up at the cafeteria. After we got our food and began walking over to our usual table, I glimpsed something strange. Two men were already sitting down there, it was Zack and Adam, but Adam wasn't wearing his suit. I spun around and saw Adam behind me. Just then it registered in my mind that Adam had another twin brother. Triplets! Well, if this guy was as fun as Zack, then I couldn't wait to meet him.

"Guys," Adam said, "this is my other brother, Peter." We all shook his hand.

It quickly became apparent that while they all looked the same, they sure didn't act the same. Turns out, Peter was unapologetically gay. The feminine lisp, the flamboyant movement, he had it all and wanted us to know it. Especially when he snapped his fingers after every sentence as if to maintain our attention before fluttering his lashes under pink eyeliner. My only relief was seeing Katrina roll her eyes at me the longer Peter went on. Where his presence was hard to ignore it was the lack of someone else's that caught my attention, Wes wasn't here. I asked Katrina if she knew where he was, but she shrugged her shoulders. It wasn't like him to skip lunch.

After finishing up my food I went to see if he headed back to our barracks for a nap. When I got there, I quietly opened the door but didn't see him lying on his bed. Just as I turned around to leave, I heard heavy footsteps coming from the bathroom. Turning back, I walked over to it. The door was cracked open, peeking inside I saw Wes. He was facing the mirror crying to himself. He had a slightly wrinkled photo in his right hand.

"Wes, you okay man?" I asked as I pushed open the door.

He spun around, stuffing the picture in his pocket.

"Yes... I'm fine." he muttered, wiped the tears from his eyes.

"Ha, I guess I… um, still have some gas in my eyes from training."

I grinned. "Ya know, I probably would have believed you if I didn't already know you're a terrible liar. What's wrong?"

His eyes filled up again. After a moment, he took a deep breath, wiping them dry. Wes and I sat down on the floor.

"Remember how I said I was sent to prison?"

"Yeah," I replied.

"Well, when I got there, it turned out there wasn't enough room for me alongside the other war criminals. Days later, they told me I was going to be shipped to another prison in Siberia. It was a place where it was considered a miracle if you didn't go insane within a year. All that ran through my mind was, I can't do this. I can't go there. I have a wife and a kid. I've got to take care of them. I asked God to explain to me what I did to deserve this! But he didn't give me an answer, and I was sent to Siberia.

"I was locked up in a concrete pit and left out in the cold like a dog. It was agony, but the worst thing about it was all I could think of was my family. I wondered if I would ever see them again. About a month later, three men arrived at the prison searching for me. They knew who I was, where I was stationed, and that I was EOD. They told me they might have a job for me. So, I asked him what the job was. He said, 'Community service,' and I asked him; 'Where?' He gave me a surprising answer... 'Space.'

"He told me he wanted me to be the replacement demolition supervisor for the off-world miners as they extracted gold and other metals out of asteroids. I figured he was joking but he was serious. I thought to myself, 'Anywhere is better than here.' So, I took him up on his offer. Two weeks later, they put me and two armed guards on the rocket Arktores in Russia, and we began our flight to the asteroid. Once we were off-planet, I took one last look at earth through the window of the shuttle. One last look at the planet and the family I was leaving behind. All for something I didn't do. At our fastest speed, it took four months for us to get there. We landed on a massive black asteroid loaded with metals like iron, nickel, and gold.

I was on that rock for nine months and worked with over 200 other miners. I was under constant watch by the guards and wasn't allowed to talk or even look at anyone, and no one ever looked at me. Everyone there thought I was a murderer. A war criminal. But I saw myself as a prisoner of war, held down by my own country. Just when I thought it couldn't get any worse, I got a call."

"What did the caller say?"

"He said, 'I regret to inform you your wife has passed. Due to extreme depression and the effects of an overdose, her body succumbed to the harmful toxin, and she passed away by her own hand.' But Jim, she wasn't the only one I lost. The man on the phone told me she was also seven months pregnant. They said the thought of me as a murderer and a war criminal was too much for her to bear. Under the pressure of it all, she somehow thought it would be better to take her own life. The neighbors found her in the bathtub fully clothed, and they said her face was blue."

"She died one month after I had landed on the asteroid, and I didn't get a call about it until seven months had passed. I never even got to see my second child. The first time I ever heard of him, he was already long dead. And on top of that, my first born blames me for the death of his mother. Then about nine months later the S.O.A.S. proved me innocent and I was sent home. Now here I am. This is all that terrorist's fault. I know Oddball sent someone to kill Thomas and frame me. He's the reason my wife is dead and why my son hates me." Wes pulled out the photo from his pocket.

"This is the only picture I have of my family. Jim, just for one day, I wish I could wake up two years before everything fell apart and stop myself and Thomas from going into that building. But I can't and all I can do now is tell myself that everything's going to be okay… Sometimes that's just not enough."

"Wes… I am so sorry." Wes shook his head and asked bluntly,

"Jim. Why did God do this to me? Why did He make me suffer like this."

"Wes I could never say enough to make up for what you've lost. I can't even pretend like I understand the feeling of losing a wife and son. And to be honest I don't know how you've kept it together this long. But I do know God is not trying to single you out. I can't say for sure what the exact reason is, but it's certainly not because He hates you. We're all going to suffer in this life because we live in a broken world. A world in desperate need of saving, where tomorrow is not guaranteed. But one thing that is, is the promise God made when He said he would never leave nor forsake us. If God hated you, He wouldn't make promises like that," I stated.

"Then what kind of loving Father would put His children through this much pain?"

"Have you considered that your son might think the same about his father?"

"What? Jim, I didn't intend for this to happen. I didn't want this. I want nothing more than to be at his side and tell him I love him. That I'm there for him."

"Wes everything you feel for your son, God feels for you." Wes shook his head.

"Then why did He still let it happen this way?"

"I've spent most of my life asking the same question about all kinds of things. And I've never gotten an in-depth answer that could satisfy my heart ache. So, I stopped asking; 'Why?' And I started asking; 'What now?' Because trying to change the past will destroy any hope for the future."

"What's the point Jim, if the things in my past were the hope of my future?"

"The point is this life is beyond our control, which is why we need a Savior. What I mean is, our hope is not in this life but in the next. For now, find peace in knowing you haven't lost everything. You still have a son, and even if he hates you right now, life will still be worth living for the day he comes around. And I pray for the moment you see him running back into your arms the way he did as a child. The same way God wants us all to when He returns."

Wes smiled. "I hope you're right… It's just not how I thought things would turn out. I feel like the whole world and everyone in it is working against me."

I placed my hand on his shoulder. "Not everyone."

Wes's eyes began to tear up again. "Thank you."

He leaned over, putting his arms over me, and we just sat there for a short moment in silence.

"Jim, you're the best friend I've ever had." he said.

"Same here man," I added smiling.

Suddenly the bathroom door swung open, and Adam stepped into the doorway. He stared at us with wide eyes.

"Well, I guess I was wrong when I thought Katrina and Trent were the only couple on our team."

Wes and I immediately stopped hugging and scooted away from each other.

"Shut up, Adam, you're interrupting a private conversation," I expressed.

"Oh, private, I gotcha. Well, when you're done being *private*, we got to go! Training continues after dinner."

He closed the door. Wes and I glanced at each other and began laughing.

"Hey, Wes, everything's going to be okay." He nodded at me. "Come on. Let's get something to eat!"

Taking his hand, I helped him to his feet. We headed for the cafeteria and moved on with our day. After getting my food I found my path was once again blocked by Joi.

"Hi, Jim!" she said.

Joi did not have the same schedule as me, so her availability to come and eat came later them mine.

"Hey! Joi… what- what're doing here?"

"Well, my shift got changed around so now I have dinner at the same time as you, and I was thinking that we could eat together and catch up."

Her eyes twinkled as she said this, and I remembered just how beautiful she was.

"Um, yeah sure. I'd love to," I forced out, even though I really didn't want to talk about old times. I ignored my better judgment as she smiled and walked me over to an empty table. She brought up all sorts of happy memories of the old days. I went along with it, and we talked together as though nothing bad had ever happened between us. After about ten minutes, Zack wandered over to our table and sat down. Peeking over to our usual booth I could see all my friends were staring at us. I didn't even have to ask because I knew they most likely dared Zack to come over and see what Joi and I were talking about.

"So, Jimbo, who's your girlfriend?"

"Hey! Woah! We're not dating!" Joi and I proclaimed in unison. Zack smirked at us with disbelief.

"Ya, sure. So why don't you guys stop being strangers and come sit down at our table? Then we can all get to know each other."

He eyed Joi up and down as he said this. I still wasn't sure about including Joi in with my new friends, all they've heard were bad stories. But I went along with it to see how things might go. We got up and walked to our booth to finish eating, and at that, all three of the empty seats were filled.

At first things were a little awkward, but as the days went on, we got used to each other and I started to notice something strange about Joi. She was a lot nicer than I remembered. She didn't get annoyed or angry as easily as she used to. She was especially friendly to me. That alone made the remaining four months of training a lot more pleasant. Still, none of us had any idea why we were called back here in the first place.

All we knew was we were training for a top-secret mission and the only clues we had were the monthly training courses we were constantly put through. After the gas tunnels, we trained with dogs and scaled down buildings while being shot at with more live ammo followed by three-on-one hand-to-hand combat drills. In the final month, we did it all again to refresh our skills. And finally, after five months of intense training, it was time to start the mysterious mission that was long unknown to us, until now.

Chapter 9- Execution Orders

Three days before the mission, the six of us were called into a small dark room at 4 AM. Before us was a big table with a map of a series of buildings arranged together inside a square wall forming a compound. General Abner entered the room holding a folder underneath his arm.

"Good morning." He slapped the folder on the table next to the map.

"You were called here for one specific mission. And for five months you've trained in preparation for it. I would just like to say you all have done very well. And today we will be discussing the details of the operation. Any questions before we begin?"

"No sir!" Dirk answered, speaking for the rest of us.

"Alright, let's get started. At O four hundred hours this Friday, you and the entire S.O.A.S. infantry will be engaging a hostile enemy compound. The compound itself is located on a beach surrounded by a horseshoe-shaped mountain range. Half of the S.O.A.S. divisions will separate from the main strike force before reaching the beach. Trent and Adam, you two will leave the U.S.S. Orishea in a fleet of F-23 Super Hawks. Halfway to the compound, your fleet will split in two. Adam, you and the Air Jumpers will increase to an altitude of eight thousand feet above sea level over the compound. You will then wait for orders to engage.

"Trent, you and the Scout Snipers will decrease in elevation and take point on top of the mountains surrounding the compound. Your job is to overwatch all those operating on the ground.

"Katrina, you will leave the U.S.S. Canaveral with the Water-to-Ground teams on skiffs. You will position yourselves one minute out from the beach at the doorstep of the compound and wait for orders to engage.

"Wes, Dirk, and Jim, you three will take part in a Humvee drop out of an Kodiak AC9. You will land on an open pasture just outside the mountains of the compound. You three will leave with the convoy and enter the main road leading toward the entrance of the compound. Before you get there, you will see steep ridges on both sides of the road. Upon reaching them, your teams will form a barricade with your Humvees. Then Beta squad will stay with the Humvees in defensive positions with their weapons aimed downrange toward the direction of the compound.

"Alpha squad, which is you three, and your assault teams will walk single file down the road through the mountains and approach the target area. Once you get inside you will be searching for a high-value target, and I'm sorry, but the identity of that target is at this moment still classified. You will be informed on just who it is when you are already on your way to execute this mission. Our intel shows a high number of insurgents living in the compound. All of whom are assumed to be hostile, and your orders are to kill on sight with extreme prejudice. But the target is not to be killed, we need them alive. So, no sonics, anything over six decibels will set off reverb panels within the structure. And were not risking any collateral damage or friendly fire. This will be an old school gunpowder and lead mission."

"Also, there is a high probability of women and children inside. You are not to engage them in a hostile manner unless you find yourself in a situation where you absolutely have to. Once you capture the target, escort this person to the nearest helicopter, and they will be extracted back to the U.S.S. Orishea."

"You will all exfil in the same manner as you entered. After we grab this person and return to America, they will be "questioned" by the CIA, and our job is done. This is an extremely important mission, and probably the most important one of your lives. We're going to be able to put a lot of bad guys in the ground if this goes right. And I believe you six are the key to tipping this fight in our favor. I have complete faith in your ability to succeed. So... no pressure."

We all smiled.

"That's it. You can return to your room and in three days you'll embark on the most important mission of your career. May God be with us all."

At 8 PM it came time to depart from the now-familiar comforts of base and embark on our mission. We slipped on our suits and set out to the main landing pad in front of base. But before that, I met with Joi to give her a last-minute hug goodbye.

"Be safe." she voiced in a worried tone as our eyes met.

Nodding, I quickly got back with the others, and we proceeded to the tarmac. Once there, we boarded a Super Hawk and waited about twenty minutes for the entire S.O.A.S. infantry to exit the base and enter their planes. Once given the all-clear, the pilot flipped on the rotor. Immediately, dust began to blow from the pavement in every direction. The rest of the aircraft followed suit, sparking there engines to life ascending one by one into the sky. We flew away like a swarm of bees leaving the hive, our fleet of thirty aircraft headed east passing over South Carolina. Over the coast, we flew high above the crashing waves. The wind blew through the open side door of our hawk. The salty air was foreign but still managed to be one of my favorite smells, bringing a smile to my face as I gazed into the blood-red sunset.

Setting in the west as we flew further east, the light seemed to slide off the edge of the world until it was gone. Now it was dark and time to go to work. We flew about three more hours on the same heading until finally arriving where we saw the twin pair of aircraft carriers, the U.S.S. Canaveral and the U.S.S. Orishea. They were stationery in the Atlantic, midway between North America and Africa. Our fleet split and the S.O.A.S. infantry landed on their assigned ships.

The six of us landed on the U.S.S. Canaveral, were landing lights illuminated the ship's deck. After all the aircraft were directed where to land, a sailor exited the ship's observation deck and stepped out onto the runway. It was the captain. She walked over to us; we all stood at attention and saluted her.

"At ease," she said, returning our salute. "I'm Captain Elisabeth Carson, and this is my ship. Follow me; we will discuss additional details of this operation."

We followed her inside as she took us up to the observation deck. We stood in a crowded room of about fifteen other men and women. The captain invited us around a rectangular metal table. She swiped her finger across the table screen and a digitized image appeared. It was a compound on a beach surrounded by a U-shaped series of mountains. The compound looked like a tiny white speck on a dark sandy coastline. The captain zoomed out to a wider shot showing the relatively small size of the beach in comparison to the ocean.

"We will drop anchor twenty miles out from the shore. Rogers, Mason. You will leave this ship and consolidate on the U.S.S. Orishea. From there, you two will gather your teams and fly to your assigned locations around the compound."

Trent and Adam nodded.

"Now the rest of you will stay here. Mis Mires, you and your teams will go to the coast near the beach at the foot of the mountains. Wilson, Richards, and Phillips, you three will board the Kodiak AC9 and wait for my cue to take off after everyone else is in position. You all know the rest. Any questions?"

"Yes ma'am. Who is the target?" Katrina asked.

The captain chuckled. "Isn't that the question of the day. General Abner informed me that I do have clearance to tell you. You're all probably familiar with his name, the target is Oddball."

The room went silent as we stood looking at the captain. I knew they had picked us for an important mission, but I never expected they would pick us to capture the biggest terrorist in the world.

Adam crossed his arms and stated, "I knew it."

"That's right. This operation right here, right now, is the mission to catch Oddball. He is the foundation of worldwide terror, and you six are our end game for the war against that terror."

Wes got a big grin on his face as he heard this. In fact, we all started to smile.

"Don't get too excited yet. We still have to go get him," the captain reminded.

After sharing a little more discussion on the matter, we were all released. Everyone went off to do their own thing, but I went to the front of the deck to listen to music. I sat down with my legs hanging over the edge and pulled out a twenty-dollar handheld recorder I'd used ever since high school. All my favorite songs were on it. Though the music I listen to most were vintage classics from eighty years back. The older music got the better it was compared to the AI garbage that's called music today.

As I listened to a new track Adam walked up beside me. I looked over to see him facing the ocean with both hands on his hips.

He glanced down at me then back at the ocean before undoing the buckle and zipper on his suit. I immediately turned away as he began to pee off the front edge of the aircraft carrier. As he did this, the oncoming wind wouldn't allow the urine to reach the water, so it just blew backward onto the front of the ship trickling down each side like melted butter on a hot knife.

"What are you doing?" I asked.

"I am relieving myself," he announced, with a voice filled with unwarranted pride. "We're going on a stressful mission, and I'm going to need all my concentration."

"You know there are bathrooms on the ship," I remarked.

"Are you kidding, I'm not using those industrial toilets that sound like they're going to suck your guts out when you flush." Adam explained. "Besides, in there, I don't get the wind to cool off my- "

"You're starting to sound like your brother," I pointed out before he could finish.

Adam chuckled. "Yeah, I've heard that before."

"That's not a compliment, ya know."

"Believe me, I get it, and I don't expect people to understand, but Zack has always been my hero. I've never been in a situation where he hasn't had my back. And if you want me to have your back on this mission, then Zack better not find out I said that." Adam warned.

"Your secret's safe with me, but you better hope the captain doesn't find out you peed on her ship."

"The captain's not going to find out!" Adam zipped up his pants and sat down next to me with his legs over the ledge like mine.

"Dirk's up there keeping her busy. They're talking about the mission or something boring." Adam raised a brow at me.

"So, what are you doing out here all by yourself?"

"Oh, I'm just listening to music," I replied. Adam pointed to my recorder.

"On that?"

"Yup."

"Why don't you just get a phone and buy songs?" Adam asked.

"Do you know how many people have asked me that?"

"I'm guessing a lot. What do you tell them?" he asked.

"That I'm a huge dork, and can't be normal to save my life," I stated, not at all joking.

"Boy, ain't that the truth?" he mocked.

"Hey! At least I'm not afraid to use a toilet." I mocked, Adam laughed.

"Where's everyone else?" I asked.

"Wes, Trent, and Katrina are eating in the lunchroom with the other soldiers. You want to go join them?" he asked.

"In a minute. I'll just stay out here for a bit longer." Adam put his hand on my shoulder as he stood up.

"Alright. Well, I'm going inside, and I think I'll try out one of those real bathrooms you're nagging me about."

"See you later."

I sat there flipping through songs till I found something to get my blood pumping. I needed to be in the right mood before we set out. This mission above most others meant so much to so many. Though for me it wasn't fueled by revenge, it was to keep on course of the work God spared my life to do. To defend those in need and prevent the terror that fell upon my family from reaching others like them. So, before it all began, I made sure to pray that God watched over all of us.

Chapter 10- Operation Neon Bravo

Hours later, Trent, Adam, and their men departed from the carrier. Two dozen stealth choppers flew high over the shores of the compound. Halfway there, Trent's teams split from Adam's and headed low toward the mountains. Adam rose higher in elevation; the batting sound of the rotor blades rumbled in his ears as he leaned halfway out the open door of the helicopter. He gazed down toward the approaching compound signaling for his teams to hold their position the moment they flew directly overhead.

As Trent approached the drop zone for his men, he radioed in.

"Touching down."

The surrounding trees on the rocky hillside whipped around from the intense downward draft of the main rotor blades. Hovering thirty feet above the ground, Trent tossed out a rope and led the way to the bottom.

The following choppers did the same, each dropping their men and flying off leaving no traces of their presence other than the dozen snipers now in position and awaiting orders.

Katrina and her teams boarded small skiffs with front-mounted machine guns. As they left the carriers, Katrina sat with her knee up on the front of the boat and one hand on the gun. The waves knocked her up and down as the ocean spray drizzled across her visors. She ordered her teams to hold position as they got close and waited for permission to engage.

Dirk, Wes, and I sat with our troops in the belly of an Kodiak AC9 as it rumbled on our way to the drop zone. A road was in an open desert just before the mountains leading into the compound. As we approached it and began to descend, a voice over the comms alerted us we were getting close. We stood up preparing to make our jump, but we were not the first to go. Before us there were three fully armored Humvees ready to drop.

As we came into position, a green light lit up over the back door as it lowered down and filled the hull with turbulent air. The Humvees released their parachutes one by one, sucking them out of the plane and slowing their descent to the ground below. Following behind, we dove out the back quickly pulling our chutes and touching down around the vehicles. After packing up our chutes and stuffing them into the back of the Humvees, we unstrapped the wheels from their air-droppable platforms and drove away.

I sat next to Wes as he drove the lead car. Before long we came upon the base of the mountain pass that led through to the compound. Wes stopped the convoy at the entrance of a narrow rock pass that wound through the range. We parked the Humvees next to each other, completely blocking the pass. The rocks on either side were high and steep; this was the only road to the compound.

"Everyone out. We're going on foot from here," Dirk ordered, then faced the soldiers on the turrets of the Humvees.

"Stay here. No one leaves down this road."

"Yes, sir," the men replied.

About thirty troops followed Wes, Dirk, and me through the passage. I was constantly checking the rocks above us for snipers and scouts but saw no one. Eventually, it opened up and as the compound came into view, the land became flat and filled with tall grass. On either side of us in the mountains above were Trent and his team of snipers. I radioed him.

"Are we clear?"

"I see you," he said. "You're clear. Keep moving to the wall."

Wes, Dirk, and I led our men through the grass and held positions at the base of a twelve-foot wall. Wes turned to me.

"What's your plan for getting in?"

Dirk answered before I could. "I'll go up," and he pointed to one of the support soldiers who had backpacks with gear.

"I need a ladder."

The soldier nodded and took off his pack, pulled out a folded-up aluminum ladder, then passed it to Dirk.

"When I'm up, I'll signal you to follow when it's clear." No one knew exactly what was waiting for us over the wall. There was only one way to find out, and this was our only quiet way in.

"Hold position." Trent's called out over comms.

I held still, seeing the others do the same as the sound of footsteps passed by from the other side of the wall. They were calm and steady, probably from a guard making his nightly rounds around the perimeter.

"Proceed." Trent said as the steps faded away.

Dirk braced the ladder against the wall and made his way to the top. Almost ten seconds went by before Dirk signaled for us to follow. The soldiers scaled up first, then Wes and me. Once at the top and behind the rim, there was a steel walkway with a railing. Beyond the walkway and throughout the compound there were buildings and sheds that housed men, equipment, planning rooms, and probably more weapons and ammo than we could carry.

Dirk pointed to the nearest building, a two-story complex with a window on the second floor facing the railing.

He whispered to us, "I've got this one. Jim, take your men down the right side of the wall and clear out those buildings. Wes, you and your men come with me, and I'll tell you where to go when we get to the end of the walkway."

"Yes, sir," Wes and I replied.

Dirk took Wes and their teams down the left side of the walkway, and I led my team down the right and over to the closest building. There was a low balcony on the second floor with a rusted railing around three sides of it. We crept toward it, all the while scanning our surroundings for hostiles. The balcony was only a short jump from the walkway where we stood. Upon reaching it, I noticed a closed wooden door on the right side. One by one, I led my team across the gap and onto the balcony. I waited by the door, the nine men behind me, once in position, touched the shoulder of the man in front of them until reaching me. I knew then that they were ready to breach, I reached down and turned the doorknob, it was unlocked.

Letting go, I whispered into my radio, "Alpha Three entering building one through unlocked door on second-floor balcony. Entering now."

I eased the door open and scanned the room with my rifle as I went inside. The room looked clear. I signaled for my team to follow in behind me. Inside the room there were metal cabinets and furniture with foreign patterns on them. There was also a set of stairs going down to the first floor.

The decor was very similar to the gas chambers we trained in back at base. Once my entire team was in, we decided to split up into two teams of five. Myself and four other men stayed upstairs while the other five searched downstairs. I noticed a hallway to our left. In this corridor, there were two doors on both sides facing each other. The four remaining soldiers then split up into groups of two leaving me by myself since I had a distinct advantage due to my suit. Two soldiers moved into the first door on the left and the remaining two men entered the first door on the right. I was left with the last two doors at the end of the hall. Quietly approaching the first one I eased open the door and highlighted the room with my night vision. Clear.

I rotated back and approached the second door on the other side of the hallway. Leaning forward I grabbed the metal doorknob. With extreme caution, I twisted it, relieved to find it was unlocked. I proceeded inside. The room was dark, messy, and had a sweaty locker room smell to it.

Scanning left, I could see a dirty pile of white and black robes piled up next to a bed. Then I saw them, lying under the sheets, a man and a woman. They were undressed, next to the bed on the man's side was an AK-47 leaning up against the wall. Aiming my gun at them, I walked up along where the man was sleeping. He rested on his back with the woman lying on her stomach next to him, her face pointed at the man's head and her left arm stretched over his neck. I looked down at him to see if the man was Oddball, but this guy was way too young to be him. I had orders to kill on sight and so that's exactly what I was going to do.

Walking over to the side of the bed where the woman was, I stopped and turned toward them both. I unclipped my suppressed pistol and aimed at the man's head, firing two shots into the left side of his skull. Blood sprayed over the woman's face, half-waking her up. I watched in silence as she slowly raised her arm off his neck and began to wipe her eyes in the darkness. Not knowing it was blood, she rolled over and sat up trying to figure out what was on her face. But then her widened eyes snapped to me and before she could scream, I grabbed her and held her mouth closed. I forced her to the ground so I could zip tie her hands and tape her mouth shut.

Snatching the blanket off the bed I covered her naked body. As I did, she rolled toward the wall away from me, her muffled voice shrieking from underneath the tape. There's nothing pretty about this job, but it had to be done. I was tired of watching news reports of dead children. I had to get this girl out of here and take her somewhere where my team can keep an eye on her. Reaching forward I picked her up and carried her out the door, closing it and marking it with chalk to signify this room was clear. That done, I took her down the hall to where my team had gathered.

"Was she the only one in the room?" a soldier asked.

"No, she had somebody in bed with her. I took him out. It's a little messy, but the room's clear."

"Did you check him to see if he's the target?"

"Yes. He's not even close. Let's move on," I ordered.

"Alright," he replied in a doubtful tone.

"Radio for the status of downstairs. See if they're clear."

The soldier did so, and the downstairs team called back giving us the all-clear.

"There's a balcony in the next room," another soldier mentioned. "I think we can jump across to the next building, clear out the second floor and meet up with the ground teams in the middle."

"Let's go," I said.

The other two soldiers picked up the woman and proceeded downstairs with her. Another followed and my last man led me to the room where the balcony was. His name was Clark. We walked through an old wooden door and onto the balcony. He was right, there was another balcony attached to the building right across from the one we were on. From here I could see deeper into the compound. There was a large dirt courtyard surrounded by white buildings, most of which were three stories high.

"I'll go first," I said.

Facing the balcony I slung my rifle to my back and climbed over the black metal railing. The jump wasn't far, about six or seven feet from the look of it. I tried to decide on how best to grab onto the edge of the other balcony. It didn't have a railing like the one I was holding onto. It was just a concrete wall with nowhere to land my feet. I just decided to go for it. Kicking off the edge of the balcony I shot out my arms in front of me to grab onto the top edge of the wall. As I did, I tucked my legs up to my chest plate, the weight of my body held my feet in place against the wall. I pulled myself up and over, landing on the balcony of the second building. Now it was Clark's turn. I leaned over the wall and held out my arm to help him up.

He jumped and with both hands he latched onto my arm. I reached down with my other arm and pulled him over the wall. There was a door next to us, Clark quickly got into position and rolled the doorknob. It was unlocked.

"Alpha Three," I announced over the radio. "Unlocked door second-story balcony, building two."

I nodded to Clark, and he eased open the door and stood to the side so I could enter. Once inside, I found myself positioned at the end of a long, dark hallway. Mounted on the wall beside me was a hexagonal metal plate with circular rings placed in sequence down to the center where a speaker sat. A reverberation panel. It faced down the corridor ready to reflect any of our high-pitched weaponry back at us. Guess Abner was right about no sonics'.

Then I heard a faint tapping sound and saw a small light at the end of the hall on the floor. I made a hand signal for Clark letting him know where the light was. He nodded, and we quietly walked toward the light at the end of the corridor. Once there, I could tell it was a blue light creeping out of the crack under a door. The tapping noise was louder and more frequent now with an occasional pause in between taps. The door was about an inch open. Clark peered into the crack to get a peek through, as he did this, the blue light from inside created a horizontal beam up and down his mask and helmet.

"There's a man inside sitting down at a desk on the far side of the room. He's typing on a computer... It's definitely not Oddball. I got 'em,"

Clark raised his barrel through the crack and fired two suppressed shots into the back of the man's head and neck. Blood spread all over the computer screen as he fell forward onto his keyboard. His head pressed down onto the H key, repeating it after whatever he was typing. Clark entered the room with me right behind. We scanned for any other targets. It was clear, but there was another open doorway to the right of the dead man. I signaled Clark to check it out while I inspected the computer screen. Pulling back the man's head, or what was left of it, prevented the H key from repeating any further down the page. I clicked the backspace and deleted it all until I could see all of what he had written. Just as I got to the top and read the word Ragna, I heard quick heavy footsteps coming from the next room.

I grabbed my gun and faced the doorway only to see Clark get tackled by another man through the second-floor window. It shattered as the two burst through it and crashed down onto the slanted metal rafters before impacting the dusty dirt floor in the courtyard. I sprinted over to the window, jumped through and slid down the rafters onto the ground next to them. Clark had landed on top of the man, and with zero hesitation stabbed him three times in the throat. My eyes pinballed around the courtyard to see if anyone had awoken from the sound of the crash. Just then, a sudden light from behind us cast our shadows across the yard. We spun back at the sound of a little girl screaming.

She stood in the first-floor doorway of the building where we had fallen from. She darted away from us and ran inside. I bolted after her, jumping onto the wooden porch and running into the house. I caught up to her just as she pounded one tiny fist on a door, I assumed it was her parent's room. Quickly snatching her up I carried the screaming girl back out the front door. I stood on the right side of the doorway pinning the girl underneath my arm, holding her mouth shut to keep her quiet. Clark dragged the dead body of the man he had stabbed underneath the porch and jumped up, running to the left side of the doorway. With my left hand, I unbuckled my tomahawk and held it ready. Looking around the courtyard, I could see that one building's third-floor window had begun to light up, and at that, I knew that things were about to get loud. Wes's voice came up over the radio.

"Alpha Three, status."

"Halt operation," I uttered as quietly as possible.

Where was the rest of my team? They were supposed to have cleared out the downstairs. I heard the creek of a door opening and a faint voice whisper.

"Jemma?" I assumed this was the little girl's name.

"Jemma?"

Then I heard the inner workings of a rifle being cocked. The footsteps got closer and once more the man called out. He was close now, about two feet from where we were hiding.

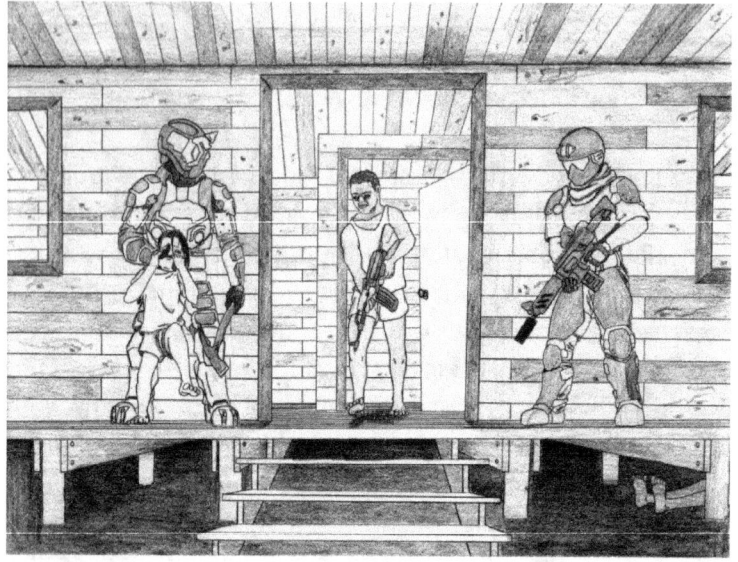

He took a step closer, and the barrel of his gun was now just inches over the threshold of the doorway. The small child Jemma tightly pressed under my hand saw his gun and tried her best to scream. The man heard her muffled cry and stepped through the doorway onto the wooden deck. Raising my tomahawk, I hurled it down into his neck. He fired out into the courtyard in reaction to the sudden pain. I used my right hand to grab the gun out of his, but by doing this, I lost my grip on Jemma. She broke free and ran screaming to the next house. Clark immediately bolted after her as I pried my tomahawk out of the man's neck. Just before Jemma reached the next house Clark tackled her onto the wooden porch. He began duct taping her mouth and zip tying her hands and feet together. As I ran over to them, I got a call from Wes.

"Alpha Three! Status!"

"Engaging! Go loud!" I said in response.

Arriving at the house, Clark opened the front door. I jumped onto the deck and rushed inside. At the end of the living room, a man was running down the stairs toward us. I popped two in his chest, and he dropped down the stairs like a rock, banging his head on the last two steps as he fell forward. I turned back to the doorway just as my team caught up with Clark and me.

"Where have you been?" I asked.

"Clearing rooms, you and Clark were supposed to meet us in the middle." I wanted to knock his teeth out. Snapping back at the stairs I heard a woman scream and remembered I had more important things to do.

"Sweep this floor, I got upstairs." I ordered.

Darting up to the sound I saw her huddling down against the wall screaming with her hands covering her face. It was clear now that the operation was in a potential crisis and Oddball could escape. I rushed up to her and quickly zip-tied the woman's hands to the railing and left her there. Heading to the left I rushed up a second flight of stairs that led to a long hallway. There I knelt and peered through my night vision. A man ran down the hallway and cut down a second hall to the left. He was quickly followed by another man going in the same direction. I got up and chased after them, bolting around the corner to see where they were going.

At the end of the hallway, there was a metal ladder that appeared to lead up to the roof. The first man was already stepping off the ladder and onto the roof. The second man was only halfway up. I shot him, once in the thigh and once in the torso just under his armpit. He fell about six feet on his back and cried out in agony. Running to the base of the ladder I shot him again. This time in the face, blowing his screaming head apart. I reached for the ladder and proceeded after the first man.

Once at the top, I stuck my head through the square opening and saw the man running away toward another building. I leaned back to hold myself in place as I raised my rifle aiming at him. He reached the edge of the roof and jumped toward the next building. I fired one shot, drilling him in the lower spine. His body continued to fly in the air until he smacked into the wall of the next building and tumbled down into the alley below. I lifted myself onto the roof and ran over to where he had fallen to see if I could confirm the kill. As I stared down into the alley, a man climbed up the ladder behind me and was aiming an R.P.G. straight at my back.

Trent caught sight of him through the lens of his scope and sent a round blasting straight through the man's right shoulder blowing his torso into pieces and spraying blood everywhere. The reflexes in his arm, however, reacted and he unintentionally fired his R.P.G. into the rooftop two feet behind me. The sudden blast robbed me of my balance and sent me off the roof slamming into the side of the next building. Tumbling down into the alley, I landed on the metal lid of a dumpster. Lying on my back, I took a second to catch my breath before slowly rolling off of it. Having only the wind knocked out of me, I took view of the three-story building I had just fallen from.

Thank you, God, for letting me still be alive.

I leaned back on the wall and checked the condition of my rifle. It appeared to be okay, so I stood up to check myself for injuries. Suddenly, something out of the shadows lunged at me. I fell back down as a large black dog pulled violently against its chain, being the only thing keeping the beast off me. The sound of rattling chains overtook my ears even more so than the barking. Fear entered my body, and it was like I was back in my nightmare. Though it was a big dog, it wouldn't do much against my suit. Still, the fear that this animal triggered in me was just as bad, but I couldn't stop. I couldn't stay here. I had people out there relying on me to get this job done. I closed my eyes and pulled out my pistol, standing up I walked around the dumpster and aimed at the dog's head. POP! Silencing it forever along with the fear in my heart.

I limped toward the mouth of the alley and leaned on the wall to reload as well as catch my breath. Looking across the courtyard, I could see Wes crouched down behind a building. His team was pinned down by an onslaught of lightning tracers streaking around them. The rounds would impact into the wall and the ground kicking up small puffs of sand. Every now and then one would ricochet off the ground and skip into the blackened sky like a little shooting star. I glanced around the corner and could see the tracer rounds were coming from a white truck. One of Oddball's men had a machine gun mounted on the back.

I spun back into the alley and noticed a door on the side of the wall I had passed. It led into the building in-between me and the white truck. Running over to the door I grabbed the knob, trying my best to turn it. Locked. Stepping back, I shot three rounds into the deadbolt blowing shards of metal and wood into the air. Kicking it open I rushed inside only to see five armed men raising their guns preparing to fire. I took one glance at them and charged, setting my rifle to full auto, emptying the remainder of my mag into the group until my gun clicked empty. I managed to kill three before my rifle went dry.

I slung it around my back as I continued at the rest. The last two men backed up as they fired at me. Reaching the closest man I front kicked his chest, with the added strength of my exo mesh under my armor he flung backward through the door that led outside. Passing the second man I spun around, whipping out my pistol and shot him once in the forehead. Spinning back, I rushed out the now open doorway that I had made passible with the first man's body. Leaping over him, I fired twice into his torso as I rushed forward to the next building.

I kicked down the door and proceeded inside with meager caution for myself. The only thing on my mind was to stop that truck from hurting my friends. This building seemed clear, so with no threat in sight, I hurried to the next door I could see passing a metal desk along the way. Stopping at the door, I eased it open, laying eyes on the truck. Reaching to my back I grabbed my rifle and pressed the magazine release dropping the empty mag to the floor. Smacking in a full magazine of thirty rounds, I loaded a bullet into the chamber and pushed open the door firing a hailstorm of glowing tracers at the gunner on the back of the truck. My bullets pierced his body. He keeled over and let go of the machine gun as he tumbled off the left side of the truck, gasping for life as his body hit the sand.

Switching targets, I aimed toward the driver's seat and shot up the man inside. A well-placed round uncapped his skull, and his head broke through the shattered window, spilling his brain down the side of the truck. Ceasing fire, I called Wes over my radio.

"Alpha Two, status?"

There was a moment of silence and a hiccup of static.

"All clear. Zero casualties. We are beginning our sweep of the compound adjacent to your position."

"Copy that. I will consolidate with my team and signal for Adam's men to drop in. Over."

"Copy, over."

I let go of my radio and took a quick peek around before reloading my rifle. Leaning back against the inside of the door frame, I finished loading my gun and put a fresh round in the chamber. A quick flash lit up over the courtyard and caught my eye.

BANG!

I was blown back inside, tumbling across the floor and slamming upside down into the metal desk, denting it beyond repair. Stunned by the sudden blast backward, my mind quickly cycled through several explanations as to the cause of my current state. Maybe it was someone's funny idea of telling me to get a desk job, but in truth, I was starting to get really annoyed by RPGs blowing me into things. This is the second time these guys caught me by surprise, and I was going to make sure they didn't get the chance to do it again.

I rolled onto my knees, stood up, and unbuckled my tomahawk as I bolted upstairs. Once on the second floor, I searched around for a ladder or staircase, anything that could lead me to the roof. I would have to get up there if I wanted to call in the cavalry. I darted to the end of the hallway, but right before I could make it to the end, WAAM!

A door swung open and collided with me at full speed. My back met the ground, and I looked up to see the cause of my new engagement with the floor. Then from behind the door stepped a massive dark brown hairy leg. The door closed behind him and towering before me was a man whose sheer size rivaled Wes'. He wore nothing but a white wife beater and stained pair of underwear, but in his hands, he gripped an AK-47, which he cocked and aimed at me.

Without warning, he fired, sending rounds ricocheting off my suit and into the walls around us. I got to my feet pushing the gun aside and raised my tomahawk. The man quickly swung back his rifle, snagging the underside of my ax head, flinging it out of my hand and onto the ground. I stepped back as he swung at me again, ducking underneath his reach. I scooped up my ax, and swung backward, slicing the back of the man's calf. Groaning as he limped away from me.

Enraged, the man yelled violently as he raised his rifle like a bat. I stepped forward aiming low and sunk my blade into his gut. A deep horizontal gash split across his stomach, just as he slammed his rifle onto my backplate. Kneeling from the impact of his blow I slouched from the weight of his intestines dumping overtop my shoulders and spilling onto the floor. He dropped the rifle, and I stood up as he fell to his knees where I placed my hand on his throat.

Spinning the ax in my hand, I stuck the spike end into his sweaty forehead. His large body fell backward to the floor pulling my ax with it. I let it go and stepped back, taking a deep breath. After a short moment to cool off, I pulled down the strand of intestine still hanging from my shoulder plates. Looking back at my ax, I knelt and with both hands tried to pull it free. Realizing it was stuck, I stood up at the sound of gunfire and small explosions outside. My friends could be in trouble. Turning away, I quickly bolted down the hallway leaving my tomahawk behind. Rounding the corner, I found exactly what I was searching for, a ladder.

Running to it I climbed to the top and pushed open the hatch. I stepped up onto the roof and hurried to the center now reaching into my back pouch to pull out a single flare. Breaking off the top ignited red flames. My arms waved toward the sky hoping they would see the signal, but there was only a starry black night. I waited and watched, but nothing came. Did they not see my signal? Just as I feared my flair had been missed, there was a flash. One after the other as dozen soldiers dove into the now full-blown war zone. Yellow flames spewed from their jetpacks as they descended onto the buildings within the compound. Once most had touched down, I spoke into my radio.

"Viper 1, move-in! We need heavy support along the coast."

At that moment Katrina and her team, about one minute out, were given the green light to engage by landing on the beach and stopping anyone from getting away by sea. The Air Jumpers stormed the compound from above and the Water-to-Ground teams quickly shot up anyone who tried to leave through the exit gates bordering the walls around the compound. Trent and his teams took out the strays and Dirk, Wes, and their teams rounded up the prisoners and held them at the center of the courtyard.

I noticed several trucks leaving the compound through an exit gate to my right. The trucks escaped down the road and sped off into the mountain pass. They were quickly stopped in their tracks by the barricade of Humvees positioned at the mouth of the ridge. The

American soldiers fired simultaneously into the oncoming vehicles tearing them into a jagged bloody mess that went careening off to the side of the road. Another truckload of enemies tried to leave by water and board escape boats. Katrina saw this and moved in to take them out before they made it to their vessel.

Their truck drove parallel with the tides. Katrina flipped off the safety on her .50 cal machine gun mounted at the front of her gunboat. Her craft bounced along the waves as her driver steered her alongside the escaping truck. She lined up the target and unloaded a vicious barrage of speeding lead into the truck as they drove alongside each other.

The truck driver was shot to pieces and the truck gently slowed and drifted into the water. With our combined efforts we quickly got the situation under control just as the sun peeked above the horizon.

By 0700 we had rounded up all the men, women, and children into the courtyard. Every soldier had a picture of Oddball. They searched through the crowd asking the people where he was, but not a single person opened their mouths. Our worst fear had become a reality. He was gone - Oddball was missing. We upended the remainder of the compound, but there was no sign of him, even in the house we suspected him to be living in. Hours passed and still, he was nowhere in sight. At this point, I, along with many others, was getting furious. There's no way we did all this for nothing.

Then one of our younger soldiers, Allen, came running out of a building next to Oddball's supposed house, yelling,

"HEY... HEY, I FOUND SOMETHING!"

Chapter 11- Echoes of the Past

All eyes fell upon him, even the prisoners had a worried look on their faces. That's how I knew the soldier had found something important. Allen showed us what he discovered inside the building. He led us to a dead man's body lying on a thin brown carpet.

"I was about to drag out his body, but then I noticed something strange," he explained.

Observing the body, I saw an exit wound in the throat where he had bled out on the carpet, but around the man's neck there was almost no blood whatsoever.

"How can a man bleed out through his throat, but only lose a small amount of blood?" Allen asked. He smiled as he knelt and picked up the carpet. "It's because he bled through the carpet and in between the cracks of the wooden hatch underneath."

"Ha ha. Way to go kid!" Wes exclaimed. "Come on, Jim. Let's go catch this-"

"Hold on," I Interrupted. "We don't even know what's down there. We can't just go rushing in after him."

"Jim, you can't stop me from catching this guy!" Wes replied in a dismissive tone.

"Wes I'm not trying to stop you. For all we know that hatch could be filled with C4 rigged to bring this whole building down the second you open it. Let's wait two more minutes to get it x-rayed before we go in," I insisted.

"Fine," dismissed Wes.

Two soldiers were sent out to retrieve the x-rays. It was a black mat they unrolled over the hatch. It had a digital screen on the top side so when it began to x-ray the area beneath, we could see through the mat like a digital window. The second it lit up everyone huddled over it in an anxious attempt to see what was below. Underneath the hatch was a man with his feet on a ladder leaning up against the wall setting explosives directly beneath us. He didn't seem finished, and it appeared he had not attached the tripwire to the door yet. If we were going to go in, now would be the time.

"Well, Jim, looks like you were right." Allen remarked. I turned to Dirk who nodded.

"Take off the x-ray," Wes ordered.

He unclipped his .45, lined up the shot, and sent two rounds into the hatch where he saw the man's head. Wes knelt down and slid his hand into the handle of the hatch swinging it open.

"After you," he said.

I leaned over to see down into the chamber. There was a ladder that went about fifteen feet to the floor where there was now a dead body lying. It was dark, but I could still make out where things were at the bottom.

"If you don't hear from us in ten minutes, call it in and send a team after us."

I looked back at Wes. "Ready?"

He nodded; I stepped over the open hole and dropped in unintentionally landing on the dead man's body and definitely broke a few of his ribs. Not that it would matter to him anymore. I brought up my rifle and aimed down the sights, finding myself once again positioned at the end of a long dark hallway. Red lights on the ceiling filled the air with a crimson glow. It looked like I had just dropped into hell, but I knew this place was anything but. I gave Wes the all-clear signal. Seconds later, he jumped in after me and for a moment we just knelt there, silently watching and waiting. Nothing happened; it was just a long silent hallway.

Wes placed his hand on my shoulder, letting me know that it was time to go see for ourselves what was down here.

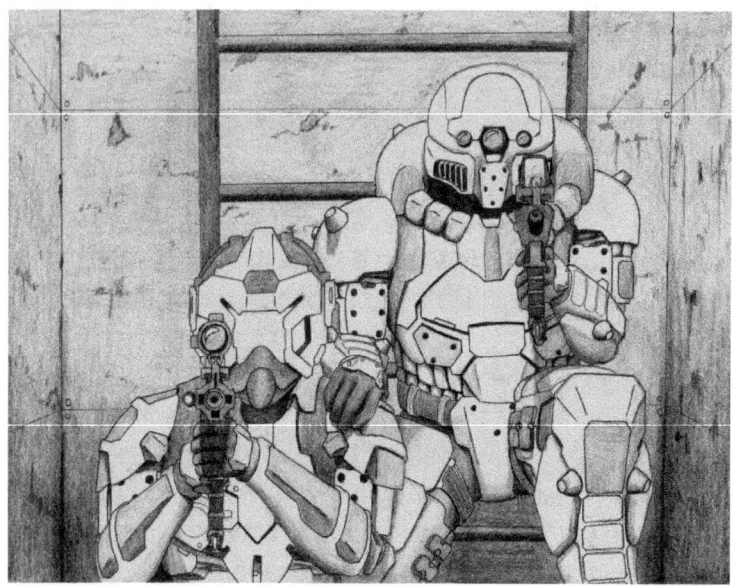

Standing up we began walking down the hall but quickly found it was hard to stay silent because there were small puddles of water all over the ground. At least, I thought it was water. Eventually, we made it to the end and found that the hallway split off in a capital T shape. There were several Reverb panels mounted on the walls. They must have expected us to blast this tunnel with sonics' since the acoustics would be magnified in these echoing halls. But we weren't falling for that.

Still, this wasn't looking good for us as now Wes and I would have to split up. Without saying a word or giving any signal, Wes headed left and I headed right. Now I was alone in an unknown area with limited ammunition and any number of enemies lurking around these dark halls.

Peering down the passage a door sat to the right midway down the hall. I proceeded toward it all the while aiming down the sights of my rifle ready to drop anything that might come at me. There was something different about this door. It was white and sealed on all the edges. Almost like a big refrigerator.

Stepping closer I reached down with my left hand grabbing the metal latch. It pulled open, breaking the suction inside. Mist engulfed my feet as the door swung to the left. I flipped on the strobe light attached to my rifle's front rail hoping to see frozen food inside, but unfortunately, that's not what I found. Hung by a chain attached to the ceiling was a dead man with his stomach stitched closed as if he'd have had a C-section. It appeared as though there were large bricks inside his abdomen. Behind him were metal shelves with arms and legs laying on them, scattered around the ground surrounding the man was a pile of pills wrapped in saran wrap and duct tape.

I could only assume they were trying to hide drugs inside the bodies. Exiting the room, I closed the door behind me. As I glanced down the hall, a bare foot stepped around the corner and out of view. I raised my gun and ran after him. Reaching the end of the hall I turned the corner coming face to face with a man pointing his gun at me. It was Wes. He stepped around the opposite side of the hall the same second as me. We stood facing each other for a moment, then with my left hand, I gestured down another hall that branched off to my right. Wes rejoined me and together we silently continued down the hallway. At the end was a door directly below a bright red light.

Wes and I proceeded toward it. Locked again. I stood aside as Wes faced it. He raised his gun and shot three rounds into the door lock, shattering its inner workings. Wes kicked it in, and we both rushed inside flipping on our strobe lights. The flashes rapidly lit up the room. This place was filled with an abundance of exotic plants. It was an underground greenhouse with plant life I had never seen before. All of which were enormous in height, some about fifteen feet tall. Wes and I walked down a path between the rows of cinderblocks holding in the dirt. Sprinklers hung from the cracked ceiling over top the blooming flowers. Once again there was no one in sight, this room though massive, was clear.

I continued forward seeing a red light on the adjacent wall overtop another door. Halfway there I stopped, Wes was no longer at my side. Turning back, I squinted as he stood still now facing the base of a tall green stem. The plant loomed over him as he gazed intently down at the dirt it was planted in. Wes collapsed.

"Wes, what's wrong?" I asked.

He raised his head and pointed to the soil. I walked over and took in a sight I was not expecting. Reaching out toward me was a tiny human hand no bigger than my thumb. Chills shot down my spine. Wes held out his hand; slowly uncovering the rotting flesh of a dead baby.

"What kind of twisted place is this?" he muttered at the horrific sight of its dismembered corpse.

Wes had two children; one was only sixteen and the other he had lost in the womb when his wife took her own life.

"Wes, we have to keep moving or Oddball's just going to get away. I know this might bring up bad memories for you, but we need to move on and put an end to this."

Wes slowly turned his head at me; he nodded and placed the baby back in its hole. Raising his rifle, he stood and walked hastily over to the next door. I could tell his sense of shock had dissipated and transformed into the rarest and most uncommon emotion Wes could ever express, rage. With all his might he kicked open the door like it was cardboard and rushed inside, but what he saw next only brought him back to his knees.

The room was clear, but not of everything, the second we entered, we were engulfed by a horrific stench. This was a large rectangular-shaped room filled with shiny aluminum tables covered with surgical equipment and unlabeled chemicals. Scattered around the room were what seemed to be rotting organic materials like dissected organs from small animals. It was the cause of the terrible smell.

This room was some kind of hospital, but not one to help people. This one was to take them apart. All the small intestines I thought to be from animals were actually the rotting corpses of hundreds of aborted human babies. They were scattered around the room like trash at the dump. Some of them were no bigger than the palm of my hand. Buckets of them hung from the ceiling by chains. Could this be what my nightmares were warning me of?

Wes fell to his knees in the center of the room. After my initial shock had passed, I ran over to him. As I got closer, I heard him sobbing quietly under his helmet.

"Wes?"

His hands were shaking; in fact, his whole body began to. I placed my hand on his shoulder. He turned to me.

"I'm going to kill him."

Wes took my arm rising to his feet and aimed for the next door where another red light sat on the ceiling. Wes began sprinting toward it, and I quickly followed. We entered a hall; it was longer than the others and had huge

120

cracks on the ceiling. They looked recent due to how sharp the edges on them were. Wes was running in front of me and when he reached the door at the end of the hall, he slammed his enormous body through it. We found ourselves in a much smaller room about the size of an average living room. There was no one inside but us, and this place was cluttered with desks, filing cabinets, and all sorts of computers. The most distinct observation was there were no other doors to go through. It was a dead end.

"No. You've got to be kidding me... don't tell me he got away!" Wes yelled.

I lowered my rifle and set it down as I stepped over to one of the desks. I sat down in the chair and rested my head on my hands. How could he have escaped, five months of training only to come up at a dead end? Staring at the paperwork scattered about, I noticed in the center of it all there was a small white card, completely blank except for a black symbol printed on the center.

Curious, I picked it up and flipped it over. A phone number was scratched off the back. I put it in a pouch on my belt for later examination. Now sweaty and frustrated, I took off my helmet and faced the wall, mumbling aloud.

"Maybe he was never here. He might have left days before the attack. Maybe our satellite photos of him were actually some kind of body double."

"I don't believe that. I know he's here," Wes affirmed.

"Where then? Where could he be? Wes, there's nowhere else to look, he's gone. I'm sorry, but it's over, we've lost him."

Wes took off his helmet and sat on a collapsed pile of rubble that had fallen out of the ceiling.

"Jim, I did not come all this way just to lose him or be stuck at a dead end."

"I know but-"

"No, Jim!" he shouted. "You don't know! I lost my life because of this guy. You didn't lose a wife and two kids. What could you possibly know about loss?" I was silent for a moment nodding in appreciation of his harsh words.

"Wes... I lost my parents." Wes's eyes snapped to mine.

"What? What are you talking about?"

"It doesn't matter," I uttered softly.

"Yes, it does. What happened?" Wes asked.

"Some psycho influenced by Oddball's propaganda walked into my parents' church and shot up the place. He killed nine people, my parents included. Blew a fat hole into the back of my dad's head. An eyewitness told me he saw my mom grab my dad's sidearm and fire back while everyone else ducked in cover, but the shooter was faster and my mom died, too. She's more of a hero than I will ever be."

"What do you mean?" Wes asked.

"I was going through a rough time. You were gone, then Joi left me, and I wasn't feeling up to going with them to church that day. If I had, then maybe I could have done something."

"I'm sorry." he said.

"Me to."

"Why didn't I hear about this on the news, this wasn't long before I got back right?" Wes asked.

I shook my head.

"BNC didn't cover it very well. I guess a church shooting isn't considered priority news. Even though the police report mentioned something I can't explain."

"What?"

"There was this one victim whose body was so shredded to the bone they couldn't identify him. He was missing an eye and a leg and they never found it. His DNA didn't match anyone on record either… I don't know what to think about that, and I'll probably never get answers for what really happened that day."

"Looks like we both have reason to hate these people, huh?" Wes presumed. I shook my head again.

"No. I don't hate them. I um- I'm trying my best to forgive him but places like this don't make it easy. And somehow, I thought that catching Oddball would make all this feel worth it, but I guess that opportunity is long gone."

"That can't be true, he's got to be here somewhere." Wes still insisted. I didn't know what else to tell him at this point.

"Maybe you're right, Wes. Maybe Oddball is still here, maybe he's in the walls or he downloaded himself into these computers."

In my anger, I began grabbing things off the desk and throwing them around the room.

"Do you think he can hear me? Get it through your head, Wes, he's gone!"

As I yelled, I threw my helmet at the wall next to Wes and sat down on the chair glaring at the floor as a tear dropped from my eye. There was a short silence before Wes spoke.

"Jim... do you see the light."

"Wes, I am not in the mood for jokes."

"No, Jim there's a light coming out of the wall!"

I looked up and saw Wes staring at a beam of light shining out of a small hole about the size of a quarter where I had thrown my helmet. The entire right wall of this room was fake, made of drywall, and disguised to look like rock. Wes tossed me my helmet as he strapped on his own. Pulling out my pistol I headed toward Wes who busted his leg through the wall followed by the rest of his body. I raised my gun and crashed in after him. What we saw next was truly heart-stopping.

Staring straight at me, with his one good eye was the terrorist, Adon Mocalla Bol. He was behind a low three-foot stone wall holding a knife to a crying child's throat. To his right at the far side of the room was another man trying to dig out the rubble of an exit door so they could escape. The doorway must have collapsed from all the explosions above ground during the battle. I couldn't believe it. This whole time he was just fifteen feet away in a secret room concealed by drywall. The second Wes and I entered, the man on the ground grabbed his rifle and held it with the barrel pointed at the floor.

"DROP IT!" Wes yelled.

The man started yelling at Oddball in Armenian before holding up a reverb panel as a shield. Oddball yelled back, and the man aimed down the sights and pointed his gun at Wes from behind his shield. Before the man could shoot, Wes fired once, blowing through the reverb panel and into the man's head. He fell backward on the rocks. The child was now screaming uncontrollably. Oddball pressed the knife closer to the boy's throat. He then hid his face behind the boy's head and began yelling at us in his language, but then he switched to English.

"DROP WEAPONS! DROP YOUR WEAPONS! NOW!"

Without a word to each other Wes and I split in opposite directions, surrounding Oddball on both sides so he couldn't hide behind the child anymore. At this point the knife he had to the boy's throat was starting to dig deeper into his skin. Blood ran down into his clothes as he cried toward the ceiling.

Oddball glared at me, and I could see the intense hatred he had for us in his eyes. He tightened his grip and pressed the knife deeper into the boy's throat as the traumatized child screamed in agony. Never in my life have I ever wanted to shoot someone so badly, but I was trusted with the ridiculous order not to kill this man. Just as I thought Oddball was going to slice this boy's life away, he did the unthinkable. He dropped the knife and pushed the boy off the low stone wall, landing him on his stomach.

"I surrender!"

Stunned, Wes stepped forward to zip tie his hands. He grabbed Oddball's right arm and spun him so he would be face to face with Wes. Oddball's back now faced me, and I noticed an irregular bulge under his shirt on his lower back, it looked square with sharp angles. Wes had control of Oddball's right hand so for a brief second his left hand was free. He quickly reached back and revealed the peculiar lump under his shirt.

A gun!

I lunged for him, but I was too late. Oddball raised it toward the boy and shot him twice in the chest. Wes and I forced Oddball against the wall. I snatched the gun away from him as Wes swung the back of his hand into Oddball's cheek, tearing off skin with the small jagged bolts protruding from his glove. I stepped over to the boy to see if he was still alive, but neither breath nor pulse could be found. Turning to Wes I shook my head. Immediately, Wes forced Oddball to the ground and viciously began beating his face into the cement. With each swing blood drained from his split cheeks. As this went on, I watched knowing that Wes was going to kill him.

He raised his fist while choking Oddball's throat as Wes spoke down into his face,

"Remember Thomas!" and bashed his fist into his nose.

"This is for him!" Again, he punched Oddball. "And my wife!"

I looked on knowing that I couldn't let Wes take his life.

"And my sons! THIS IS FOR ALL OF THEM!"

Wes reached back, pulling out his knife as the lost voices of his past cried out for vengeance. He raised the blade over his head. I stepped forward.

"WES, STOP!" I grabbed his arm and held it back as I pulled Wes off Oddball who laid still.

"We can't kill him!"

Wes shook in my arms as he stared back at Oddball who slowly breathed in and out. Eventually Wes dropped the knife and leaned against the wall as he calmed down. I rushed over to Oddball and securely bound his hands and feet together. I flicked on my radio and spoke on all channels.

"Attention! All stations, target acquired."

I radioed the men waiting above the hatch asking for assistance to get Oddball out of here and into more secure hands. As we waited, Wes raised his head at me.

"I'm sorry, Jim." I knelt down.

"I don't blame you, Wes. For a second there, I almost let you kill him. But his death wouldn't bring to life all those we've lost. There will probably be a day where I'm too blind by rage to turn away from my need for vengeance. And I know you'll be there to pull me away."

Wes stared at me and nodded; I reached out my hand. Grasping it we stood together and glared down at Oddball who glared back. Moments later, two soldiers arrived to help. They entered the room and saw the condition Oddball was in.

"What happened to him?" Wes looked away. I faced the men and quickly explained as I pointed to the dead man lying on the rubble.

"Oddball was in a dispute with that man who shot this boy. We heard the shot from the other room, and that's how we knew it was a fake wall. By the time we got through it, he had nearly beaten Oddball to death. But we stopped him."

Wes glanced at me and hid his bloody fist behind his back. He turned back to the men and nodded in agreement. Soon the four of us carried Oddball out of his secret room down the hall, beyond the hospital room and the green house. We made it to the ladder and the soldiers up top sent down a rope so we could tie it around Oddball and hoist him to the surface. After doing this, we brought him into a more controlled location and cut his feet loose, walking him out the front door of the building and into the courtyard. The second we stepped onto the yard; we were surrounded by an eruption of cheering and joyful applause.

All our soldiers clapped and shouted our names. It was like being at a concert after the last song. I couldn't help but smile. To look around the crowd and have the satisfaction of knowing you did something really good. This would have probably been one of the best moments of my life, but after failing to save that kid, I just wasn't in the mood. I did have to admit though; I felt a sense of relief that it was over. This worldwide spread of terrorism was finally over, and my friends and I were the ones to end it. Wes and I escorted Oddball to the nearest helicopter, and once he was onboard, we backed away so the aircraft could take off. Before it could, Wes stepped forward and looked Oddball in his eyes.

"I forgive you." he declared.

My eyes shot at him as I was taken back by his words. Wes had lost so much and if he could find the strength to push out those words, who was I to hold them in. The man who killed my parents was no worse than Oddball, so what was stopping me?

As we stood to watch the chopper ascend and transport the prisoner to the U.S.S. Orishea, I took one last look at Oddball. Expecting to see the humiliated look on his swollen face. I saw something else instead. It was a look of something far more disturbing, a cheeky grin followed by the wink of his eye. They then placed a black bag and a pair of headphones around his head before taking off, never to be seen by my eyes again.

Later, a man came up to me and placed his hand on my shoulder. It was Clark. Turning to see what he wanted I found that he didn't want anything but instead wanted to return something. My tomahawk I had left behind during the battle. As he handed it back to me, I shook his hand, grateful he had returned it.

Then I walked over to Wes and he and I boarded a Super Hawk now beginning our return to the aircraft carriers. Our time in Africa had come to an end and now began our long venture home. While in flight over the ocean, I began to think about Joi. For the first time since I had come back to base, I was actually excited to see her again. But I couldn't help but wonder if things would turn out the same as the last time I returned from a mission?

Chapter 12- Hellbender

The trip across the Atlantic was spent mostly sleeping. We were all tired after a long night of unrelenting stress. The hours quickly went by, and we soon found ourselves stepping off the plane and setting foot onto the familiar tarmac back at Skymont Air Force Base.

General Abner was the first to greet the six of us, and we all stood at attention and gave him a well-deserved salute. He did the same, smiling as he congratulated us on a job well done. Out of everyone I'd seen, he by far was the happiest of them all. He informed us how grateful he was and stated how the last real threat in the world was now gone. That's great and all, I thought, but I was focused on one single thing.

The first chance I got I left the company of my friends and raced to the barracks. I quickly unclipped my suit and stuffed it into my trunk. Standing, I left my room, casually walking down the hall to her office in the file sector. I found her door and stopped before I entered. The last time I had returned to her from a mission, I found her in the arms of another man. I wanted to believe she had changed; this would be the first test. I took a deep breath and stepped in. She was sitting there alone typing on the computer, her eyes lit by the screen, but then even more so as she saw me.

"Jim!"

I couldn't hold back the smile as she jumped up to hug me. For the first time in what seemed like ages, I didn't feel sad, worried or even scared. I was relieved knowing everything that had been ruined was now reforged into something better. Even happier knowing that Joi, the woman who had broken my heart so many times before, was now someone I could start placing my trust in again.

I spent the remainder of the day with her in her office. I didn't even realize how time had rolled by until I looked out her window and saw that it was night. Not wanting to keep her from sleeping as well as finishing her work, I said my goodbyes. Before I left, she stretched out her arms to offer me one last hug goodnight, and before it ended, she leaned forward kissing my cheek, and uttered softly, "Good night, Jim."

I smiled as we parted ways and walked down the hall, holding back the urge to shout with excitement. I rounded the corner, already replaying the best moments in my mind of the past couple of hours. I made it to the barracks where my friends were sound asleep. Careful not to wake them, I quietly snuck over to my bed and laid under the covers. The first thought that entered my mind was to thank God for all the drastic changes He'd made in my life. I wouldn't be here without Him and that night I slept without a single nightmare.

The next day, to our surprise, we were called to partake in an urgent and mandatory assembly, except this time we were being called in to celebrate a job well done by attending a party in our honor. The day before nearly one hundred workers were called into the cafeteria to strip it clean and decorate it for the celebration. However, a part of me didn't want to go to this event. Once it was over, I would have to say goodbye to all my new friends. We did what we came here to do. We put an end to Oddball's crimes. In all this time, I had really come to love the people in my new team, but now that our job was over, everyone who was called here would be sent back to the bases they came from.

At 7 PM, we were given word to enter the cafeteria for our farewell party. Trent and Katrina arrived first. They were wearing their class A uniforms of the military branches they were representing. They held hands as they walked through the front door. Adam entered next with his brother, Zack. The two of them joined Katrina and Trent exchanging hugs with them saying how much they would miss each other. Soon after, Wes arrived with Joi and me and together the seven of us stood saying our goodbyes. I noticed Katrina was wearing a new necklace, a silver heart with diamonds inserted on its sides. Trent had given it to her as a going-away gift. Seconds later, Dirk entered the room, and we all fell silent as we faced him, expecting the usual. He stopped walking and glared at us.

"Ladies," he announced, tipping his hat before walking on his way.

We all laughed. It would seem underneath all that grumpiness there was a nice man with a sense of humor. Even Sergeant Ford congratulated us on the way in. After finding a place to sit the room quickly filled to capacity. While we waited for the announcements some people stood and began to slow dance in the center of the room. Katrina and Trent got up and invited Joi and I over to join them on the dance floor. There was a long list of things I could do but dancing sure wasn't one of them. Thank God it was a slow dance. I glanced at Trent as he held Katrina, and whatever he was doing looked right so I just tried my best to copy him, acting as if I were a professional. Wes knew I had no idea how to dance, and I eyed him laughing to himself from over my shoulder. Thankfully, the song soon finished and so did my robotic dancing skills. I walked with Joi back to the table and sat down.

Wes leaned over and whispered in my ear.

"That was painful to watch, man."

"Nobody asked for your opinion." I said.

Seconds later, Trent took Katrina over to the most popular table at the party, a long slender buffet littered with steaming seafood and all kinds of roasted meats drenched in their own juices. Trent and Katrina filled their plates.

"What do you want to drink?" Trent asked.

"Just water for now," she stared, watching him walk away with a twinkle in her eyes.

"Well, sweetheart," Zack said, walking over, "Ya enjoying yourself tonight?"

"Oh yes," she answered with a grin.

"So, where's your boy-toy run off to?" Katrina rolled her eyes.

"He's not my boy-toy. We're not some bimbo couple who don't have any respect for each other. Oh wait, that's not something a person like you would understand."

"Oh really. And what kind of person am I?"

"You're the kind of guy who sleeps with any girl he can trick into bed," Katrina presumed.

"Well, you're not wrong," Zack admitted.

"You're unbelievable," she stated.

"I agree," he said, smiling back.

"Forgive my curiosity, but how many women do you claim to have slept with? I'm sure the number is over a hundred?" she asked.

"Well, that depends, would you like to join me tonight and become the one hundred and first?"

"Gross." Katrina said, disgusted with his comment.

"Katrina, you should be honored. I only offer myself to the sexiest girls," Zack assured.

"You're a real romantic," she said sarcastically.

Zack smiled. "I do try."

"Well, not hard enough because it's still a no. Goodnight, Zack."

She walked back to our table, leaving him frozen in his ego.

Trent returned to where he had left Katrina and saw Zack stuffing his face with whatever food he could get a hold of.

"Where's Katrina?" he asked Zack.

Zack simply pointed in her direction. Trent and Zack wandered over seconds later and sat down with us while we waited. Zack wasn't the one who seemed to be looking for a good time though. Peter finally joined us and seemed to be more alert and energetic than usual. As we talked Peter never failed to twist normal things like food and meat into a dirty joke or reference to a sexual act. Eventually, he stood up and left after locking eyes with another man waving in his direction.

Finally, General Abner entered from a back door. He set up a microphone onto a temporary stage the cadets had built for the party. This was it, the moment I was dreading, the moment we would have to say goodbye to each other. I took a deep breath as the general switched on the microphone.

"Everyone, please take a seat, we're about to begin. Today is a beautiful day worth celebrating, and I'm so honored to have the privilege of congratulating these six brilliant soldiers who led this mission. Please stand and welcome to stage, Wes, Adam, Jim, Dirk, Katrina, and Trent, your Special Ops Armored Soldiers."

Everyone clapped as we got up from our table and walked on stage. It was almost funny because half of them didn't even know the real reason why we were being congratulated tonight. People like Joi, Peter, Zack, and everyone else who wasn't on the mission had no idea we had just taken out Oddball. They were all told we had gone and cleared out hostages in a Somalian-controlled bunker. Obviously, that's not what we did, and they would all find out eventually when the president broadcasts it on the news in about three months. The delay would give the military time to ensure our identities are safe from the public. For now, it was our little secret.

"Over the last five months," Abner said as he started his speech. "I've been watching the six of you train for this mission. In that time, I've seen you grow together as more than just a team. I can see you all have a love for each other like a family. I can't imagine how hard it will be to say goodbye. So, with that in mind, just ten minutes ago I spoke with three very big sponsors of the S.O.A.S. program. After hearing their proposal and with a great deal of debate, I have decided that if you six truly desire to stay here as a team, you may. Along with any other S.O.A.S. members who wants this as well."

Our mouths dropped as we were instantly overwhelmed with relief and unexplainable excitement. Katrina immediately jumped into Trent's arms, passionately kissing him. The rest of us looked at each other thrilled at the idea we didn't have to say goodbye. Even Dirk seemed pleased, and he turned to Wes.

"Well, looks like we're stuck together."

Wes stood over Dirk glaring down at him, "Fraid so." he said then warned, "Just watch your back, old man." The two then shook hands. General Abner chuckled.

"I'm going to take that as a yes. If any soldier chooses to leave you may do so with no questions asked, but you will be sworn to secrecy for what you've seen here. Oh, and one other thing. A cadet came up to me today with an appropriate name for you six. Hellbenders, because you're hell-bent on ending the war. It's a little corny, but I think it fits."

Then Katrina stepped over and asked for the microphone. Abner handed it over and Katrina smiled briefly as the room fell silent.

"I just wanted to say this mission has meant more to me than I've let on. I um… I know most people here have lost someone close to them. And that's true for me too. I lost my brother five years ago and I was not expecting to come here and find five more to make up for that lost time. So, I just wanted to say thank you guys and say this was all for you Ben."

Katrina handed the mic back to Abner as the tears fell from her eyes. Trent was the first to take her in his arms then one by one Wes, Adam and I wrapped around her. Dirk placed his hand on Katrina's shoulder. She glanced up at him seeing that he was standing off to the side. Katrina reached out, taking hold of his uniform as she pulled him into the final gap of our group. Once again, the crowd exploded in a grand eruption of cheering and applause. Standing before it, all I could think was, it's amazing how one's life could be changed so much just by opening a letter. As our hug came to an end Wes stepped over to me.

"I guess you were right, Jim. Things are starting to turn out alright." I stared out into the crowd and saw Joi smiling up at me.

"I guess they are."

Chapter 13- Test Tube

December 31st 2098 - Three years later...

It was New Year's Eve of 2098. Trent and I were on an explosive ordnance investigation mission in the heart of Mexico. For weeks now, a bomber with an unknown name has been terrorizing a town near a jungle region of the country. That's how the bomber remained so elusive, by retreating there after each attack. He would sneak into the low-security town, blow up what he wanted and then disappear into the jungle. The only flaw in his routine was just that; he had a routine.

About once a week, he would sneak into town and stock up on supplies like food and household ingredients to make explosives. No one really knew how he acquired these things except a handful of store clerks waking up and finding several key items missing from their shelves. The bomber's most common act of terrorism was to brew up a gallon bucket of homemade napalm. He would hide in an alleyway and wait for unsuspecting civilians to pass by, then hurl the burning jelly into their faces. This wasn't enough to kill most, but it was enough to permanently scar his victims for life.

Now the true reason Trent and I were stuck here searching for this man wasn't that the Mexican police couldn't handle it. It's because after we took out Oddball, there wasn't any major threat left in the world. Everyone seemed to handle their own problems and stay out of the way. The American government, however, still wanted to reinforce the necessity for Hellbenders after the threat of Oddball was eliminated. So, by sending us here, they were sending the message - we'll handle your problems as long as it still makes us look relevant. I didn't agree with it, but I did as I was told and followed my orders.

Our, now famous, operation to take out Oddball had become a marketing tool to encourage new enlisters. An unofficial slogan arose as the years went by. When a Hellbender's fight ends on Earth their war begins in Hell. It was even more cringe then the Hell-Bent one Abner used. But to the general public it was an enticing phrase used by edgy volunteers seeking to make a name for themselves. I hated it, and the fact that we were being used as a symbol of propaganda.

Trent and I were on the main street of the town. The road ended at a three-story building. Located on the top floor were two windows facing the center of the road. Trent was positioned at the left window with the best view of the street. An array of buildings ran down both sides of the road from where Trent was located. He set up his compact sniper rifle at the back end of the room. Strung up before him were several 10x10 black screen sheets, so it was easy for him to see outside, but hard for anyone to see in.

I, on the other hand, was not concealed by a building, but instead exposed on the open streets.

We had been in this town for about a week now, and this morning, we got word the bomb maker was spotted last night digging a hole in the center of the gravel road. Fearing that it was an IED, the Mexican police had the witness walk with me in search of it. He escorted me twenty yards down the evacuated street and led me in between two four-story buildings. There, the man held out his hand in front of me.

"Stop! Bomb in this area."

He moved his arm in a circle gesturing to an area about the size of an average living room. As he did, I marked the ground with powder. I spoke to him in Spanish, asking him to point where he saw the bomber dig. He shrugged at me, expressing his uncertainty, mainly because it had rained this morning and the downpour had covered up any trace of disturbed gravel the bomber may have left behind. I nodded and told him to run back to the safe area so I could get to work. He did so and I pulled out my handheld retractable metal detector. I inspected the target area before me and knew that this would take a while to find.

"So, Trent," I said, calling him over the comms. "Is this how you expected to spend your New Year's Eve?"

"No. I was planning on taking Katrina to the top of the mountain to watch fireworks from base," he said.

"Well, by the time we get back home, fireworks will be illegal!" I joked.

"Yeah." Trent chuckled in agreement.

While I was at base a few months ago, the new presidential administration led by Leslie Carter, a lesbian, outlawed all traditional firearms. I had gotten the news that the ATF searched my house and confiscated my parent's antique rifles. They were all replaced with the new smart guns that ran on batteries. The idea behind this was in the scenario of someone using a smart gun for illegal purposes, the government could hack into the gun and shut it off before any real damage could be done.

The military had also adopted these new guns. Personally, I absolutely hated them. I like things that I could rely on even if the batteries run out, and I also don't like the idea of someone behind a desk deciding for me whether or not to pull the trigger. Now the most recent rumor is that all U.S soldiers at home and on deployment will have to sport a rainbow flag patch over top of the American flag.

"Our new president is going to ruin the last few good things we have left in America, though I find it hard to imagine anything worse than the Civil Race Wars of the '80s," I stated.

"Katrina was saying that same thing the other day! What gets her the most is this new president's support of satanic teachings in schools. And I'm not superstitious or religious in any way, but even I know to stay away from that stuff," Trent replied.

"Well, Katrina believes in God," I remarked.

"Yeah, don't remind me. She tried to convert me a while back. It was cute that she tried but I told her it will never happen," Trent declared.

"Why do you say that?"

"Because God's not real. There's no science to back that up. The more we learn about the world, the more we can see God had nothing to do with it. And the simple fact of the matter is if I can't see it or touch it then why should I believe in it?" Trent stated.

"So, you're saying science can explain everything?"

"Not everything, not yet." he admitted.

"Well, all I know is the science theories are always being rewritten but the truth in God's word has always stayed the same. But you shouldn't just take my word for it, if you're looking for answers then you should read the Bible for yourself... and besides, Katrina agrees with me, so you're out numbered."

"So what?" Trent questioned.

"So as her squeeze, you should at least make an effort to learn about her beliefs. You got nothing to lose by giving her your ear." I suggested.

"Not if it means joining a cult," Trent mocked.

I laughed.

"Well, answer this then, how do you know you love Katrina?"

Trent was quiet for a moment, probably taken back by my strange question. Or maybe just pondering a thought he'd never rationalized before.

"Because I feel it." Trent answered.

"How does science explain that feeling?" I asked.

"Um, with chemicals in our brain?" Trent uttered, uncertain in his answer.

"Well, if that's true, and love is nothing more than chemicals then I guess love can exist and be measured in a test tube. But it can't, so, the fact that science can't quantify love is proof enough for me that it can't explain the important things."

"If science can't explain love, how does it make more sense that God made Leslie gay?" I fell quiet for a moment thinking how I should answer.

"It doesn't, if your assuming God wants her to be a lesbian, but He doesn't and He didn't make her to be. God says homosexuality is a sin but allows us all be born with a sinful nature. God doesn't make us sin; but He does make us into a new creation and become born again through belief and repentance. It's through Jesus' saving work in our lives to change us in ways we can't change ourselves, that we come to know His love, grace and mercy."

"You know you can just say you hate her; you don't have to give me a sermon." Trent dismissed.

I chuckled. "I don't hate her; I just hate everything she stands for."

"How did we go from banning fireworks to gay marriage?" Trent asked. I laughed.

144

"I guess that's just another one of life's endless mysteries. But speaking of marriage, last night before you went to bed, you left our room. And I noticed something peeking out of your bag. I didn't go through your stuff, but I could tell that what was inside was an engagement ring in a little fuzzy box. And I couldn't help but wonder how you were going to pop the big question to Katrina."

"Well, the thing is I already did... And she said no." Trent replied, reaching down and grasping her heart neckless he wore around his neck.

"What?"

"Yeah. She mentioned something about not being equally yoked. Whatever that means, I know it's some Bible thing."

"She meant that she can't marry someone who doesn't believe in God."

"Why does that matter?" Trent questioned, his tone was noticeably angrier. "After all the work I've put into proving that I love her, she still says no. I've never cheated or kept secrets. I love her more than any girl I've dated before. So, what does it matter if I don't believe in God?"

"Because marriage is a big deal. Katrina's not going to marry someone who she can't trust and rely on."

"What have I done to make her feel that way?"

"You don't believe, Trent. That's the only thing holding her back."

"But again, why should that matter?"

"Let me put it this way. Could you, as a sniper, trust your spotter to call out your shots if they covered their eyes with a blindfold?"

"No."

"Marriage is the same way. That's what it means to be unequally yoked. She believes and therefore sees the world for what it truly is, and you don't. She can't rely on you to call the shots. This isn't just about carrying the weight financially or physically. This is a spiritual partnership, and if you're not able to meet her at her level then you're dragging her down which is the opposite of love."

"Is this why you still haven't asked out Joi." Trent asked.

"Pretty much. I already made that mistake once and as bad as I want to, I can't and… Wait, I've got a hit."

I began detecting all around the target trying to see how big it is. The data appeared as a rough holographic rendering formed above the search coil. The object was about a foot long and it seemed more oval, like a really big pill. My first guess was it could be a mortar or an unexploded tank shell. The only problem with this theory is the bomber wouldn't have access to live military ordnance, but I've been wrong before. I started to dig with a small trowel attached to my belt. Gently scooping small trenches around the gravel before me brushing away the soil a little at a time.

I didn't want to dig too deep and accidentally ignite the bomb, so I set my trowel to the side and reached for my brush, lightly feathering away the somewhat loose dirt revealing the scalp of the ordnance. It was dark green and from what I could see, it had a studded metal shell encasing it. I knew the second I saw it that it was military-grade ordnance, but not any that I recognized from past experience. In this case, caution was a practice that could not be underemphasized. I brushed away more of the gravel revealing the now obviously rigged contraption.

Having uncovered the majority of the device, I quickly snapped a few pictures and then reached to my pouch for my explosives in order to detonate this bomb. Then a scratchy disturbance in my radio caused me to jump.

"Contact! Six o'clock!"

In one fluid motion, I spun around and took hold of the rifle strapped to my side. Facing the center of the street I aimed down my scope and saw the unexpected. A small boy dressed heavily in raggedy stained clothes stared at me through a ripped cloth slit around his eyes.

For a moment, he and I were fixed in silence just staring at one another. I switched to sonic ready to incapacitate him with a low frequency from the speaker under my barrel.

"Go back," I said in Spanish, gesturing to the building behind him, but he didn't go, he just stood still staring back at me. I lowered my gun and shook my head.

"Go back kid."

The boy remained motionless. Trent examined him through his scope, observing his body for anything suspicious. I stood up and nudged the kid's chest. He stumbled two steps back, then took three steps forward, nearly stepping on the I.E.D. I lunged down to stop him from getting any closer when suddenly Trent yelled.

"Jim, stop!" I froze in place; the boy's eyes zigzagged across my helmet.

"There's micro-fibers running out of his bottom right pant leg."

I leaned over and saw thin black wires trailing across the road and into an open door of the building behind him. I locked eyes with a man who stood with a gaping mouth. Wires as thin as hair spilled down from his split jaws leading across the road back to the boy. Glancing down at him I-

BANG!

I was thrown backward, smashing through a boarded window on the building behind me. The blast wave blew off the dust of the surrounding buildings before reaching the sediment encasing Trent's floor. Dust filled the streets, but Trent could still see the faint silhouette of a man sprinting out of the same building the boy had walked out of. He ran out the opposite end into a second street that paralleled the main road Trent had been aiming down.

Trent flipped off the pressure release on his rifle, retracting the barrel inward, converting it to a close-quarters rifle. The scope folded to the side popping up a pair of holographic sights. Trent stood, slinging his rifle over his back, and began sprinting toward the open window in front of him. Trent had a 1080 rig attached to his lower back, a rope mechanism that was designed to slow the rate at which someone falls. Before Trent leaped out the window, he hooked the steel carabiner (attached to the end of the rig) to a metal railing that framed the window. He slid down onto the roof of a smaller building beneath the one he was in and detached from the rig. Trent darted to the right edge of the roof and saw the assumed bomber frantically sprinting away. Trent radioed me.

"I have eyes on target, respond."

Through the thick dust and rubble, I faintly made out Trent's message, and I mustered out one word,

"Engage."

Trent cut the mic and bolted to his left, sprinting on top of a series of rooftops that paralleled the street. The bomber had a short head start, but Trent was gaining fast. The rooftops were cluttered and multilayered. Trent had to weave in between A.C. units, satellite dishes, and piles of junk as he leaped up and down the many levels of the building's sun-scorched roofs. Trent was the fastest runner in our squad, and he quickly caught up to the bomber, running parallel with him. He sped up ahead of the man, passing him by at least two buildings.

Suddenly his path was obstructed by a three-story drop off into an alley. Seeing the oncoming gap, Trent noticed a stairwell zigzagging down the other side. With his high momentum, he reached the edge of the building and jumped. His body flew fifteen feet, and he dropped one story down to the second-floor staircase on the adjacent building. He landed hard as the force brought him to his knees. His shoulder plate scraped paint off the wall next to him. From here, Trent could see a short way back down the road and noticed the bomber about to run out of view.

Before he lost sight of him, Trent got up and searched for a way to get back down to ground level. Other than jumping or taking forever on the stairs he decided to go inside through the door next to him. He rushed in and was greeted by a woman's scream as he ran past her and her husband hiding underneath a table. Trent ignored them as he hurried to their window. Below it was a white supply truck parked in front of a garage next door to an old bakery. Trent forced open the window and jumped out landing on the truck. He faced back down the road and swung his rifle into firing position. Trent aimed at the bomber and fired three rounds, one just clipping the man's ankle as he stumbled into a nearby alley.

Lowering his rifle Trent gazed toward the alley across from his position.

The thick dust from the explosion had begun to clear, I crawled out of the rubble surrounding me. The structures within the proximity of the explosion still appeared to be somewhat intact, but all of them had their windows and paint blown off. On the ground in the center of the street was a two-and-a-half foot-deep crater. Above it, dangling from the power lines, was the sparking child's dusty mutilated corpse. The blood dripped off his body before a narrow gap between two buildings in front of me. I stumbled over the now uneven, rocky ground and straight into the gap. Sparks flashed through the opening in the left wall. Glancing inside my eyes landed on the man with the gaping jaws. An android. The bomber must have sent him to trigger the boy and clear his getaway. Which means the

I.E.D. was just a distraction to draw us out. Turning away I stepped onto the second street that Trent was on.

A gust of wind blew the remainder of the dust cloud past me until I emerged on the other side. A quick flash lit up from out of an alley. Catching my attention, I began sprinting over to it. Just as I made it there, Trent stepped out from around the corner. I came to a stop as he just stood still for a moment and stared at me. He looked down and continued walking as he dragged something behind him. It was the bomber. He was dead. Trent dragged the body along with him by the collar of his jacket. Once he reached me, Trent dropped the man face down in the dirt.

"Ready to go home?" I smiled and nodded.

A short time later, the Mexican police called us over to their trucks where Trent and I loaded in the body. Taking off my helmet I glanced at the bomber lying in the truck. A small white piece of paper was peeking out of his pocket. Looking closer, I saw the edge of a black symbol printed on it. When no one was paying attention, I pulled out the paper. My eyes shot open. It was the same white card I had found beneath Oddball's compound three years ago. Just like that one, the number on the back was scratched off.

Then the sound of a small crowd began to form, and I stuffed the card into my pocket. At the center of the crowd, a woman was on her knees, sobbing. She was weeping into a bloody rag, and it suddenly dawned on me that the rag belonged to the boy who tried to blow me up. I assumed the woman was his mother. I wanted to say something to make her feel better, but I didn't know what to tell her. As I thought of what to say an old woman hobbled up to me and Trent.

"Thank you both. We can all sleep easy now the Americans saved the day."

"We're just happy to help," Trent expressed.

"Well, in that case, I'm sure you'd be happy to help rebuild our town as well," she said.

Clearly, she wasn't happy with us or what we had done, so I redirected the conversation.

"Who's that woman?"

I gestured to the girl crying on her knees. The old woman took a deep breath.

"That is the older sister of the boy you killed. He went missing three days ago. Thanks for finding him. As you can see, she appreciates your efforts here."

I was reminded of the little boy down in Oddball's compound I was unable to save as well.

"Glad we could help, Abuela," Trent said. "You have a happy new year."

"Safe trip," she announced as we left.

Later on, Trent and I packed up our stuff and drove about an hour out of town. As we went along, traffic brought us to a stop just before an overpass. Below the beams of the bridge Trent and I could see a man, woman and child hung by the neck as their naked bodies swayed by the passing cars overhead. Even though our mission was complete, we had made no difference here.

Trent leaned over and gestured up at them,

"Jim be honest. How can you look at that and say God is loving. If it sounds ridiculous to you for me to say that love can exist in a test tube, think about how ridiculous it sounds to me when you say God's love exists in all this?"

I gazed up at those bodies and said,

"Why does God allow violence?"

Trent nodded.

"Trent, the world is like this because of us. Humanity's disobedience. God first made a perfect world with no violence or death, but sin entered the world through one man and was passed down to all of us. If God just came down and whipped out every bad thing He saw, He would take you and me out too, because were also guilty of sin. It is a testament to God's great love and mercy that we even exist at all. God also uses tragedy and violence to reveal who you really are. Evil people glorify evil. The cowardly shy away. But those who know God is in control can stand in the middle of all this and be unafraid. So, maybe you should be asking yourself, what kind of person are you? Because whatever your answer is that was the man Katrina saw and said no to."

Trent was silent.

"If I'm being totally honest, Trent. I would say to forget about your relationship with Katrina and start your relationship with Jesus." Trent took a breath.

"I don't know where to start." he admitted in a low voice.

"I am more than willing to show you. You have to be willing to listen."

"Alright." he uttered.

Eventually we made it to the nearest airport. Now that our job was done, I was happy to say I didn't have to spend the New Year's stuck in Mexico. We boarded a Super Hawk that was waiting for us and began our flight home. While in flight I sat with Trent and opened my Bible to the New Testament. I flipped to the book of John, and we began reading. He had many more questions but after he actually read the words for himself his questions weren't so harsh. He sounded more curious than dismissive. And it was his newfound interest in the Word of God that brought a smile to my face, despite the horrors of our mission.

But even still something was scratching away at my mind. How did the bomber have the same white card as Oddball? Upon my arrival to base I rushed to my room and pulled out the card I had taken from Oddball's compound, comparing it with the one I had found on the bomber. They were identical! Who was handing out these cards? And why did it turn up now?

Chapter 14- Eyes of The Inferno

January 1st 2099

All was quiet along the grassy expanse of the southern wind turbine valley near the coast of northern Burma. The brown frosty grass crunched underneath the treads of four tanks. A party of forty American troops followed behind as they escorted two Super Stinger pilots to the U.S. airbase, now only a mile away. The brisk mountain air stung as it kissed the bare faces of the two pilots. Julia, the main pilot and Isaac, her co-pilot. She was accompanying him to train in an aircraft he had never flown before.

"About thirty more minutes!" yelled a man resting on top of a tank that crept forward on their left.

"Julia, let's say if I crash this plane, how much trouble do you think I will get in?"

"Isaac, you're only nineteen. I think because of your age they would take it a little easier on you," she assured.

"You really think so?" he asked.

"No," she replied bluntly, then added, "but in the scenario that you do screw this up, I would say your best option is to go down with the plane because your discharge from the military will not be pretty."

Isaac stared at her with concern.

"So, you're saying it's better to die than to get in trouble with the military?"

Julia shrugged her shoulders.

"More or less, but remember Isaac, if you die, there's nothing afterward. It's just absence and oblivion, the purest form of nothing there is. So, enjoy your life for what it is now- with all its ups and downs."

Squinting, Isaac turned his head at this.

"But hey, you've got nothing to worry about; you're a great pilot, and I'm willing to bet that in the next few hours you're going to have crowds of people clapping and cheering your name. You have a bright future ahead of you, Isaac."

Isaac grinned at her uplifting comment.

Minutes later, a thick pillar of black smoke began to form beyond a hill in the far distance. The party came to a halt as one man crawled out of his tank and leaned out the hatch. With a pair of digital binoculars, he examined the peculiar sight ahead and adjusted his zoom, bringing the picture into focus.

"Is that the airbase?" one man asked.

The soldier lowered his binoculars.

"Something's coming."

"Julia, what's going on?" Isaac asked.

"I don't know. It's probably nothing."

As she said this, three black indistinguishable silhouettes came rolling over the distant horizon. Tanks. They rode forward with clouds of black, ashy smoke to their backs. The mysterious vehicles slowly crept closer, but eventually stopped and just sat there, watching the American soldiers. From this distance, the dark silhouettes appeared like ordinary tanks except for two upward facing protrusions on the sides of its shell like a capital V.

"Do you think those are ours?" one man asked.

There was a flash from the center vehicle, and before they could blink, they heard a piercing whistle zipping over them. The round impacted a distant wind turbine behind them. Shock filled the men as the soldier at the top of the hatch yelled down inside.

"FIRE!"

The tank rocked back as a round blew out of the breach and snatched everyone's hearing along with it. The glowing streak made impact in the ground near the strange vehicles just a few feet off target.

"JULIA! WHAT'S HAPPENING?" Isaac yelled as he tightly grasped his ears.

"JUST STAY WITH ME AND YOU'LL BE FINE!"

She took his arm and began running with him out of the line of fire, heading toward the back of the closest tank.

"Stay here!" she ordered as she peeked around the corner of the tracks.

The tank next to her was lining up its shot when Julia snapped back at Isaac.

"Get underneath!" she shouted.

Suddenly, a hailstorm of five-foot-long rods rained down upon them, piercing the ground. Julia forced Isaac under the tank and quickly followed behind as the barrage continued. Seconds later, it stopped. Isaac rose from the frost and stared out from beneath. One of the rods was out there. It was as thick as a baseball bat with four drag flaps at the top, and in the center was a cylindrical cover. Isaac stared at it for a moment, then watched as the cover quickly slid down about a foot, revealing a series of holes, as well as a sudden and constant clicking. All at once, a yellow, odorless mist hissed out from them and accumulated on the ground as the clicking continued.

Isaac and Julia watched in silence as the rod let out a loud ding. Suddenly, the metal cylinder around the rod slid back up, casting down a glowing spray of sparks igniting the yellow gas to flame. The fire expanded across the ground, reaching like fingers underneath the tank. The two hid their faces and heard nothing but the desperate screams of the American soldiers being burned alive all around them. The icy grass had become black soggy ash, and the young Isaac, now terrified, began frantically crawling out from beneath the tank as the fire thinned out.

Julia grabbed his wrist and yelled, "STAY HERE!"

"FORGET THIS! I'M GETTING OUT OF HERE!" Isaac yelled back.

Julia tugged harder, trying to keep him from running out to his death. Isaac grabbed her hand trying to pry it off when suddenly he was blown back twenty feet as the tank was obliterated.

Stunned, but still miraculously alive, Isaac struggled to sit up. He stared at the twisted burning wreck and remembered that Julia was still under the tank. Isaac staggered to his feet and yelled out her name, but his attention was brought to the ground as he noticed something fall out of his lap. It was Julia's mangled arm. Horrified, Isaac turned away from the battle and ran. His heart sank as he saw four more ominous silhouettes of the mysterious vehicles coming from the opposite direction.

They quickly approached, and with no hope left, Isaac wept as he slowly walked backward into the bloody inferno. Due to the ever-present ringing in his ears Isaac couldn't even hear the many screams and pleas for help from his fellow soldiers. He stumbled over mutilated bodies and charred tank parts as he desperately searched for a place to hide.

The flash from a distant blast to his left threw his attention up only to see a nearby wind turbine being struck with a tank round. The turbine shaft shattered midway to the top and sent its rotating fan blades hurling to the ground in front of Isaac. The force of the impact knocked

Isaac on his face as the ground shook beneath him. As he hit the dirt, he screamed from a piercing pain throbbing in his right shoulder. A jagged metal spike of shrapnel protruded from under his collar bone. It must have been lodged there when the tank he was under exploded. Until now, he was in too much shock to notice.

Isaac picked himself up and tried to look beyond his fear and saw a second fallen turbine in the near distance. In this flat field, it was the only place to hide and wait out the slaughter. Isaac held his injured arm and began sprinting faster than he ever had in his life, but it felt like he was running in slow motion. The world seemed to blow up around him. Gasping in the cold air his lungs ached as his airways tightened. The remainder of the American troops ran around in senseless chaos as the enemy tanks slowly picked them off one by one. Isaac, just barely dodging the oncoming fire, finally made it to the downed turbine. He jumped inside, now watching through a rip in the outer shell of the metal exterior as he saw a continuous scene of unmerciful horror.

He looked on as the last two American tanks were obliterated. Suddenly, Isaac was hit by something from his left and saw more shrapnel protruding out of his left calf. Isaac was so deaf he couldn't hear his own scream from the pain. Glancing up he saw the sender of the jagged debris.

Fear filled him again as he witnessed another rod just feet from him that had been fired into the hull of the collapsed turbine. The cylinder slid down and the odorless yellow mist dispersed all around him. Isaac knew what came next. In desperation, he ran toward the nearest gap in the torn walls of the turbine shaft. He jumped through, stumbling to his feet as a fiery blast torched the crippled shell, leaving nothing but a burning rib cage of its interior steel support beams. Isaac rose at the crushing sound of an enemy tank tread slowly rolling past him.

With a clear view of the strange vehicles, he saw, stamped on the side, a solid white rectangle with a strange black symbol printed in the center.

Above that was the name K-10 Goliath, the two objects mounted on the top of the tank angled upward like a V now became clear as well. They were two giant ammo magazines that held the five-foot-long rods. The tank unloaded its mags, firing at more U.S. soldiers. Then the empty magazine shot out from the top of the tank, ringing like a bell as it flew over Isaac. It landed behind him, and Isaac realized it was his only chance. He quickly crawled to it and kicked in the ammo spring. It was very hot, nearly burning his skin through his clothes. He only pushed in the follower far enough for his body to fit inside, once in, he tried to push it back further, but the spring was too strong for him to overpower.

He laid there, staring out the opening trying to cover the entrance of the mag with the now blood-stained dirt. Moments later, a sudden blast from behind launched the tank magazine into the air with Isaac still inside. It landed some feet away falling right side up onto the rim of a crater. Isaac, now unconscious, rolled out of the mag and tumbled down into a puddle of shallow bloody water. Hours passed, day became night and at 6 AM, January 2nd, Isaac awoke from his mild concussion to the cold dark of morning.

The entire right side of his head was masked with a flaky layer of blood from his head injury. It was difficult for him to open his eyes. The icy frost held them shut. Then one by one they snapped open, blinking rapidly as they adjusted to the cold air. For a moment, Isaac just lay still, slowly coming in and out of consciousness, but eventually, his hunger became too overwhelming for sleep. He tried to move, but realized he was stuck. He opened his eyes fully and noticed his legs and upper right torso were submerged under a half-inch thick sheet of ice. The fingers on his right hand were protruding out of the ice about a foot in front of his face. He tried to move them, but nothing happened. Squinting, he tried again. Still, they would not move. This was strange because Isaac could feel and move his legs, but it seemed that all the nerves in his right arm had just shut down.

The puncture wound from the shrapnel damaged his flight suit causing its internal temperature gauge to malfunction in his right arm. Overnight, as the ice froze over the water, Isaac's arm had become too exposed to the cold and his hand had nearly frozen. A thin layer of frost coated the fabric of his glove. Once Isaac realized this, he stopped trying to move it, and he began breaking through the thin ice as he stood up. Some small sheets stuck onto his clothes and one big piece was still encasing his fingers.

Isaac smashed it on the frozen dirt wall beside him. He removed his glove and touched his now free hand and felt how stiff and cold it was. It was as if someone else's hand was attached to his body and the feeling wasn't his own. Isaac put his glove back on and peeked out of the crater gazing at the dark blueish world around him. The crater wasn't too deep, so Isaac easily crawled out and saw a sight that made him wish he had never woken up.

The once vast and grassy field had become a scorched black wasteland littered with the charred and frozen corpses of over forty Americans. The smell of burnt flesh was thick in the air. A cloud of dread loomed over him like the haze of a graveyard. He was the only survivor of the sudden attack and now in the middle of the horrific aftermath, he was left with no options and had no idea what to do next. The morning fog concealed the mountain bases in the distance. Isaac focused in on the sound of a flock of birds flying overhead.

They landed in a nearby forest to his left. His stomach growled once more, and the thought of catching food brought ease to his worried mind. Isaac tried again to curl his fingers but still had no feeling or movement in them. Again, his stomach growled, and Isaac knew he would have to find a gun to catch food, so he began limping around, scavenging for supplies.

The dismembered bodies were hard for him to look at. These were people that he had once shared conversation with. The frozen puddles ran thick with blood, and the foggy white and red color would, under different circumstances, seem beautiful in a way. Isaac searched around for a gun, one that still appeared functional, but everyone he saw had either a bent barrel or was empty.

Then a sudden blast to his right caught his gaze like a deer in the headlights. Isaac stood motionless as he watched two men in the far distance burning the American corpses with flamethrowers. These men were wearing identical black combat uniforms that Isaac had never seen before. He squinted as they knelt to the corpses and pulled out a strange spike from the heads of each body. He also noticed the end of the spike had a green light on it. Slowly Isaac crept backward wondering who these people were and why they had attacked.

As Isaac fixed his eyes on the two men, he didn't notice the stock of a rifle protruding out of the ground behind him. It caught his heel and sent him quickly to the ground. Isaac frantically sat up and locked eyes back on the distant men trying to see if they had noticed him. They didn't seem to, so Isaac reached forward grabbing the rifle. He rapidly wiggled it back and forth trying to free it from the icy ground. Once it came loose, he stood up and checked its condition. Chills shot up his spine as he saw a frozen arm still clinging onto the handle. The skin on it was scrunched up to the wrist like a sock and frozen in place. Bone and muscle were exposed under a coating of dirt and ice.

Another blast made Isaac's body jump as he glanced up again at the enemy soldiers. In fear and without thinking he dropped the gun and ran toward the nearby forest. Once at the edge of it, Isaac glanced back to see if he was being followed. He wasn't. Looking ahead he was brought to his knees as his heart stopped. Standing before him were two more men who had just stepped out of the forest.

The enemy had found him.

Chapter 15- Cades Cove

January 14th 2099

Sitting on the couch in our barracks I sat eating lunch when Trent came and sat beside me. He placed my Bible on the cushion between us and stated,

"Okay Jim, I've been reading, and I get what you're saying to some extent, but I've got another question."

"Alright." I said and quickly prayed in my mind for God to help me in this conversation.

"To put it bluntly, why should I even care? If God's real, then so what? Why should I care about some guy who lived over two thousand years ago. What has He ever done for me? Because so far, I can't think of a single time I ever really needed Him. I've always had myself, and I've gotten by just fine."

I thought for a moment then answered.

"So, you and I are what God defines as sinners. Meaning, in our broken, imperfect, state of being we have fallen utterly short of God's perfection and holiness. That means we have broken His law and have to pay the penalty. But there's good news." Trent chuckled.

"Wait so, if He's God why doesn't He just lower his standards of perfection." Trent interjected.

"Since He is God, we have to acknowledge His authority and conform to Him not Him to us. If our level of perfection was the standard by which we are saved, we'd all be doomed and Heaven would look as sinful as Earth. God takes sin very seriously and so must we. Since we are sinners and are guilty of sin, we are therefore incapable of entering Heaven by our own imperfect human effort. God says on our best day our good deeds are like filthy rags. So, where does that leave us then? If we don't deserve to be in Heaven, there's only one other place."

"Were going to continue our war in Hell." Trent joked.

I shook my head.

"On Judgment Day we will stand completely exposed before God, to whom we must give an account. Before Him we will have nothing to hide behind, nothing to barter with and no way to prove ourselves to be righteous. And I believe the most common thing spoken on that day will be, 'Please Lord just give me one more chance.' But there will be no more chances, by then the doorway of Grace has closed and without that our final destination is a one-way trip to Hell where we will experience complete separation from God. In Hell there will be weeping and gnashing teeth day and night without rest or hope of escape."

"Wait, I thought you said this was good news?" Trent asked.

"Here's the good part and it's from Him. Because God loves us and doesn't desire any of us to be in Hell, He offers us a way out. He came down in the form of a man and lived the perfect, sinless life we could not, and took the punishment on the cross you and I deserved. Jesus paid the price for the sins of your life, my life, even the lives of the very worst of us. 'He was pierced for our transgressions, He was crushed for our iniquities; the punishment that brought us peace was on Him, and by His wounds we are healed.' 'God made Him who had no sin to be sin for us, that in Him we might become the righteousness of God.'"

"Okay well; since He did all that for me, what should I be doing?" Trent asked.

"Repent." I answered. "Which means to turn away from sin and seek only after Jesus, trusting that He will forgive you. 'For God so loved the world, that He gave His only Son, that whoever believes in Him should not perish but have eternal life.' 'If we believe in our heart that God has raised Him from death, if we confess with our mouth that Jesus is Lord then we will be saved.'"

Trent was quiet for a moment thinking over what had been said.

"The truth is we need God more than we can even imagine. He did everything for us, while the devil is trying every day to make it seem like we can rely on ourselves as if we don't need God. And without God we have no hope in this life or the next."

"What if your wrong about all this and none of its real? And all you're actually doing is trying to scare me into adopting your beliefs." Trent asked.

"If you're afraid, it's because you have an expectation of punishment and your trust is not in the finished work of Jesus. I can't sugarcoat the severity of sin and water down the sacrifice Jesus made to save us from what we deserve. Because at the end of my life, if I'm wrong and all this is fake, then I've lost nothing. If you're wrong and what's written in this book is the truth, how could you ignore it and gamble with your place in eternity."

Once again, Trent was silent.

"Now the next thing you need to consider is, are you asking about this because you think by knowing about God it will get Katrina to like you more? Or are you doing this because you believe and trust in someone greater than yourself. This is a lot bigger than trying to impress a girl. This isn't some kind of after-death insurance plan which kicks in just in case God turns out to be real but, this

168

is assurance that when we die and stand before God, His promise to save us is certain."

"So, if questioning all this is nothing more than a mask you're trying to put on then know Katrina will see right through it and so will God. Trent, I love you guys and want you two to stay together, but Katrina is a one in a million girl. And if you say that you love her, either step up to become the man she can follow or step aside so she can go find him."

The next day, Trent walked to our room. Opening the door, he looked inside and saw Katrina there reading a book on her bed. Trent walked over and sat down next to Katrina; she closed her book.

"Are you hungry?" Trent asked and Katrina nodded.

"Well, today I was thinking we could eat somewhere off-base."

She peered at him suspiciously.

"Oooh, and will Abner have a problem with this?"

"I don't think he'll mind," Trent noted.

He had already gotten permission from General Abner to leave for the day because it was a special occasion.

Preparing to leave, Trent and Katrina changed into warmer clothes. They stepped into Trent's truck, drove down the Sinavo Highway next to the base, and headed through Pigeon Forge. As usual, they passed by many tourists in town on their way south into the Great Smoky Mountain National Forest.

Eventually, they pulled up to a park called Cades Cove. The sky was blue; the air was still and the world around them was taken over by a pale frost. In every direction, a thick layer of snow covered the vast landscape, and the best part was, there was no one in sight. A herd of deer shot up to see them drive past as they rode along the tree line onto the paved street that guided their way through the valley. They passed by old farmhouses and watermills. The leafless branches were coated with frosty snow that dumped on the road as the truck brushed under them. Soon, they arrived at a picnic table near an old log building.

Trent stopped the truck, and the two of them got out, grabbing the food. They walked to the table and wiped the snow off the seats before sitting down. Trent placed the thermal container on the table; he reached inside pulling out two toasted and still steamy sandwiches. He handed one to Katrina and sat his own on the table as he reached back in to grab a pair of sealed cups. Trent watched as Katrina bowed her head and prayed over her food. Smiling he closed his eyes and did the same.

As the two sat there they talked softly to each other while they ate. Once finished, they decided to take a walk through the snowy wilderness. They held hands and drank hot chocolate as they went along. There was an old trail that led up the mountain. After several minutes they came upon a cave. It was a low dropping hole that sat beneath a fifteen-foot-high rock face.

"Well, you first," Trent offered as the two of them faced it.

Katrina glared at him.

"You're so brave."

She stepped forward then stopped as something peculiar caught her eye on the stone surface.

"What's that?" she asked, pointing at an old carving engraved into the rock.

Trent glanced at it seeing the shape of a circle with a smaller circle inside it.

"Hmm. Caveman doorbell?"

Katrina laughed and shook her head.

"Let's keep going."

They proceeded inside. Ducking under the low ceiling they stood up in a larger room gazing at a wall of steel bars that blocked the way in.

"Well, that's disappointing," Katrina said.

There was no way to explore the chamber any further. Trent touched the thick steel as he peeked through them seeing only darkness.

"I have a question." Trent announced.

"Jesus was buried in a tomb, right?"

"Yes." Katrina said.

"And His tomb is empty, huh?"

"Yeah, unlike buddha or muhammad, Jesus rose again." Trent smiled at her as he pondered her words.

"Come on, let's go," he said.

Katrina squinted curiously as Trent led her out of the cave.

As they continued through the woods a sudden creak from above caught their gaze. A large clump of snow plummeted through branches and landed flat on Trent's face. Katrina laughed, and Trent wiped his eyes as a squirrel jumped from branch to branch causing more snow to fall throughout the woods.

"Oh, you think it's funny?" Trent said, smiling.

Katrina nodded, continuing to laugh before Trent did as well. He glared back up at the squirrel and a sudden thud to his side shot his gaze back at Katrina. She had thrown a snowball at him.

"What! You're on his side?" he said, pointing at the squirrel. She nodded.

"Oh, you're in trouble now!" Trent stated as he grabbed a handful of snow.

The two began hurling as much as they could at each other. Trent threw his faster and Katrina began running away from the incoming icy hail. Trent ran after her as she quickly darted behind a tree. He ran to it and turned the corner, but the second he did, she jumped out, tackling him onto the soft snowy ground. Trent pushed off the snow with his feet and rolled on top of her. She moved the hair out of her face and gazed into his eyes, he looked down into hers and kissed her.

The world fell silent around them, only the distant chirps of the birds could be heard in their solitary moment of happiness. For a while, the two of them just lay there underneath the sparkling frost covering the branches overhead. Katrina rolled over resting her head on his warm chest.

"I have another question." Trent said, as he gazed up at the sky. Katrina chuckled.

"I'm ready."

"What made you believe?"

Katrina remained silent and exhaled before speaking.

"Well, at first it was because of my parents. But I didn't truly start to believe until I hit rock bottom after my brother died. I relied on him for everything, and he was suddenly gone. I was at the end of my ropes asking God, why him? Why Ben? Why not someone else? It took me a few years to finally realize God took him away to spare him from the world we have to deal with. A world that loves evil and hates good. Also to show me I can't do all this myself. So, what made me believe was knowing God gave us a way out that the world couldn't and it was through His Son Jesus."

Trent lay quietly contemplating what she had disclosed. Then sitting up he said,

"Come on there's another spot I want to show you."

He helped her up, and walked back to the truck, they packed up what they had brought and left their lunch site. Trent drove a bit more down the edge of the valley until arriving at a clearing in the trees to their right. He stopped the truck for a brief moment and just sat in silence. Katrina turned to him thinking this was strange.

"We're here," he stated.

"Where?" she asked.

Trent winked and gestured for her to follow him out of the truck. She did and they walked together from under the trees onto a trail leading through the woods.

Eventually they reached a waterfall. It was covered in a draping skirt of white icicles. Katrina took two steps more and spun around to face him. Trent stopped and held out his phone. The two took a few pictures standing beside it.

"Thank you for taking me here, it's so beautiful." Katrina said as she flipped through the photos. A light breeze fluttered her hair, and Trent gazed at her red nose and rosy cheeks knowing in his heart this was the right choice.

"I have one last question."

"Why are you asking me so many questions?" Katrina smirked.

"Because you give me answers, the rest of the world gives me theories. And I don't want to keep guessing my way through life." Katrina smiled.

"What's the question?"

Trent reached into his pocket and pulled out the little fuzzy box with her engagement ring inside. As Katrina's gaze dropped upon it, she fell more still than the cold air around them.

"Will you marry me?"

Suddenly, the door to our room opened and I snapped to face it along with all our friends who sat in the room as well. Trent stepped inside. He glanced at us, and we saw the heartbroken look on his face. Then Katrina stepped in and slammed the door behind her. Trent closed his eyes, squinting tightly as she did this.

"Katrina, wait."

"No!" she yelled. "Just leave me alone," quickly walking over to her bed.

She grabbed some of her things and aggressively stuffed them into a bag. Then she walked past Trent and out the door, Trent followed her pleading.

"Wait!"

Joi shot me a look of shock. Even Dirk looked concerned, but no one jumped up faster than Zack who darted for the door. The rest followed and rushed after him. Once in the hall, we turned right only to see Trent and Katrina standing there smiling at us.

"What's going on?" I asked.

"Were engaged" Katrina proclaimed with a smile as she showed off the ring on her finger.

"Gotcha," Trent gloated.

As some laughed and others went after Trent for tricking them, I looked at Katrina as Dirk gave her the biggest hug and saw the look in her eye. Staring at Trent she gazed at him with a twinkle that wasn't there before.

"You guys are weird." Zack uttered.

"You'll understand one day." Trent put his arms around Katrina.

She giggled and kissed him. We all smiled too and congratulated them on their new engagement.

Chapter 16- Hunted

"Who are you?" Isaac asked, hesitantly staring up at the mysterious soldiers standing before him.

The closest looked to the man next to him then back to Isaac. He took a step closer.

"Well, who are you?" he asked back.

His voice was low and calm, his eyes locked onto Isaac's and his expression was still like the cold air around them.

"I... My name is Isaac. I'm an American," Isaac stuttered.

"Really? Well, in that case. We're the good guys," the man implied, barring a toothy smile.

"The what?" Isaac asked. The soldier looked back at the other.

"Get him."

Isaac's eyes widened. He stumbled backward as the second soldier charged toward him. Isaac rolled over, trying to stand and run, but as he set pressure on his right arm the throbbing pain from the shrapnel returned. A sudden kick to the ribs sent him rolling onto his back as he choked on the cold air. The soldier knelt down, plunging his knee onto Isaac's stomach as he repeatedly pounded Isaac's face into the frozen ground. Isaac grabbed the man's shoulder trying to make him stop, but a second kick to the ribs brought his arm down as the first soldier had now joined in.

Again and again, they struck Isaac's body, splitting and welting skin as the brutal beating continued. Isaac turned his head at the wrong second and his face was met with a boot to the nose. It immediately broke and began bleeding heavily.

"Enough. Help me pick him up. He should be alive when we burn him."

The two of them knelt down, grabbing the now bloody and motionless nineteen-year-old. They dragged him away from the tree line and back onto the charred battlefield. The sun was peeking over the distant mountains. The warm light touched Isaac's face. He was unable to open his swollen left eye. Isaac glanced up with his right to see its rays for what he assumed was the last time. The two men carried him over to a steep crater and tossed him inside.

Isaac rolled down, tumbling over dead bodies to the sheen icy floor beneath, his body slid across to the center. The cracking ice cooled his wounds. As the blood drained from his face, it slowly gathered from under his nose and mouth into a scarlet pool on the calm marbled-like surface. Isaac's heavy breathing rippled the thick warm blood. The sounds from one of the men igniting his flamethrower came up from behind while the other soldier pulled out a strange gun. Defeated and hopeless, Isaac peeled himself off the bloody frozen ice and rolled over to face his enemy and accept his fate. He moved his arms backward to support his back, but as he did, he grazed over something rough in the ice. Glancing down at his left hand he saw his way out.

Protruding halfway out of the ice was a Glock .45 handgun. Isaac, with what little life he had left, leaned over, and smashed his frozen right hand through the ice. The freed gun dropped several inches to the shallow floor beneath. Isaac fell through with it and the icy water engulfed his legs and hips. He grabbed the gun and aimed at the two soldiers quickly firing round after round at the men. But after the first five shots, he realized their body armor was too strong for the bullets to penetrate. He took a second to settle down as the men stumbled back, flinching from the sudden impacts. Isaac sighted in on their heads and with a pull of the trigger, he blew their lives away.

Once again, Isaac's hearing was gone, but he didn't care, he was too relieved to be afraid now. As quickly as he could, Isaac crawled up toward the rim of the crater and stood over the soldiers' bodies. One of them was still alive and bleeding heavily out of his mouth as he stared fearfully up at Isaac, struggling to breathe. Isaac saw the man had another gun strapped to his boot. Quickly, he tried to move his frozen hand, happy to see he now could, even if the movement was slow.

With no time to lose, Isaac tried to take off the man's gun. In his panic, he couldn't figure out how to free it from the holster, so he untied the boot and took the whole thing. Isaac examined the second man. He was dead, so Isaac grabbed his knife and sat the first soldier up to take off his armored vest, but then the man did something that sent chills down Isaac's spine. The soldier began laughing, a sinister gurgling croak. Fear and anger returned as Isaac tore off his bloodstained vest.

"What's so funny?"

In response, the soldier pointed his shaking arm straight out in front of him. Isaac rose back. The first two men he had seen burning bodies when he had woken up were running toward him. They must have heard the gunshots. Isaac tucked the boot under his left arm and grabbed the Glock with the other. He dropped the dying

179

man on his back and fired at the new attackers, using up the remaining rounds from the Glock. As he fired back, he could tell that one of them was a woman by her pinned up hair.

They ducked behind cover giving Isaac a few seconds of precious time as he dropped the now empty gun and began running toward the forest. The two soldiers quickly got up and ran to their doomed comrades. Coming to a stop they checked the two of them. The soldier that was still alive coughed up more blood as he pointed upward behind him in Isaac's direction. The man's brows lowered at the soldier and then flared up at Isaac running in the distance. They knew the soldier was done for, so together they gave him a quick nod followed by a spike to the head from one of their strange rifles. The end of the spike glowed green, and the soldier knelt saying to his fallen comrade.

"Sweet dreams."

The two soldiers peered up at the forest and began their pursuit. Isaac stumbled and tripped several times as he desperately tried to escape the devils hunting him. He flinched only to have a whistling bullet clip his ear as he tried to get a look at their position, one soldier stopped the other.

"Don't shoot his head."

Isaac continued running faster as he tried to put on the armored vest he had stolen. He managed to get it around his left arm but realized he wouldn't be able to slip his injured right arm through due to the spike of shrapnel still protruding from his shoulder.

As Isaac ran, he bit down on the collar of his flight suit and pulled open the tear in the fabric made by the shrapnel in his shoulder. He moved the boot under his right arm, wrapped his left hand around the crooked metal spike, and gnawed harder onto his collar. He tried for a moment to pull it out, but the pain was too immense. He glanced back at the soldiers seeing how far ahead of them he was. With a fare gap between them he took the opportunity to stop and grab the shrapnel with both hands. He groaned and yelled into his collar as he slowly pried it out. Small chunks of torn skin and muscle came with it as blood gushed out of the now open puncture wound.

Isaac threw down the jagged spike and glanced back again at the two soldiers. He only had a few seconds left before they got too close. Isaac dropped to the ground and frantically cut his shoelaces with the knife and tossed off the boot. He pulled off his sock, scrunched it up, grabbed a handful of dirt, and packed it into his wound. Then he pressed the sock against it and held it there as he slipped his right arm into the vest. Sliding on the new boot he tried once again to detach the small handgun but still couldn't figure out how to pull it free. Again, Isaac took note of the soldiers and saw they had gotten too close for his comfort, about thirty feet away.

Jumping to his feet Isaac continued running away from them as they fired at his back, ricocheting the rounds off the armored vest. As they ran, they soon began rising higher in elevation. After about five minutes of constant chasing, Isaac found himself staring at a vast rock bed before a steep cliff. It was in a U shape and there was no way around it. Isaac had just cornered himself. He couldn't go back, and he couldn't hide. All he could do was sit down and wait to die or try his best to climb up the hundred and fifty-foot rocky cliff.

Isaac checked back at the soldiers running toward him from inside the distant forest. For a brief moment, Isaac closed his eyes and thought of all the slow and painful ways in which the soldiers would torture him. He peered up the bluff ahead and thought death by falling was probably better than whatever these people would do to him. Isaac began running again, trying not to trip over the massive boulders framing the base of the cliff. Isaac's blood dripped onto the rocks as he jumped across them.

The soldiers stepped out of the forest and saw Isaac reach the base.

"Wait, stop! I've got an idea," the woman announced.

Isaac put his foot on the wall and brought his hands up to a groove above him. He pulled himself up and began his way to the top. The soldiers stopped and watched as Isaac rose higher and higher up the wall. Almost halfway up, Isaac began to get tired. He was hungry, injured, and all he wanted was to go home. The soldiers took their time as they climbed over the large boulders on their way to the cliff. Once there, they stood on top of two large rocks as they sprayed the base under Isaac with their flamethrowers. The fuel kept the flames burning and the woman set down her weapon and picked up rocks. They looked up at Isaac.

"When he falls, make sure you have the gun ready."

The woman nodded and began to throw their rocks at him in an attempt to make him fall into the flames below. Isaac's legs shook as they struggled to support his own body weight. He reached to the left trying to get to an easier section to climb.

BANG!

A bullet smacked the surface just inches away from Isaac's hand.

"Not that way!" the man shouted as he lowered his gun. The soldiers laughed. Isaac examined a two-foot-wide ledge just above his head. It was approximately at the halfway point up the cliff. If Isaac could reach it, he would be able to sit and rest for a moment. He reached up grabbing onto the ledge just as a rock struck the back of his head. His mind rang and a white flash blew across his eyes. Isaac knew this couldn't be good for his vision, but he didn't care; he just wanted to get up to the ledge and rest. He wrung the strength from his body as he used what little was left to push himself up and onto the narrow gap. Isaac scooted himself around and dangled his exhausted legs off the side where he gazed down at the two soldiers who gazed back at him.

"There's nowhere to run to now. You're stuck!"

Isaac surveyed a potential route toward the top of the cliff. He still had a long way to go.

"Why don't you just shoot me!" Isaac yelled.

"Why waste the ammo, you're just going to fall!"

"And what if I don't? Isaac asked.

"We'll wait and shoot you then!" the women yelled back.

Isaac thought for a moment.

"Fine! But since you have guns, if I make it to the top, you give me a one-minute head start, then you can shoot me!"

The two laughed and nodded in agreement, it was clear Isaac would never reach the top and they wanted to watch him fall to his death. The soldiers sat down on the big rocks and gestured for Isaac to resume climbing.

"You'll never make it kid. You can't do this!" the woman shouted.

"Watch me." Isaac whispered.

He bit down on his teeth and squinted at the sun. It was higher in the sky and beginning to melt the frost covering the rocks. This would make climbing the rest of the way a lot harder. Isaac looked to his left and saw two small icicles hanging. He broke one off and began sucking on it for water. Once ready Isaac stood up and faced the cliff. His legs were still tired, but what little energy he had gained back would have to do.

The fire below Isaac died down and the cold air slowly engulfed him again. Facing back up to the peak of the cliff Isaac began to do the best he could to proceed upward. The rocks were wet and cold, but Isaac was a good climber and knew to always keep three points of contact. He clung to the wall knowing that every inch he gained in height was another inch he gained in distance between him and his enemies.

The soldiers watched in anticipation, waiting for Isaac to make one wrong move and plummet to his death. Though as Isaac came closer to the top, the two soldiers grew nervous. Isaac's legs had begun to shake again. Above him was an overhang stretching two feet over his head.

"Here it comes, he'll never be able to climb over that."

Isaac positioned himself so that his head was just under the overhang. He took a deep breath. If he made even the slightest mistake, then it would be game over and his life after death would be nothing more than a black silent absence, void of everything he had come to know. This thought filled him with fear and gave him an intense drive to succeed. Isaac grabbed the cracks underneath the ledge with his left hand. He kicked off the wall as he reached his right hand over the ledge

and slapped it down on the top of the cliff. He brought his left arm up and as his face turned red, he pushed himself over the overhang. His legs dangled and the two soldiers stood up in shock that Isaac had reached the top.

"He's gonna make it," the woman said.

"No, he won't," the man stated, grabbing his gun and shooting at Isaac.

A bullet struck Isaac's back right calf. He dropped down to his elbows, and spit flew out of his mouth as he tried to hold himself up. With his fingers clawing into the ground, he grabbed the dirt ahead of him and pulled himself forward utilizing the last ounce of his pulsing adrenaline until he was finally lying face down on the top of the cliff. Isaac, exhausted and out of breath, had made it. He quickly crawled toward the trees in front of him and laughed to himself as he heard the two soldiers yelling from below him.

All Isaac wanted was to rest, but the smart thing to do was to get as far away from these people as possible. Standing up he stumbled into the woods. Isaac limped on and walked until the sun was high in the sky. Hours passed and Isaac, still with a smile on his face, found a large patch of moss to lay in as the sun warmed his body. He laid there and soon fell asleep; receiving a long-awaited rest, but his horrors had not yet reached an end.

When he awoke, he stared up at the sky and saw the faint twinkle of the stars forming across it. It was nearly dark. Isaac was once again awoken by his growling stomach. Standing up he almost immediately fell back down as he became dizzy from tunnel vision. He had lost a lot of blood and had no nutrients in almost two days. Isaac took a second to get his bearings and began walking. Not long after, the pain from his frozen hand became unbearable. Though he could now move it, it had become a burden in a whole new way. Isaac knew he had to warm it back up but had no means to make a fire. Nor would he risk lighting one in fear of the attention it would draw.

Isaac unzipped his jacket and removed his glove, stuffing his hand under his armpit allowing his body heat to warm his fingers. Soon it was completely dark, and Isaac's natural night vision was fully adjusted to the world around him. He kept an eye out for anything to eat but saw nothing.

Suddenly, a bright flash to his left caught his attention. He dropped to his knees and witnessed a sight that made him want to lay down and cry; the two soldiers were back and searching the forest for him. Isaac didn't want to move, but they were walking in his direction. They were still a good distance away but since all the animals were still hibernating, Isaac would be the only thing making noise in the woods.

Isaac stood up and slowly walked backward as they got closer, but trying to move silently in the woods was impossible. Everything made noise when touched. The frost crunched underneath his feet and the dead leaves and sticks cracked and snapped. Isaac stared at their flashlights which quickly took away his night vision. Turning away from them Isaac tried to walk forward but now couldn't see the woods around him. It was complete darkness.

Isaac stumbled, making more noise. The soldiers heard this and walked faster in Isaac's direction. Isaac held his arms in front of him so he wouldn't run into anything he couldn't see, but the icicles hanging from a low branch caught his head and snapped off causing the branch to vibrate and drop all its snow. This created a loud thud and Isaac immediately froze in place. He slowly turned around and saw the two flashlights aimed right at his face, Isaac's eyes widened.

"There you are! Shoot him!"

Bolting further into the woods, he frantically sprinted away from the soldiers. They cursed and yelled at him as they ran, but because Isaac had rested earlier, he was able to quickly sprint ahead of them. At least for a while. Soon Isaac got lightheaded and faint from his blood loss. He leaned on a tree and looked around for a place to hide but saw nothing. Isaac took two steps forward and fell on his face from exhaustion. Rising from the dirt he saw the gaping mouth of a hollow log in front of him.

Isaac crawled inside and laid on his back. Listening close as the two soldiers ran through the woods looking for him. They cursed and shot off their weapons into the forest, but Isaac remained still hoping they wouldn't find him. While they searched, Isaac grabbed his nose and struggled against the pain as he snapped it back in place from when it had broken earlier.

Soon, the soldiers did as Isaac hoped and moved on. Isaac was tense as a stone deep within the log for the next hour, listening intently to every sound the forest made in fear that it could be the soldiers. Eventually, his tense body fell limp as his tired eyes began to pull him into sleep, but just before dreams of a better place could overtake his mind, Isaac snapped alert again as he heard the soldiers walking back to his position. They both then sat down on the log Isaac was hiding in and began dumping wood they had collected into a pile. Isaac watched through a thin crack in the log as one soldier used his flamethrower to ignite the pile of wood into a fire. The two soldiers sat together.

"We'll continue our search in the morning."

There was just silence for a moment and Isaac listened close.

"Do you think we'll recognize each other after we change?" the woman asked.

"How could I forget you?" he assured.

She slowly slid her boot over to touch his.

"I'm still cold."

Isaac heard the wood above him creak as the man leaned over.

"Well, come here and get warmed up."

Isaac thought this was a strange thing for him to say since they had a fire right next to them, but then he heard kissing and soon after, the two quickly undressed. The

189

part of the log above Isaac's face began cracking as the man and woman became more intimate with each other. Isaac held up his hands trying to give the log more support so it wouldn't break and reveal his position. Again, Isaac reached for his boot to grab the small gun, knowing this was probably the best chance he would get to kill these people. He lifted his leg feeling for the gun, but the interior of the log was too narrow for him to grasp it. Isaac pressed his face up to the top of the log and reached down to his ankle as he lifted his leg. Grabbing hold of the gun Isaac messed around with the straps trying to free it from the holster.

He felt a metal latch on the side and touched two buttons. Pressing them both the latch slid upward on the holster but still, the gun wasn't free. The wooden cracks touching Isaac's cheeks grew wider and Isaac continued to mess with the latch, now desperate to get it free. He began shaking it inside its holster and as he did this his hand unintentionally nudged the latch and twisted it to the side releasing the clips and freeing the gun. Isaac fell backward and held the gun over his face.

With zero hesitation, he pressed the barrel to the wood over him and screamed as he blasted the entire magazine into the naked soldiers above.

Chapter 17- The Wedding

February 14th 2099 - Valentine's Day

The doorbell rang and I jumped to my feet. The time had come to begin preparations. I could hear voices as I passed the stone fireplace. Reaching the large door, I took a moment to swing it open. My eyes widened as I looked across the faces of about fifty men and women standing at the front door of my hillside mansion.

"We're ready," a man said.

"Great, let's get started."

It felt like yesterday that Trent asked Katrina to marry him, and now only a month later we would all be gathering at my house to see it through. General Abner, who still was very appreciative of our services in taking out Oddball, generously paid for the entire thing. He called in for a large team of wedding planners to set up everything around my house that was needed for the day. It was 7 AM and by 12:30, they were finished and out of sight before the first guests arrived.

An enormous ornate tent was erected to the left of my house near the woods. As the first guests arrived, they parked near it in my front yard. I stepped out to meet them and soon my property was populated with people from Trent and Katrina's families. Trent was one of the first people to show up. It was my job as the Best Man to keep him away from Katrina until the ceremony. Katrina was taken into an upstairs room in my house to get ready. I took Trent downstairs to a party room with a large wall screen TV and a small bar in the back. He and I sat below the screen in the first row.

"So, ya nervous?" I asked.

"Ya know, I thought I would be, but now that I'm here, I don't have any cold feet; in fact, I can't wait to call Katrina my wife."

"I'm glad to hear that."

Trent grinned as he looked away, and at that moment, I received a message from Wes on my phone. I glanced down at the screen.

Jim, come outside. Katrina's friend Meghan is looking for you.

I got up and told Trent that I would be right back. Leaving Trent with his thoughts I made my way outside. Once there I took view of the massive tent where the majority of the guests were already seated and indulging in conversation. Small children ran past me as I locked on to Wes. He stood inside the tent talking to Meghan. I stepped over to them and at first sight of me Meghan immediately took my arm.

"There you are. Katrina's been asking for you."

"Why?" I asked.

"I don't know. She wouldn't tell me, come on," Meghan demanded.

I left with her as she took me back into my house and up the stairs, we rounded the corner and proceeded down the hall. I noticed faint voices as Meghan led me to the room at the end. We stopped at the door and Meghan opened it for me; I stepped inside and smiled as I looked upon Katrina's face. She was all dressed up wearing a long, white gown that was draped across the floor. She twisted in her dress smiling at me and asked for everyone to leave the room for a moment. Meghan shut the door after everyone had left.

"Hi, Jim."

"Wow. Trent's going to lose his mind when he sees you." I noted.

She laughed. "Is he nervous?"

"No, he sounds excited," I said.

"Good I am too." she stated. "I um…" Katrina paused searching for the right words.

"Ya know, not that long ago I was going to leave him. The longer I dated him the more I knew I shouldn't have been. He was so stubborn, and hardheaded, especially when it came to God, but now I see all these changes in him. So, when Trent told me you were telling him about God… I just wanted to say I really appreciate that."

"I just told him the truth. God did all the real work." I admitted. Katrina nodded.

"Jim, you're one of the best friends I've ever had, and I'm so grateful God put you in my life."

Then she walked up and hugged me unable to hold back her tears of joy.

"Great," she said, stepping back. "Now I have to fix my makeup. Thanks, Jim."

I laughed.

"Oh, before you go, I want you to tell Zack to stop flirting with my cousins."

"I'll make sure he gets the message."

I left the room and made my way back down to where I left Trent. I found Wes and Zack down there with him and soon we were accompanied by Adam and his new girlfriend. Her name was Amy, and it was very clear Adam was head over heels for her. She was nice, and she spent the next few hours with us as we kept Trent busy. We laughed, told stories and as the day rolled by, soon it came time for the main event.

Trent's dad came into the room and said it was time to start. Exiting my house, we headed toward the wooden walkway that led over a small stream. The boardwalk crept down the nearby rock face at the back of my house. At the top of the stairs leading downward was a wooden arch. Seven arches led down to the lowest platform at the end of the boardwalk. Each arch had ribbons wrapped around both pillars and at the top was a complex assortment of branches with flowers growing on them.

I walked with Joi and the dozens of other guests down to the lowest platform. Once at the bottom, Joi found a seat and I stood beside Trent at the altar. Wes and some of Trent's family members were the groomsmen. Meghan was the Maid of Honor and standing beside her were all the bridesmaids. We all wore identical suits for the men and dresses for the women and in my pocket was Katrina's wedding ring. Everyone soon filed in, and Katrina's family sat to the right and Trent's to the left.

Even Sergeant Ford was here to congratulate them. Dirk held hands with his wife and the two of them sat with Adam, Amy, Zack, and Peter.

Standing beside Trent was Katrina's dad. Being the pastor of her church, he stood with a Bible ready to perform the marriage. He stepped forward and invited everyone to stand. It was 7 PM and as the sun began to set above the distant mountains behind us, all our eyes simultaneously gazed up to the ridge above. Then, slowly appearing underneath the first arch was Katrina and two children, her niece and nephew. She held a bouquet of flowers gazing down at us.

All the women gasped as they saw how beautiful she was. Music began to play, and Katrina slowly took her first steps down the stairs. I glanced over at Trent, and his

194

eyes were completely locked onto her. As she descended, her eyes were just as equally fixed onto his. People among the crowd were commenting on her immaculate beauty and as she stepped onto our platform her white teeth could be seen through the veil as she smiled at Trent. She walked up to him and stood at his side, Trent now seeing she was wearing the silver heart necklace he had given her years ago.

"Hey," she said,

"Hey," he said back.

We all laughed, and Meghan took her bouquet. Trent held Katrina's hands out in front of him and Katrina's father began.

"We have gathered in the presence of this company to witness the union of Trent Brian Rogers and Katrina Harmon Mires in marriage. We begin the ceremony with prayer. Dear Heavenly Father, we thank You for Your grace, mercy, and love that makes this joyous occasion possible. Most of all we ask for a special blessing for Trent and Katrina as they enter into marriage, may their life together and their love for each other become a true reflection of Your perfect love for each of us. In the name of Jesus, we pray amen."

The crowd said amen, and Katrina's dad continued.

"In the beginning, God created the heavens and the earth, on day six of creation He made beings in His own image. They were not only made to reflect his image, but they were in His image. So, God created man in His own image and the image of God created him; male and female He created them. Genesis 1:27."

"Man was not complete when he was alone, so God created the perfect complement for the male, the female. Together, they were both to be companions for life and collaborators in fulfilling the creation mandate of God. Be fruitful and multiply and fill the earth and subdue it, rule over the fish of the sea and the birds of the air and over every living creature that moves upon the earth. In the time of man's innocence, God instituted the state of matrimony between the first man and woman. He designed and intended marriage to be between one man and one woman."

Hearring this Peter rolled his eyes and checked his watch.

"Marriage is very serious; God does not treat it carelessly and neither should we. It is not to be entered into lightly or half-heartedly. He desired our marriages to be successful, fulfilling, and to endure. Haven't you read the scriptures? Jesus replied, they reported that from the beginning God made them male and female. He said this explains why a man leaves his father and mother and is joined to his wife and the two are united as one. Since they are no longer two but one, let no one separate what God has joined together. Matthew 19:4-6."

"In order for a marriage to last, it must be built on a solid foundation. Love is a very strong foundation. It can withstand even the most difficult trials. Love is patient and kind, love is not jealous or boastful or proud, or rude. Love does not demand its own way. Love is not irritable and it keeps no record of when it is wronged. It is never glad about injustice, but rejoices when truth wins out. Love never gives up, love never loses faith, is always hopeful, and endures through every circumstance. First Corinthians 13:4-7."

"This kind of perfect love comes from God Himself. For anyone to be able to share this true love with their spouse, we must first possess it for ourselves. Dear friends, let us continue to love one another. For love comes from God. Anyone who loves God is born of him and knows him, but anyone who does not love does not know God for God is love. 1 John 4:7-8."

"These verses give wise counsel to all those who want to spend the rest of their lives being in love with their spouse. When we put God first in our lives and in our marriages, we will be truly fulfilled in every way. God does not disappoint; He also does not leave us without instructions on how to achieve true satisfaction in our relationship with one another. The apostle Paul describes some very clear ways on how to achieve true satisfaction. He devotes twice as many words to advise the husband as he does the wives. He starts with the wives first.

"Wives, submit yourselves unto your own husbands as unto the Lord. For the husband is the head of the wife even as Christ is head of the church and He is the savior of the body therefore as the church is subject unto Christ so let the wife be in everything."

"Alright, husbands, here's our part," Katrina's dad said as he squinted at Trent.

"Husbands, love your wives even as Christ also loved the church, and gave Himself for it; that He might sanctify and cleanse it with the washing of the water by the word. That He might present it to Himself a glorious church, having no spot, or wrinkle, or any such thing; but that it should be holy and without blemish. So ought men to love their wives as their own bodies. He that loves his wife, loves himself, for no man ever yet hated his own flesh but nourishes it and cherishes it even as the Lord did the church. For we are members of His body, of His flesh, and of His bones. For this cause shall a man leave his father and mother and shall be joined to his wife and they two shall be one flesh. This is a great mystery, but I speak concerning Christ and the church. Nevertheless, let every one of you in particular so love his wife even as himself and the wife see that she respects the husband, Ephesians 5:22-33."

"So, you see, marriage is far more than a simple union between a man and a woman. God also uses it as a secret symbol for the true love He has for us. God's greatest demonstration of that love is shown in the sacrifice of His only son Jesus who died on the cross to pay for our sins so that we will receive eternal life."

Katrina's father took a deep breath.

"Now, Trent and Katrina will exchange their vows they have made to each other."

He gestured for Trent to start first. By now the sun was low and the orange light was touching their faces.

Trent pulled out a card, and tears filled his eyes as he read.

"To my best friend and to whom I owe my love. I promise to live every day happy only in your arms. I know if ever a day were to come where I…"

Trent paused for a moment trying to hold back the tears. He then wiped his eyes and continued,

"If ever a day were to come where I was to stumble, I know you'll be there for me just as I will be there for you. Katrina, for you I would sacrifice everything, because nothing this world can give me, is worth more than my life with you."

Tears filled Katrina's eyes and her father gestured for her to say her vows.

"Trent, we've been together for three years now and from the first day I saw you, I knew through our ups and downs we would ultimately share something special together. I promise to look at you every day with the love I will feel for no other. I will stand beside you through all your hurts and missteps, and not a day will go by that I will have regretted this decision."

Katrina's face rose. "I love you, Trent."

"Do we have the rings?"

I stepped to the side facing both of them and handed Trent Katrina's ring. Meghan stepped over and gave Katrina Trent's ring. They both smiled as they held the rings in their hands. They placed them on each other's fingers and Katrina's dad faced Trent.

"Trent, do you take this woman to be your wife in holy matrimony? To love her, to honor her, to comfort her, and to keep her in sickness and in health, forsaking all others for as long as you both shall live?"

"I do," he said.

"Katrina, do you take this man to be your husband in holy matrimony? To love him, to honor him, to comfort him, and to keep him in sickness and in health, forsaking all others for as long as you both shall live?"

"I do," she said.

"Now, by the power vested in me, I pronounce you husband and wife. You may kiss the bride."

They leaned forward and kissed; holding each other more lovingly than I had ever seen them do so before.

"I now present to you Mr. and Mrs. Rogers."

I, including the entire crowd, clapped and cheered for them. Then Trent and Katrina turned and held each other as they smiled back at everyone. The sun dropped behind the distant horizon and as night fell, we all followed behind the newlyweds and headed back up to the tent. An array of glistening lights strung up on the canopy above lit our way. Twenty round tables draped with white cloth filled the inside of the tent. To the left was a massive buffet which is where Zack spent most of his time. At the front of the tent was a long table with white cloth and green ribbons draped up and down its front side. This is where the bride and groom sat alongside the best man, bridesmaids, and groomsmen.

Music played all around us, and the time had finally come for me to do my big part. I stood up, tapping my hand on a microphone, gazing across the crowd. I now had their full attention. As everyone went silent, I turned to Trent and Katrina, speaking into the mic.

"Three years ago, I was sitting inside my house just about thirty feet away, and at that time I was truly regretting the idea of returning to Skymont Air Force Base. But as I stand before the two of you now, I realize just what a blessing it was to go back and meet you all. Trent, Katrina, you both are two of my best friends, and I can't imagine a life where I would be happy without you in it. I can only hope the impact you've had on me will be the same for everyone you meet. May your life together and your love for each other be a true example of what this world desperately needs more of."

I held my cup to them, and the crowd once again clapped and cheered. Soon, after a series of other speeches and funny stories, everyone received their food and had a great time. Nothing negative was spoken or even brought up, that is until Wes strolled over to me. He pulled up a chair and held out his phone.

"Jim, you should read this, it's from BNC."

I took the phone from Wes and read the article opened up on screen.

"Hellbender spotted killing children in Mexico!" I looked up at Wes.

"Are you serious?"

I continued reading.

"Jim Phillips, one of six white-skinned Hellbenders was spotted crossing over national borders in one of Mexico's most peaceful towns. The Hellbender is known for his old-world Christian beliefs and explosive ordnance disposal skills. Though on this particular outing those "skills" seem to have been left at home. For when the Hellbender was placed before a young boy rigged to blow, Jim Phillips did little to disarm the device. Eyewitnesses say the Hellbender stood and watched as the boy begged for his life, hoping in vain as his final seconds ticked by. It is up for debate whether the Hellbender allowed the boy to parish based on a lack of the necessary qualifications or racial religious discrimination!"

"Are you kidding me?" I said, glancing at Wes.

"Keep reading, it gets better."

I continued on.

"This latest offense calls into question the necessities for the Hellbenders in a post war era. Terrorism has seen a rapid decline since the death of Oddball in 2096. But the rise of white injustice and perceived superiority has been increasing, and it would seem the white Hellbenders of America are no exception to this hateful delusion."

I handed the phone back to Wes.

"Well, I got to hand it to them, that was slightly less deranged than the last time they wrote about me."

Wes shook his head.

"I wish I could say that was all, but there's something else, too."

"What?" I asked.

"Did you hear about what happened in Burma?"

"No," I replied.

"Apparently, back in January, there was an American airbase that got blown up just outside a wind turbine field where an entire tank patrol was demolished as well. No one knows who led the attack, but the Chinese are involved in some way, along with the Koreans and Russians. But that's just a few. I heard nations from all over the world are joining against us daily."

"Really? How come the news isn't reporting on that?" I asked.

"It's not politically relevant yet." Wes noted. "Don't be surprised if you see another one of our territories get blown up soon. To be honest, Jim, I think we might be going to war soon, a real war."

"How do you know all this?" I asked.

"I overheard Abner talking the other day at base. Remember that rumor of the ugly rainbow flag patch, well, it's not a rumor anymore, it's on its way. I heard Abner himself express his support of it. But hey, what's it matter? The world and its problems are no match for us, right?" Wes joked as he walked away.

I wanted to tell Trent and Katrina about all this, but I didn't want them to worry about anything on their wedding day, so I didn't try to find them. Then I thought about their marriage certificate. It would have to be signed before they leave for the night. So, I got up and walked toward my house. Once inside, I had to make my way in between dozens of people as I searched for them. I asked around and one man suggested checking upstairs. On my way there I ran into Peter coming out of the bathroom. He peered straight ahead without even looking in my direction.

"Hey Peter, have you seen Trent and Katrina?"

He glanced at me with a blank stare. His nose was wet and his eyes seemed to be gazing right through me. Then he shrugged and continued on his way. Confused, I turned and headed to the second floor. Searching around I saw no one and was about to leave when I heard a faint giggle coming from my room. I walked over to it and reached for the doorknob. But just before I could touch it the door opened, and a young woman stepped out. With raised eyebrows she mouthed 'excuse me' and walked past, I peered inside and saw Zack zip up his pants as he stepped over to the door.

"You didn't," I uttered in disbelief.

"Oh hey, Jimmy. Man, I'll tell you what, you got a soft bed."

As he tried to walk out, I grabbed his arm and glared at his face.

"Get out of my house before I throw you out."

"Whatever, Ranger Phillips. Just thought I'd give the playboy mansion some use."

He jerked his arm out of my hand and walked away. Watching him leave, I slammed the door to my room as he went on causing Zack to walk away a little faster.

I left my now tarnished house and sat with Joi as Meghan brought Trent and Katrina back from taking pictures. After everyone had finished eating, it was time for Katrina and Trent to have the first dance. They stepped out onto the wood flooring laid out on top of my yard. The two of them gently held each other underneath the twinkling lights above, dancing to some of their favorite songs.

Next up was Meghan and me. It was tradition for the best man and the bridesmaids to dance together. I don't think Joi liked this too much, so I made sure to be appropriate. I didn't find Meghan all that attractive anyway. Then, as more people got up to dance, I left Meghan and made my way back to Joi to dance with her, but as I got back to her table, she wasn't there.

I scanned around for her and eventually saw her standing in another man's arms with her head on his chest. Then I realized just who it was she was dancing with. Brock Stellar, a jerk that used to bully me in basic training when I first joined. I didn't even know he was invited, and now he's got his hands all over her. Joi knew I couldn't stand that guy, so what was she doing? And why did she look so into it.

I made sure that when I danced with someone, I didn't get intimate. It was getting really awkward now, not only because it hurt to watch, but also people who knew Joi and I were sort of a thing were watching. They shook at me like, aren't you going to do something about it? I couldn't tell what was more demoralizing, causing a scene at my friends' wedding, or sitting and watching as Joi danced with another man outside my own house. And just before I was about to intervene, she left Brock and sat down next to me. I just stared at her for a moment, and she looked at me like I was crazy.

"What?" she questioned.

"Why are you dancing with Brock like I don't exist."

"Seriously, Jim, don't be so clingy. It was just a dance; besides, you were just dancing with Meghan."

"Yeah, but I didn't get all touchy like you were with him," I pointed out.

"Jim, you're not my boyfriend. I can dance with whoever I want."

Joi got up and walked away. I sat at her table alone while the party continued around me and glanced back at Trent and Katrina. Their world seemed to stand still as I sat at the round table underneath the tent. Maybe one day, I will be where they are, and the world will seem to stand still for me too. As I thought this, I fiddled around with two forks beside the plate next to me, one was about an inch smaller than the other. And at some point, a kid had stabbed one of the forks into the table leaving it standing straight up. Seeing this, I grabbed the other one and interlinked the prongs of the two forks together as I leaned them onto one another. I let go and they held each other in place on top of the table.

Then, as I stood up to leave, the smaller fork fell back down and laid still.

Chapter 18- Ways to Go Yet

February 14th 2099 - Trent and Katrina's wedding day

In the past month of January, Isaac had made his way out of Burma. He had escaped the cold forest, hitchhiked on trucks, and walked miles until he stumbled upon a river. He found a small fishing community and after stealing some of their supplies, he was finally approaching the coast. Isaac sat upon the stern of a canoe filled with dead fish heading downstream along an unnamed river.

It has been forty-three days since Isaac killed last, but the sight of their bloody faces and dying screams still echoed in his mind. The thought of killing again made him sicker than the rotting fish under his feet. The high mountain banks served as his only cover while he slowly drifted downstream. The sun was high, and Isaac hid from its light underneath a torn ragged leather coat. With all his new clothes, Isaac appeared as just an ordinary fisherman, but underneath it all, he still wore the same armored vest he had taken from the soldiers hunting him.

After the incident inside the log, Isaac had taken many supplies from their uniforms. He had also found a map inside a fisherman's house about a week ago. He knew there was a U.S. embassy in India. All he had to do was reach the coast, sneak aboard a ship sailing to India, and he would be saved.

So, as night began to overtake the world, Isaac casually approached a large town and remained on his small boat paddling through it unseen until reaching the ocean. To his right there was a wooden dock. Isaac waited until no one was in sight before paddling over to it and hid underneath in his canoe. The dock was low, and Isaac had to duck and push himself forward using the boards overhead.

He reached the end of the dock and waited for the right boat to show up. Hours passed. Boat after boat came and went, but Isaac couldn't confirm any to be going to India, but then one with an Indian flag showed up. This was his only shot. The boat had the name Darpan painted on the side. As the boat steered into position, large waves rocked Isaac up and down causing his back to lightly knock against the wooden planks above.

The boat came in and docked to the platform Isaac was under. Isaac watched as people got off and shuffled across the wood over his head. He sat patiently and waited for them to leave. Once it was all clear, Isaac left from under the dock and paddled around to the back of the boat. He placed his hands on the side of the hull for balance as he stood up in his wobbly canoe. Grabbing onto the railing Isaac pulled himself up and onto the deck. He peeked around, hoping the coast was clear.

Seeing no one, Isaac quickly snuck around trying to find a door that would lead him below deck to hide. He soon found one and swung it open. Once safely inside, he shut the door behind him. There was a short series of steel grate stairs. He went down them on his way below deck. It was pitch black, but Isaac had gotten a small flashlight from the soldiers he'd killed.

He flipped it on and the second he did, its beam illuminated the one thing he hoped he would never see again. A black symbol in the center of a white rectangular patch. The enemy insignia was stamped onto dozens of wooden shipping crates. This was an enemy supply ship, and at that moment, Isaac realized he had picked the wrong boat.

Just then, voices from above deck caught his attention. Someone was coming and Isaac had nowhere to go. He checked for a place to hide as he walked swiftly around the crates. Toward the back of the ship, he saw a large pile of fishing nets, and with no other options, it would have to do. Isaac ran over to it and struggled to pick it up due to the heavy lead weights mixed in with the strands. He managed to get some of it up and frantically crawled underneath. It stunk like dead fish, but at this point in Isaac's life, he didn't really care much. He was like a mad dog searching for a way back home.

From in between the tangled mess of net fibers, Isaac saw one man place some small boxes on the floor. Soon after that, they all left again heading back up. Isaac had to get off this boat, but before he could even think of how, it lurched forward and was already heading out to sea. He could try to leave, but he knew he would get caught if he went back on deck, so once again, Isaac had no idea what to do.

Chapter 19- Declaration of War

After Katrina and Trent were wed, they boarded a plane and flew to Siesta Keys in Florida. As they arrived at their beachside hotel, Trent and Katrina unpacked and left for the beach where they met with a local pastor. Together they went into the water where Trent was baptized. Soon after Trent carried Katrina over the threshold of their room and the two of them slept together for the first time as husband and wife.

As the sun rose on the following morning, its light shone upon their faces. They turned to gaze at each other for the longest time laughing and kissing while they laid in bed. It was as if they had no care in the world. That is, until they flipped on the TV. The islands of Hawaii were about to once again face a sudden and dire turn of events.

On February 15th at three in the morning, an attack was executed by the same unknown armed force that had attacked the airbase in Burma. Hawaii was important to this new threat only because of the island's new solar rigs. Three massive mushroom-shaped solar domes were constructed off the coast of Hawaii as a more efficient energy source.

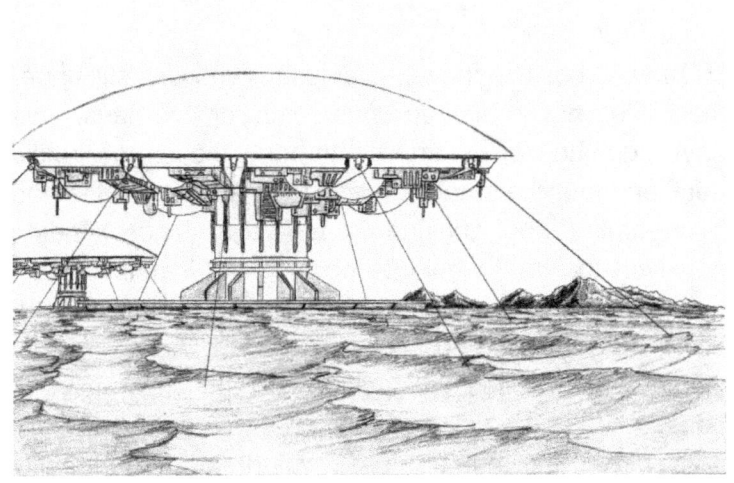

This is why the enemy desired them so much. They wanted to use them to power short-range missiles to launch at America. Almost overnight, they were taken, and production quickly began on the missiles. This day came as a shock to all of America and on February 15th, 2099, the day after Valentine's Day, Leslie Carter, the President of the United States, declared war on the new enemy.

In response to this declaration of war the enemy simply laughed, for now all was going according to plan.

Chapter 20- Anton Von Janko

February 20th 2099

Midway across the sea to India, Isaac, who was still under the fishing net, remained undetected for five days. Two days ago, he was searching through the crates below deck and found a small one with food and water. He had been eating and drinking from it ever since. Today, however, the boat would be docking in Visakhapatnam, India. Isaac would have to find a way to escape without being caught.

The ship pulled into port and Isaac grew nervous because he had no idea who or what was outside. Hours passed, and the moment Isaac was dreading had finally come. Men in black uniforms descended below deck and began to carry the smaller crates out of the ships. They left the larger ones behind, resting below massive doors on the center deck. The doors rolled open, and the men used Keylex gloves to unload them.

These devices were gloves that held a cylindrical disk on the back palm, a unique pitch of sound waves would allow the disk to levitate up to about one hundred feet. The disk itself had millions of microscopic ridges like that of a gecko hand that could lift up to one ton. These devices were used at construction sites all over the world to lift heavy objects with ease, but they were recently banned for misuse. Seeing the enemy using outlawed equipment didn't come as a surprise to Isaac who was now conditioned to expect the worst from them.

Isaac heard soldiers everywhere. He had nowhere to go; his only hope was they wouldn't look under the thick pile of netting concealing him. It took hours for them to unload all the crates. As they moved away the last two boxes in front of Isaac, he lay still, breathing in silence. He watched through the dripping sweat on his brows as the men walked away with them. The crates were hauled out, and they left. Isaac exhaled.

Suddenly, the hatch leading below deck opened again, and more men came down and pointed directly at the net Isaac was under. It seemed as though they were discussing whether to take the net off the boat. Isaac couldn't understand them. He didn't recognize their language. Then, what he had feared suddenly came true. The men reached down and began dragging away parts of the net. This was it; they were going to find him. The only thing he could do now was come out fighting.

As the closest soldier reached down again to grab more net, Isaac shot out his fist from underneath and struck the man in the nose. He stumbled backward; Isaac crawled out screaming like a wild man as he charged toward the second soldier. He looked down with wide eyes as Isaac tackled him to the floor, viciously trying to pound his face in. The first man with the hurt nose pulled out his gun and fired at Isaac's back, but due to Isaac's armored vest, the rounds did nothing. Fear overtook the two men as they thought Isaac was some kind of monster or ghost.

Isaac's apparent victory was short-lived however as men from above deck heard all the ruckus from below and quickly came rushing down. They all tackled Isaac and began to beat him to the floor. The soldiers tore off his ragged clothes and noticed he was wearing the same kind of armored vest as they were. This puzzled the men because they could tell that Isaac was not one of them.

213

After Isaac had enough, the men discussed what to do with him. It would be easier just to kill him, but they wanted to know how he got the armored vest and boot. Isaac, lying there nearly unconscious, felt the men pick him up and carry him above deck. Once again, Isaac was at the mercy of the enemy. They threw him face down onto the cold metal floor and tore off all the supplies he had on him, tossing them into the ocean. Again, they discussed amongst themselves what to do with Isaac.

The sun fell lower, and it was now very dark. A spotlight lit up the deck and soon a man walked slowly from the dock and stepped onto the ship. Isaac, who was still breathing heavily, watched as the man's feet approached him from out of the darkness. The soldiers brought Isaac to his knees, and the approaching man came and knelt so he could be face to face with him. This man was big with thick arms and broad shoulders; he must have been six and a half feet tall. Isaac stared into his eyes and saw only a face of evil.

The man was silent for a moment as he peered at Isaac but then spoke.

"Well kid, what brings you here?"

"I don't even know where this is," Isaac responded.

"Where did you get the vest?"

"I tore it off one of your men after I shot him in the face."

The man who was holding Isaac up raised his hand and bashed his fist against the back of Isaac's head. The man kneeling before Isaac raised his hand up for the other soldier to stop.

"What's your name?"

Isaac stuttered, trying to pronounce his name.

"I-Isaac," he let out.

The man chuckled.

"Hello, Isaac. I'm Anton Von Janko and I would be most grateful if you could inform me as to why you were aboard one of my ships?"

Isaac looked him in the eye and remained silent. Anton slapped Isaac, causing him to bite down on his tongue. It started to bleed, and Anton asked again more sternly this time. Isaac said nothing and Anton punched him and yelled into his face.

"TELL ME!"

"I... I'm on my way to the U.S. embassy in Odisha."

Anton bore his teeth.

"Are you really? Well, you don't mean the embassy we destroyed a week ago. You couldn't possibly mean that one."

"What?" Isaac asked.

"Don't tell me you were trying to go there because you thought they could take you back to America. Soon, Isaac, very soon, there won't even be a country for you to run back to. Everything you know, all of it, will belong to Morgan."

"Who's that?" Isaac asked.

"The man who will fix the world."

Isaac spit into Anton's face, calling him a liar. Anton calmly locked eyes with him keeping a straight face, he pulled out a rag and gently wiped it clean. He glanced down at the rag then back up at Isaac and was silent before forcing it into Isaac's mouth. Anton tackled Isaac to the floor, pinning him to the deck of the ship. He sat on Isaac's stomach as two other soldiers held down Isaac's arms as he tried to struggle free. His resistance came to a stop as he gazed at Anton who was stuffing his fingers down his throat.

Before Isaac realized what he was doing, Anton leaned forward vomiting onto Isaac's face. Isaac closed his eyes as the chunky warm mush poured over him, filling his nostrils and drenching his hair. Isaac tensed up as it spilled over every part of his face. As Anton's gagging convulsions came to an end, he wiped his mouth and spit out the rest onto Isaac's face. As Isaac cleared his nostrils and blinked open his eyes, Anton pressed Isaac's steaming head down onto the wet metal and spoke viciously into Isaac's ear.

"You see, Isaac! You are powerless here under me! And before I save you, I will have your body raped and beaten over and over until every one of your bones are shattered! Then, as you cry out for help, I will snatch out your tongue and serve it amongst the rats! Your corpse will be butchered, and I will personally deliver the rotting pieces to the whimpering whore you call a mother! Only then could you appreciate what I have done for you!"

Isaac spit out the rag as he too hacked up his last meal. Spitting the chunks from his lips he cried out. "You're insane!"

Anton leaned back.

"You're lost from home and in need of my help. Stop resisting. We're your family now."

Isaac stopped moving and went silent for a moment as he recalled his family.

"My family's gone. I don't have any parents. My mother is dead and my father's a murderer. I don't have anyone out there who loves me."

Anton got off Isaac, as did the other soldiers.

"You're wrong. Morgan loves you."

216

Isaac began to wipe his face.

"Who are you people?"

"Oh, Isaac, we're the good guys."

He then turned away from Isaac.

"Bring me a knife and prepare a neural transmitter, this boy is almost ready."

Then without warning Isaac jolted back and rolled off the edge of the boat. This was his only chance to escape and had caught them all by surprise. The soldiers immediately fired their weapons into the water after him, but their high caliber rounds didn't pierce more than several inches into the water. They dropped in grenades, before one soldier stepped over and fired a sonic rifle which did penetrate deep into the water. Seconds later small fish floated up to the surface, but Isaac was not among them. He was already underneath the boat and swimming up on the opposite side. He reached the surface coming up underneath the dock with a clean face and sucking air between his lips.

Isaac was far from safe, however. He took one big breath and quickly swam back down as the soldiers lit up the water with floodlights. Isaac swam in the shadow cast by the dock heading toward the shore. The moment he lost his breath; he would come up just for a second and quickly swim back down. The soldiers searched and screamed his name as they cursed into the air. Isaac reached the rocky shore and ran along the right side of the sea wall away from the men. He ran further into the darkness until he couldn't hear the soldiers' screams anymore. But as he reached the end, he realized he had run in the wrong direction. Before him there was nothing but more ocean.

This long stretch of stone and cement was a wave brake to calm the waters before reaching the wooden docks. Land and the cover of the forest was in the other direction, but the only way to get to it was through a construction site. Isaac shook his head as he exhaled, knowing the site was most likely populated with what he assumed were dozens of psychotic soldiers like Anton. Isaac couldn't swim around them. They were already sending out boats in search of him and blasting the water with sonic charges.

He started back, trying to think of another way, but none came to mind. Halfway to the dock, he climbed up and over the sea wall seeing there were fewer soldiers in the distance patrolling this side. Isaac scanned the uneven water to the closest point of land adjacent to his position. He got back in and swam toward it, careful not to upset the calm surface and draw the attention of the few soldiers searching for him. Once there, he climbed over another sea wall and stepped up onto the ground between two wooden docks.

The construction site before him was large, and there was still a good portion of it between him and the nearby woods. Isaac ran across the dusty ground and hid behind a stack of metal pipes, but just when he thought he was well hidden about ten flood lights lit up one by one all around the site. Isaac darted out of the light and into an open shipping container. Seconds passed. He assumed he was still undetected because he heard no alarm and saw no one coming for him. Suddenly, the screeching sound of scraping metal came before a whoosh. He peeked around the corner and saw an oval tank from a cement mixer hurling through the air toward his position.

Isaac bolted inside and jumped out the opposite end just as the tank smashed into the container. Isaac glanced back watching as both were sent tumbling over the sea wall and into the water. A disk flew off the tank and traveled into the distance, back to its user.

Someone was using a Keylex glove to hurl things at him. Really big things! They must have seen him as the floodlights switched on. He had to get out of the open. Isaac stood up and ran into the nearby office building, smashing through the glass front doors just as a pallet of cinder blocks crashed down behind him. Isaac landed on his side as glass from the door bounced all around his body. A Korean woman screamed. Isaac snapped up at her, and the two locked eyes for a moment before he read her name tag. Sara.

Isaac jumped to his feet sprinting past her. He glanced to his left and saw a stairwell, quickly charging to the top. On the right, was a red exit sign above the door at the end of the hall. The lights above were off, but the red glow lit his way to the door and upon reaching it, Isaac pushed hard on the latch. It was locked. *What kind of building has locked exit doors?* Isaac spun around as a massive steel H-beam flew up the stairs and sunk into the wall above.

He watched as the disk from a Keylex glove detached from the steel beam just as Anton stepped up the stairs and into the hallway. Catching the disk into his hand, he stared at Isaac from a distance and calmly set the disk back onto the beam.

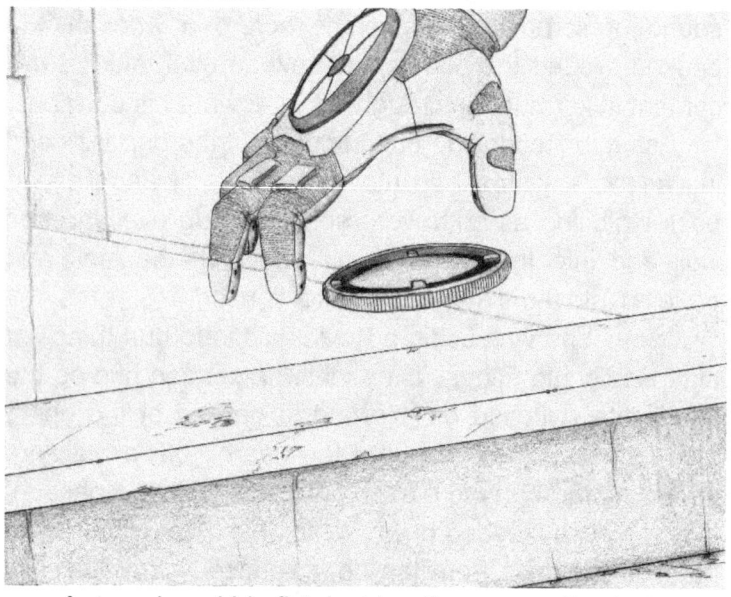

Anton closed his fist, locking the connection between the disk and the beam. He glared at Isaac with a grin and suddenly launched the steel column directly at him. Halfway to Isaac, the beam rotated as both ends tore into the office walls. Showing no sign of slowing, it hurled toward Isaac just two feet above the floor. Isaac dropped to his face, covering his head as the beam grazed his back. It crashed through the exit door and knocked out half of the wall to his right. Isaac was partially covered in rubble and dust, but the locked exit door was now completely gone.

Cracks in the ceiling began to form and Isaac knew the roof was about to give in. As he got up, the Keylex disk flew up over his head from the beam outside and landed back into Anton's hand. Small parts of the roof fell on Isaac, and he wasted no time as he ran out the new exit. Isaac jumped over the metal railing and onto a series of crates below. The roof caved in, blocking Anton's view of him. Isaac could now see that the surrounding woods were near.

He leapt down onto a wooden pallet landing on his right knee. Instantly Isaac screamed in agony as he glanced down to see an upside-down nail from the pallet was embedded into the tissue below his kneecap. Isaac had no time to stop. His body shook as he pried his knee off it.

Once standing, Isaac frantically hobbled toward the forest after crawling underneath a high chain-link fence. He ran and ran throughout the darkness and for the third time, he had narrowly avoided death from the enemy, or so he thought.

About half a mile from the construction site Isaac stumbled onto a road. He walked for hours using a stick to give support to his injured knee. Every now and then, a car would drive by, and Isaac would hide from it in the forest. As one slow-moving truck approached, Isaac watched from behind a tree. It looked old and had a wooden bed carrying small livestock.

He assumed this couldn't have any relation to his enemy. As it approached, Isaac pushed down a dead tree that blocked the road. The truck slowly came to a stop which allowed Isaac to sneak onto the tailgate and climb in.

The driver, annoyed by the fallen tree, quickly moved it out of his path and re-entered his truck. A wooden wall blocked Isaac from the view of the driver, and once again, Isaac, now injured and tired, finally laid down to rest, but this time he would rest in the company of about twenty slobbering goats. As the truck drove on, it soon took Isaac into a large town and turned left then right then left again. The truck continued to drive north till night fell, passing more small forests and eventually coming up onto an airport.

Isaac saw the runway and thought if he could get a plane running, he could take off and be out of here for good. With this in mind, he jumped off the truck and rolled into the dark forest. Isaac trekked through the woods until he reached another chain link fence. He worked his way under it. No one was in sight. He stumbled as he ran across the runway on his way to an unoccupied hangar. A small plane was inside.

A neutral exhaust twin-engine which didn't require keys or an ignition code to get it running. Isaac remembered this type of aircraft from his pilots training. All he would have to do is break into the breakers underneath the dash and reverse the negative engine connection to positive. Then Isaac could fly out of here a free man.

He searched the hanger for a screwdriver and after several minutes of stumbling around, he found one. Isaac climbed into the plane and broke open the locked hatch with a crowbar he had also found. He stepped into the cockpit and knelt down underneath the console. A curved metal panel was bolted over where he wanted to get in. Isaac used the screwdriver to get that out of the way and reach the engine breakers to flip them too positive. Once done, Isaac revved the gas and the second he did, the intake fan began to rotate. The touch screen dashboard lit up, and Isaac yelled in happiness. For the first time he felt in control. He steered the plane out of the hangar and onto the runway. No one was in sight.

Isaac hit the throttle and took off, speeding down the runway and finally ascending into the air. Isaac exhaled in relief, grateful to be away from Anton. He laughed at the thought that he actually stole a plane, but as he checked the gas levels, he realized why it was in the hanger; it was low on fuel at just under a quarter tank. Isaac brought up a map on the dash and estimated the farthest distance over the water he could reach. He saw that Saudi Arabia was the closest point in a straight line, so he started in that direction and set the plane to autopilot so he could rest and tend to his wounds.

As morning approached the horizon, Isaac awoke to the sound of an alarm ringing from the dash, he glanced over at the gas level. It was completely empty. Isaac peered out the window and saw he was over an ocean of sand dunes. Isaac switched the plane to manual and steered toward the ground. Once he got close, he leveled out and glided over the sand, releasing his landing gear.

A high dune scraped the bottom of the fuselage and broke off the front set of wheels. Isaac descended even more and slid across the sand until finally reaching a full stop. The landing was rough, but Isaac had survived. Leaning back in his seat he smiled. A sudden flashing light on the dash caught his attention and Isaac read the label below it. Clear broadcast. This meant that Isaac would be able to call for help. He grabbed the radio and locked onto a U.S. military frequency. For a moment there was only static then he heard a woman's voice.

"Aft Nab Air Force Base. Sergeant Taylor speaking."

"Yes! Hello! My name is Isaac Richards! I'm the son of Westley Richerds the Hellbender. My service number is AF26 118 765. I'm the only survivor of the O'Brien Airbase attack in Burma about a month ago. I need immediate assistance, I'm injured, hungry and I just want to go home. My coordinates are 20°58'42.9"N 50°57'07.8"E."

"Hold your position. We will have men on site in approximately twenty-four hours."

"Thank you. Please hurry!" Isaac said.

He placed the radio on the dash, leaned back in his chair and began to laugh. Help was on the way. Hours later, around midday, Isaac was resting in his plane as his radio picked up a foreign broadcast from somewhere in the desert.

"Dalara station beneath Lolsouladad is ready to receive the arrival schedule of the Kronos, Hector and Dr. Krull are awaiting green light to be-"

The message became unintelligible due to interference, but then it cleared up.

"Unknown aircraft landed seventy miles away from our position. I want it investigated immediately tomorrow morning. Until then, proceed in clearing the drop zone."

What in the world was that all about? Isaac wondered but then made the realization that the enemy was on their way here. Knowing that this broadcast had been recorded on his planes flight recorder Isaac snatched up the radio again. He called back the airbase and made it very clear that the situation may be more urgent than he had first led them to believe.

Chapter 21- Best Play

At noon, Trent, Dirk, Katrina, Adam, Wes, and I made our way into General Abner's office for a long-awaited meeting that we had demanded. We all found a place to stand or sit in the room which was filled with a couple of chairs and a desk along with pictures on the walls. One of which was of Abner in his football jersey from his college days. Placed on the wall beside this was a TV playing the news. It was on mute, but as we waited, I took note of the reporter out in the streets of a city covering a story of a rich man, Jerry Larkson throwing checks off a building. I seemed to be the only one paying any attention to this and didn't even realize as the general walked in and shut off the TV. Snapping out of it, I faced him as he stepped around his desk.

"I know why you're here and let me just stop you before you say a word because my answer is no."

Dirk spoke up first.

"Sir, respectfully, I insist that you reconsider. I believe we are a valuable resource in preventing this growing crisis, and I think we need to act now before this gets out of hand."

"Dirk, what do you plan on doing?" Abner asked. "I can't just let you go guns blazing into China. We don't even know if they're officially involved. I know that's the rumor right now, but I've heard nothing from the Chinese president about their involvement."

While Abner spoke, I shook my head and thought, if it walks like a duck and talks like a duck, it's probably a duck. Best to shoot it down now before it flies too high.

"All we know is that the majority of enemy troops we've seen are Chinese." Abner said. "But none of them are in Chinese uniforms or have Chinese weaponry. We know nothing about these people."

"And we never will unless you send us out to fight them. We can't just sit here as they destroy one base after another," Wes expressed.

"As we speak, I have troops out gathering information," the General assured.

"On what? Which bases were going to lose next?" Trent added.

"And how are we looking to the rest of the world?" Katrina asked. "I can only guess they're laughing, like always."

"Let's end this before it gets any worse," Adam said. "We're at Defcon 3 going on 2. Any lower, and it will be too late."

"And how do you feel about this, Jim?" Abner asked, turning his eyes to me.

"If you're losing the game, you don't bench your star athletes and let the rookies play."

Abner looked away and was silent for a moment.

"Well, it just so happens that I have missions most of you can commence tonight. So, Trent! There is a Russian military leader who just signed papers to join the enemy. You will be assassinating him at a company party. Katrina, there's a Korean supply ship in the Eastern Mid Atlantic. We need you to report what they are selling and then destroy the ship."

"Yes Sir," she said happily.

"Wes! There's an arms factory in China that, if crippled, will put a halt to weapons manufacturing to the enemy forces across Asia. Adam, due to Hawaii's recent disaster with its solar rigs, you and your team of Air Jumpers will perform a H.A.L.P jump above the domes."

He finished his commands and the four of them nodded in approval of their assignments. He eyed Dirk and me.

"You two just hold tight until something else shows up that I'll need you for." He added, "It shouldn't take very long. And before anyone goes anywhere you all need to pay Dr. Hammond a visit. He has a new upgrade for your suits. He wanted to wait a while before giving it to you, but since you're all so eager to start fighting, I guess you're all going to receive it early."

We went downstairs into a bunker where our suits were already laying on tables. Men wearing gas masks were working on them. Dr. Hammond saw us step in, and he came over to greet us. He explained that the men were implanting a chemical agent below every sheet of Fragmight so when connected to a unique electric current the entire suit would be obliterated.

Basically, the suits were now equipped with a self-destruct button that we were to activate if we were ever captured. Most of us, myself included, were a little skeptical about this. My job was to defuse bombs, not become one. But we were in no position to complain after the talk we just had with Abner. It was quickly coined the Hell switch to fit the superstition. When a hellbender fight ends on Earth their war begins in Hell.

Soon, they were finished with everyone's suits except mine because all the ignition buttons varied on each suit. Dr. Hammond told me that since I wasn't going on a mission just yet he would have extra time to prepare a more complicated detonation switch into my suit. He made

228

sure the buttons couldn't be pressed by accident. As my friends and I left, the workers started by unbolting the center sheet on my chest plate and cooking it in the furnace for ten hours until it was glowing white. Then they took a diamond saw to it and were able to cut it in half to create a latch that would cover a keyhole to ignite the chemical agent.

Adam's mission was the next morning. We had all gotten the gear needed for the missions out of the barracks so he could get some sleep. Wes was the first to leave with his team aboard an Kodiak AC10 for the slow, day-long flight across the world for China. Dirk left and went to the gym alone. Right after this, I got a text from Joi saying she too was leaving for some time on a trip to deliver papers to Washington. By the time she got back I would probably be away on a mission myself and would not get to see her. I took the opportunity to go say goodbye.

Meanwhile, Trent was with Katrina, trying to spend what little time they had left before the missions in each other's arms. Katrina kissed him.

"Where's Jim? He's the only one I haven't said goodbye to yet."

"I don't know. I thought he'd be here," Trent answered.

Katrina frowned.

"I hope he shows up before I leave."

"If not, I'll tell him you said goodbye," Trent softly reassured.

After some more time passed, Katrina checked her watch.

"I have to go."

She stood up, but before she left, she took off her necklace.

"Hold onto this for me."

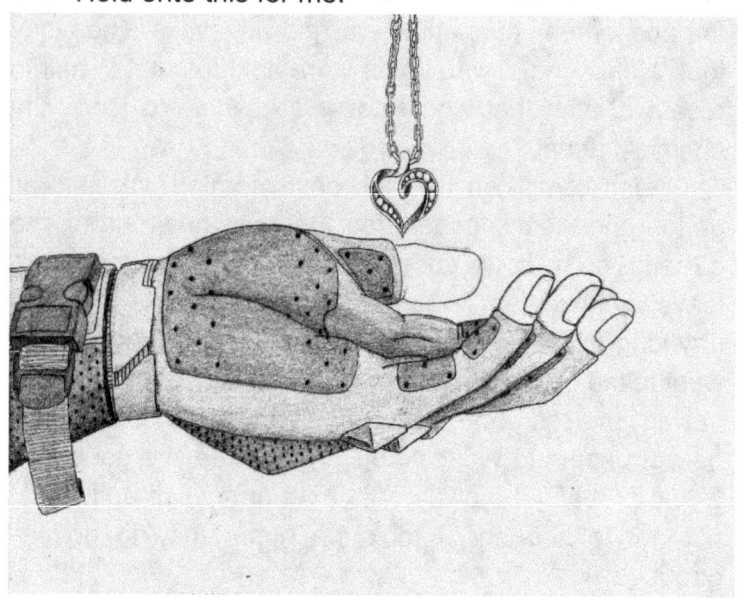

Trent shook his head.

"Why do you give me this every time I leave for a mission?"

"I have to leave something behind to motivate me to come back," she joked.

Trent rolled his eyes and lightly jabbed her side making her jump and giggle as he said, "What? Is my heart not good enough?"

"Course it is. That's why I'm leaving mine with you so yours won't get lonely." Trent reached out his hands toward Katrina.

"Pray with me." he said.

Katrina smiled and took hold; they bowed their heads and closed their eyes.

"God, please watch over us as we go our separate ways. Keep us safe and help us to stop these people who are trying to destroy the country You have blessed us with. Bring us, and all those out on deployment, back home safely. Amen."

Katrina raised her head and looked into Trent's opening eyes.

"I love you." she said.

"I love you too." Trent said back as they hugged.

Finally, she turned away to leave. Trent stuffed her necklace into his pocket and departed soon after.

I finished my farewells with Joi and went off to bed, completely forgetting about saying goodbye to Trent and Katrina. It felt as though Joi has been a little distant recently, and I didn't want to lose her again so I had to take every chance I could to see her. The only strange thing was later that night I had a nightmare, and this time it was different than the rest. I was naked in the dark standing before a tree with seven branches. Each branch became a black chain the further out it stretched.

Then the chain to the far right suddenly and without warning snapped off from the tree spewing blood upon the ground.

It was at that moment I awoke.

Chapter 22- Operation Orbital Hammer

February 20th

The next day, Peter, Zack, and Adam along with the other Air Jumpers sat in the rumbling belly of their plane as it approached the drop zone over Hawaii. The fleet flew in formation as the piercing blasts of oncoming AA fire became barely recognizable over the blaring music Zack was playing on the comms. Peter pulled a small box from his pocket and smeared his fingers in the white powder packed inside.

As they entered the drop zone above the three massive mushroom-shaped solar rigs, Zack flipped on the green light over the back door. It lowered down, scanning Adam's helmet with sunlight. The smoky air whipped around him and his men, and the smell of sulfur filled their lungs as the door fell open revealing the full-blown war zone below. Peter made sure no one was looking before he rubbed the powder across his gums. Adam ignited his thrusters and darted out the back along with Peter and the other six men diving head-first into the falling wreckage and burning debris of the surrounding aircrafts. High-velocity rounds zipped past, nearly smacking into Adam as it punched through a man to his left, splitting him in half and sending his torso spinning into the distance with a puff of red mist.

Below them, a bobbing grid of Maglev hover mines sat suspended in midair by a magnetic field. Any plane within fifty feet overwhelmed the field and was swarmed with mines. Since Adam and his team were so small they passed right through the field without disruption where they deployed EMP charges. This disabled the grid allowing the aircrafts to finally enter enemy occupied airspace.

Just as another plane was preparing to drop its Air Jumpers, it was struck by the artillery below, causing it to dump out the burning soldiers within as it lost control and erupted into flame and black smoke.

Peter saw the incoming artillery and spun to the left, falling behind a burning helicopter as it plummeted toward the ocean in a ball of burning ash. The twirling cloud was so large he hid inside and concealed himself from the incoming artillery. Adam glanced at Peter and did the same, following him into the smoke. Deep concussions drummed the air around them with shock charges that thundered the sky over the domes.

Fire and debris rained down as they approached the water below, but before crashing head-first, the remaining Air Jumpers leaned back, igniting their jetpacks and skipped off the water like a hurled stone now jetting across the choppy waves. Adam and Peter's headsets saw through the smoke counting down the dropping distance to the water below. As the remains of the helicopter approached it, the brothers split from one another letting the burning wreck crash into the sea with a white splash and a sudden plume of red flame.

In less than a second a large cloud of fire erupted below them and they were consumed by the flames. Almost in unison, both men leaned back, igniting their jetpacks causing water and fire to twirl around them. Shooting forward they both leapt out of the flames and continued ahead.

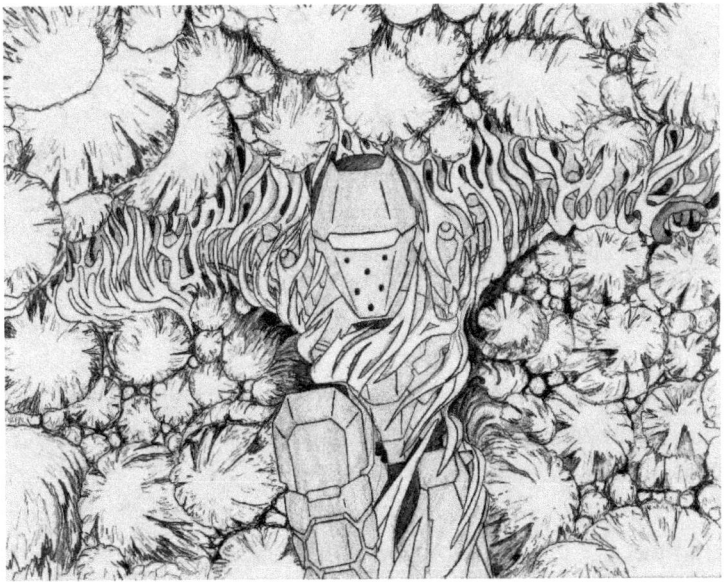

Now skimming across the open water, the base of the solar domes came into full view as were three-speed boats carrying launch codes to the nearby mainland. Adam and Peter caught up with their men heading over the water like attack jets as they approached the boats. The Air Jumper team was low. All together they raced across the ocean toward enemy speed boats that were firing rockets and machine guns back at them.

A second boat joined in as they approached the first solar rig. A falling plane impacted on the right side of the rig causing the dome to crack in half and break apart into the water. Adam saw this but was too close to maneuver out of the way, so he sped forward and dove below the rim just before it crashed into the ocean.

As Adam's men continued toward the boats, one Air Jumper got too close and was hit by a rocket, blasting him to pieces and splattering his blood across the visor of the man behind. This blinded him, causing him to lose control and tumble across the water. Seeing this, Adam and Peter gave each other a glance and a quick nod before splitting apart and heading toward the two closest boats.

Peter reached his boat first, dodging missiles as he pulled out his small gun mounted on his right thigh. He launched himself high over the bouncing vessel as he loaded the gun with a mag from his left thigh. Coming down, he opened fire on the men below. A rocket nearly hitting him as it whizzed past.

Peter fired into the men as he came into land, killing the soldier with the rockets. Upon entering the boat, he shoved his barrel into the face of another soldier, just as a second Air Jumper rushed to Peter's aid. He lit up the driver, quickly taking his place and bringing the boat to a stop. A small pack of Air Jumpers swarmed the craft, frantically searching for the launch codes. They eventually found them in a suitcase underneath the driver's seat.

Adam, who had nearly reached the second boat called Peter over comms who notified him to check underneath the driver's seat. Adam sped toward the engine while unloading mag after mag into it only to find it was heavily armored like the rest of the boat. Enemy soldiers leaned over the sides firing back at Adam sending rounds smacking into his suit finding that he too was quite bullet resistant.

Just then, an Air Jumper caught the soldiers in the boat off guard as she came in from the right, leaping over the boat and dropping in a smoke grenade. Instantly, the boat became a skipping cloud of black smoke only defended by blind potshots from the men inside. Adam curved off to his right just as another Air Jumper came in from the left side of the boat and dropped in an explosive grenade as he leaped over.

The boat hopped off the water in a ball of flame, catching the air for a brief moment as it glided like a kite from the high momentum. Then it dropped back down at a sharp angle, rapidly tumbling over and over and launching the men inside out like drops of water from a wet dog shaking to get dry. Immediately, Adam lifted his legs allowing the jets on his calves to halt his progression forward.

He shot back toward the crashing boat as it came to a stop, quickly landing onboard. Seawater began to flood in, and he had to find the launch codes fast. He checked under the driver's seat first and sure enough, they were there. He snatched them up just as another Air Jumper joined him to help. Adam handed him the suitcase and looked up to see that the third boat was now dangerously close to the shore. Adam notified his team over comms, ordering them to advance on the final boat.

Adam ignited his jetpack and blasted after them with his fellow Jumpers darting behind. They fired on the boat, but it was too late. It reached the shore, and Adam could see the men spilling out like rats trying to hide in the palm trees ahead. Seeing that they were carrying the launch codes with them, Adam touched down onshore, shutting off his jetpack as he opened fire on the retreating men. They passed the tree line, bursting through the leaves and disappearing through the thick brush.

Adam lit up his pack and shot after them, smashing through the leaves. He saw three men scattered amongst the array of pillar-like tree trunks holding up the dimly lit canopy above them. Adam landed, kicking up dead leaves and sand as he shot up the closest man with his gun, spraying his brains on the palm tree ahead. Adam shoved his final mag into his rifle as one of the enemy soldiers fired back, smacking several rounds across Adam's helmet. He aimed at the man, unloading into his head dropping the soldier to the ground. Adam spotted the last man far ahead running with the suitcase.

He launched toward him, burning the leaves on the ground as he took off. Blasting forward he passed between the palms and hurled down toward the soldier preparing to front kick him to the ground as he got close. The soldier ducked to the left at the last second. Adam kicked the air, missing him and sliding on the ground before turning to be on all fours, coming to a stop as his fingers dug into the ground while he slid backwards.

The enemy soldier glared back at Adam trying to catch his breath. Adam, still resting on all fours, slowly rose at him. The rocket boosters on his back popped rapidly as Adam flipped the switch on his wrist to shut them off. He faced the man, never once breaking eye contact. There was a brief silence between the two as they stared at each other. Suddenly, the remaining Air Jumpers burst through the canopy above, landing all around the enemy soldier. Now surrounding him, Adam stepped forward and the soldier dropped the suitcase to the ground, trembling in fear as he accepted his fate.

Moments later, Adam and his men returned to the beach dragging the three dead soldiers out by their vest collar. Dropping them as the sight of the ocean came back into view, Adam turned to the sound of an approaching helicopter. It came in low just barely hovering over the water. Beneath it was a man swimming toward the shore. The last enemy soldier by the look of it. Adam and his men saw how exhausted he was as he slowly crawled onto the shore. Just as he did, the helicopter landed, crushing him under the left skid.

The man cried out in agony. Peter walked up behind Adam, and together they approached the chopper with the suitcases. The two bore no sympathy for the screaming man. As the helicopter door slid open Zack stepped out. Wearing sunglasses and a Hawaiian shirt flapping in the breeze he sucked on a lollipop. Stepping off the helicopter, Zack planted his boot on the head of the screaming soldier under the skid driving his face into the sand, finally muffling his painful outburst. Zack wandered forward toward Adam and Peter, flicking his half-finished lolly into the waves. Taking off his sunglasses he pointed off into the distance.

"Missed one."

Adam and Peter turned around and took view of the volcanic lava fields nearby. They could see the gray dusty trail of a lone soldier running across the fields toward the launch pads.

Adam glanced back at Zack.

"Well, that would explain the empty suitcase."

He flipped open the third case he'd acquired from the man in the palm forest, now realizing he was just a decoy. The real launch codes were with the man running in the direction of the launch pads.

Putting his sunglasses back on Zack said, "I'll give you a lift."

Zack spun around and stepped back onto the man's head this time twisting his sandy boots on his hair as he entered the helicopter. Adam followed and together the two took off flying after the last enemy soldier.

He ran over the hot volcanic glass that crunched under his boots all the while dodging small superheated vents oozing streams of lava around him. He was exhausted, running with the stack of launch codes in his

240

hands. Sweat and saliva flung out from his nose and mouth as he forced himself on, knowing his destination was in sight. Just as he made it over the hill and saw the launch pad, he thought he was in the clear. Then out of the sky came Adam.

He thrust downward, driving his boots into the back of the soldier, crashing him through the thin volcanic crust. They plunged into the shallow scorching lava below. Adam quickly snatched the stack of launch codes from the man's thrashing limbs and stepped out of the burning hole. Lava stuck to the armor on his legs like a melted marshmallow. Checking through the papers to see if they were indeed the codes Adam was Happy to see they were in fact the codes. He smiled knowing the mission was a success. Glancing up to his brother Zack, Adam saluted his helicopter. He restacked the papers preparing to leave, but before he did, Adam took one last look at the enemy soldier still thrashing in the burning pool of lava.

Chapter 23- Operation Midnight Delta

February 20th 2:30 AM

Katrina was loaded under the right wing of an Olympic 8 Sea Raven. A long range naval jet. Her team sat strapped into six identical mini-subs called Lampreys. There were three on each side, mounted under each wing. As the plane approached one mile from target, it dropped them two by two like torpedoes into the direction of the massive supply ship. Four drag flaps deployed as the Lampreys made contact with the water.

The oncoming current made the back flaps spin and unscrew the end caps like a water bottle lid to reveal the hidden propellers within. The cap was there to protect the turbine from the force of the impact. Each sub held three people, one as the driver and two in the seats behind. Katrina's mission was to board the enemy ship and clear it of all inhabitants before cataloging what the enemy was shipping. Then she was to use a four-pound block of black C4 strapped to her lower back to sink the ship. A red light lit up the dark space inside the Lamprey.

"Three minutes from the target."

The six subs rapidly approached the ship and upon arrival, the company split, three to each side of the vessel. The driver of the sub saw the submerged steel wall of its hull. Using radar, he cut the engine and rolled the sub sideways so the padded magnetic rim around the bottom hatch could attach to the boat like a suckerfish on a shark. The inside of the sub rotated so everyone inside would be right-side up.

The diver closest to the hatch unstrapped from his seat and opened it. A small amount of ocean water that was caught in between the door and the magnetic rim drained inside. Next, he stuck a black x-ray mat to the wall and checked if anyone was on the other side. It was clear. The soldier took out a blow torch and began cutting a circular hole into the boat's hull. While he did this Katrina and the other men switched on their rebreathers while he cut to avoid inhaling any toxic fumes that filled the air.

Once finished, he dropped the blow torch and grabbed his small compact smart rifle. He aimed at the hatch and kicked out the plug. It fell inside the ship as fresh air filled the sub. The diver crawled through, then Katrina and lastly the man behind her entered. They all slid down the curved wall onto metal walkways below. It was dark and seemed as though they were alone. The teams from the other subs pushed out their plugs and entered the ship. They gathered up with Katrina's men.

Together, they all proceeded to a nearby door at the end of the walkway. It was locked so Katrina placed a pulse charge on the latch as her team stepped to the side. It detonated, sending the door flying open with a trail of white smoke following behind. Katrina stepped through the mist, aiming her weapon into the next room. This new area was well lit and abandoned. It must have been somewhere near the center of the ship. Two walkways crossed over them from both sides. Katrina split her team, sending six to one end, and accompanied the other five to the opposite side.

Down below in the center of the room were two closed doors that lay flat on the floor. An object was hanging above them by metal beams and industrial pulleys. Wires hung off it connecting to a generator on its left side. The object was a blunt-tipped, mechanical cone with a reflective dome on the bottom. It was surrounded by copper wires and metal paneling. Katrina directed her men down to gather any information that they could. As they reached it, a door opened at the end of the room forcing Katrina and her men to quickly hide before they could examine the thing.

The men who walked in didn't seem to notice Katrina and her men were there, then more soldiers followed from behind. They were wearing white armored vests, and together they stood around the object.

"Should we engage?" one diver whispered.

"Negative. Let's see what they do first," Katrina whispered back.

The enemy soldiers opened the doors beneath the object and lowered it into the ocean. They flipped on the generator and typed a code into its data panel. The object made a pinging sound.

"That's everything, bring it back up." One man ordered and the object was raised out of the ocean.

Katrina signaled her team and gave a quick nod. She rose and fired at the soldiers. Her men joined in and eliminated the threat, the suppressor rounds kept things quiet and the soldiers in white dropped to the floor. Katrina walked up to examine the object as a diver from her team stood next to her and read off the data panel. It was in Korean. He could make out the label at the top of the screen which read 'Neural Broadcast Terminal'.

"They're sending some kind of message using sonar to broadcast information down below the ship."

"What's below the ship?" she asked.

"I have no idea."

Just then, a faint beep caught one diver's attention. He glanced up to an overhead walkway and saw a man in white talking on a walkie-talkie. The diver quickly shot at him but missed as the soldier ran through a nearby door.

"We're about to have company," the diver said.

Katrina directed her men under the stairwell at the far end of the room where the soldier had escaped. They didn't wait long until reinforcements came rushing down the metal steps. Katrina and her team watched until the last of them made their way down the stairs before firing away shooting at their legs and back. The soldiers tumbled down the remaining steps as Katrina's men swarmed them, executing anyone who was still breathing. Katrina led her men over the bodies, proceeded up the stairs and down narrow corridors as they began clearing the rest of the ship.

After about thirty minutes of back-and-forth shooting, Katrina had lost five of her soldiers but managed to clear out the ship. As she led the remaining half to the door of the captain's command room, she stood to the side as one of her men quickly placed charges on the door. It blew open, and they filed inside. Katrina quickly scanned the interior of the room, shooting two enemy soldiers in the face leaving only the captain.

"Get on the ground!" Katrina demanded as she aimed at him.

He glared at her with a fearless smirk on his face. Katrina gestured to one of her men. He walked to the captain, grabbed him by the collar, and forcefully threw him to the floor. As he did this the captain reached into his pocket and pulled out a small remote. He pressed it and the room was immediately filled with white phosphorus.

"Everyone out!" Katrina shouted, but it was too late, they were already exposed to the hot gas.

Katrina's suit kept her safe, but she was left with the haunting screams of her men as their skin burnt away. She could only watch as they thrashed from the intense pain. Smoke billowed from their burning flesh which filled the room with the smell of garlic. Katrina stepped backward in shock and tripped, landing on one of her soldiers. The melting skin from his face stuck to her suit like gum.

Quickly, she stumbled to her feet and rushed out of the room. Once in the hall, she leaned against a wall taking a minute to process what had just happened. She was now alone and with a heavy heart she got up knowing her job was not over. Katrina began to make her way back down to the neural broadcast terminal.

Upon arrival, she stood aside the open doors leading to the ocean reflecting off the dome beneath the object. She stared at the water slapping against the sides of the door frame. *What were they sending a broadcast to?*

Without a second thought, Katrina flipped on her rebreather, strapped on her flippers and jumped in. She peered down but saw only darkness. Then, as if there was only a single star in the sky, Katrina saw a tiny flash from the darkness below. She swam under the ship to the anchor chain at the bow and followed it down. Her suit adjusted to the increasing pressure around her.

About 400 meters down the lights on her helmet illuminated the seafloor below and her lead weights sunk her between the walls of an ocean trench. The flashing light was clearer now, and she cautiously approached it swimming between the walls illuminated by the strobe light at the end of the trench. The light flashed across her visor as she drifted out of the trench and stared down off the continental shelf. The strobe was at the tip of a black antenna, but it was too dark to see where it led. Strangely, in the very moment that she locked eyes on it, the strobe began to slowly rise above her head and the lights on her helmet lit up something unexpected. A dark metal-plated wall ascended above her head. It curved around from all sides forming a massive sphere.

Katrina gazed up at it, not sure what to do. Then rising before her she saw a black symbol in the center of a white rectangle on its port side.

Katrina placed her hand on the wall of the trench to steady herself as she took pictures of it with her helmet's micro camera. As she did this, she felt something writhing against her hand. Turning left her lights lit up the face of an eight-foot eel lunging toward her visors. Its mouth latched onto her helmet and its second inner jaws snapped at her face. The eel thrashed around her neck and beneath her right arm. With her left hand, she reached down to her hip and unclipped a knife. Taking hold, she thrust it up, slicing into its green body. Blood clouded the beams from her helmet; it detached from her face and wriggled back down into the hole from where it came.

Katrina glanced back up to the mega sphere as it rose up from beneath the shelf. It was far larger than she had imagined, about the size of a football stadium. She had to stop it before it drifted away. With no way of getting inside she figured the four pounds of C4 on her back would at least do something. Kicking off the ground she swam upward, gliding above the upper dome and making contact on the top. The downward current from above kept her in place as the vessel picked up speed; rapidly approaching the surface. Probably to investigate the loss of contact with the ship.

Reaching back Katrina unclipped the block of C4 and stuck it onto the metal plating. She set the timer for forty seconds and after activating it, she darted back down. As she reached the ocean trench for cover the block detonated, stopping the sphere in its place. The dome cracked open like an egg causing large pockets of air to escape and fill the hull with seawater. It began to sink as other sections imploded. Just as it did the lower engines rolled it sideways causing it to impact the seafloor.

Like a black moon the sphere collided with the sediment below and sent out a wall of gray dust barreling toward Katrina. Dropping her lead weights, she kicked off the ground as the cloud passed beneath her. She deployed the air balloons on the back of her suit to speed up her ascension. A blast from below drew her attention back down as the round vessel detonated under her feet. A growing air bubble from inside the hull welled up from the blasts. The rising air pocket looked at least half the size of Yankee Stadium.

Katrina swam to the side, trying to get out of the way, but it was too fast for her to escape, and the bubble swallowed her up. She fell through, but her inflatable air balloons kept her afloat on the bottom. There wasn't enough distance to the surface for the massive air bubble to completely disperse into smaller bubbles. As it came up beneath the supply ship, the subtracting water between couldn't support the ship's weight, and it too, was swallowed up, falling inside as the air pocket reached the surface.

The ship fell past Katrina, nearly crushing her as it sank into the ocean below. The air bubble then exploded as it exited the ocean releasing a spitting geyser of white rain and mist. The surrounding water collapsed around Katrina. The gigantic walls of the bubble slammed together, thrashing her around on her way to the surface. Breaching the foamy water, trillions of smaller bubbles rose beneath her like a hot tub as the water calmed.

Desperate for fresh air Katrina took off her helmet and was grateful to be alive. Relieved and exhausted, she laid back as she floated under the misty light of the morning sun. After a moment to catch her breath Katrina glanced over and saw the distant shore of Africa. This was currently a neutral zone in the war, and it would be safe enough to wait there for rescue. Flipping on her tracker she began making her way to the coast.

Chapter 24- Operation Brazen Cinder

February 20th 11:37 PM

The back door to the Kodiak AC10 dropped down. Wes and his team of four EOD bombers strapped on their helmets and stood up. A green light lit up from the roof and the five of them jumped out into the black world below. Wes and his team had just dropped into China to destroy one of their main weapons factories. They touched down in the forest just outside the city of Chongqing.

The plan was to walk to the edge of town and meet up with their contact, a man working on the inside. He would be escorting them safely through the city before reaching the factory. They met halfway on an old road. Wes and his men boarded a white van and their Chinese defector, Wong, started the engine and hit the gas.

Wong had informed the U.S. that the factory Wes was here to destroy was populated with civilian workers not androids like expected (probably children) so simply bombing it was out of the question.

Wes and his team would have to find a way to clear it before the detonation, so as Wong drove the van, Wes discussed with his men the best way it should be done. The contact drove them across the Yangtze River on the Caiyuanba Changjiang bridge. They soon found themselves in the center of Time Square. This city was still very much alive even at this time of night. All the buildings were lit up like Christmas. Entire skyscrapers became TV screens and roads illuminated in various colors as cars drove over them. Even people's clothing had luminescent patterns on them.

Wes enjoyed the view from behind the tinted windows, but then his attention was drawn to the driver as the van came to a sudden stop.

253

"What's the problem?" Wes asked.

Wong twisted back to him and struggled to speak in English.

"I'm going... bring back factory plans, like... layout of building."

"Factory plans. Okay good, go," Wes ordered.

Wong opened his door and stepped out. He walked hastily to the closest building, once inside he turned to look at the van. Wes and his team watched from behind the windows as Wong stretched out a crooked smile and pulled out a small switch from his pocket.

"Everyone out!" Wes yelled as Wong pushed the button sending the van tumbling into the air in a fiery wreck.

It came back down, tires up. Wes's suit kept him alive, but the same could not be said for his team. Out of the four men, only one was still breathing. Wes dragged him to safety and put out the small fires on his body. His name was Riley, and his EOD suit was now black and crisp, but the soldier inside was more or less okay. Wes helped him to his feet and the two of them went around the burning van and searched for Wong, the double agent. As they looked inside at the spot where he had taken cover, Wes shook his head seeing no one in sight.

"This means we're dead right?" Riley presumed.

"No, we got this." Wes assured.

Then Wes was drawn to the chopping blades of an attack helicopter coming their way feeling a rising urge to take back his response.

"You were saying!" Riley said.

The streets had cleared from the explosion. All the citizens ran for cover as Wes and Riley began firing their weapons at the chopper. It fired back, cutting the burning van in half. Wes switched to his grenade launcher, firing one round after another toward the enemy aircraft. Several rounds missed and were sent into the surrounding buildings, but finally, one grenade struck the cockpit. The helicopter hurled down toward them. Wes and Riley lunged to the ground as the burning aircraft smashed into the street behind them.

Wes got up and stared at it, but then there was a sudden flash and a loud bang. Riley was obliterated in a cloud of red vapor by an enemy tank round. Wes aimed his rifle at the tank as about twenty soldiers in armored vests came around from behind it. These guys weren't messing around. The tank rotated its barrel at him and fired. Wes dove to the ground as the glowing round passed over him like a bolt of lightning. It punched through the four support pillars that stood in a row holding up the right side of a large building. Cracks quickly formed and rapidly spread up to the roof. Wes's eyes snapped up as the entire face of the building came crumbling down to the street below. Dust filled the air as it engulfed Time Square.

Wes was now hidden from view as the soldiers couldn't see him through the thick multicolored dust illuminated by the street. However, the thermal signature radiating off his body was in full view of the tank. Wes knew he couldn't hide from their sensors even with all the loose debris in the air. He had to get out of here.

Rubble from the fallen building had just cut off his only exit. The way out was blocked. Shuffling his feet as he moved slowly through the clouds of finely pulverized concrete, the toe of his boot bumped into a raised object on the road. Reaching down he felt the round edges of a manhole cover. Grabbing a piece of bent rebar lying nearby, he started to pry the cover off the storm drain. Once off, Wes jumped down and landed with a tremendous splash. He was instantly carried away by the powerful surge of sewage.

The pipes were almost full, and Wes was tossed around bend after bend as he gasped in the barely breathable air. Suddenly, the pipe ended, and Wes was dumped into the brown, murky water of the Yangtze River.

Chapter 25- Operation High Strike

Trent's pilot hovered low as he descended the Super Hawk upon the rooftop of one of Moscow's tallest buildings. The megacity was in a state of electric celebration as the country had just joined forces with the enemies of the United States. Trent had been flown in to assassinate their head arms dealer in an attempt to stall the distribution of their weapons and ammunition. He was positioned on a building that American spies had chosen several days before Trent arrived. The building was specially chosen not only for its height, but also because the entire thing was temporarily closed due to major construction on the central floors.

Three days ago, an ignited gas leak blew out all the windows from the 51st to the 58th floor killing twenty-two people. Trent didn't know if this incident was caused by the American spies or was an honest accident. He didn't ponder the legitimacy of it as this was not his mission, pulling the trigger was. Trent hooked his 1080 rig onto some railing from one of the construction cranes on the rooftop of the skyscraper.

He climbed over the edge and walked down the side of the building as the rig slowly lowered him down. A thick layer of city smog concealed the base of the building and the streets around it. Vast multitudes of color lit up the low smog as the citizens ignited thousands of sparkling fireworks from below. Trent descended into it and the city below became clear as the immense light from a woman's face on an electronic billboard lit his way.

Trent was armed with a fifty caliber zero-point smart rifle, and as he approached the 58th floor, he slung it to his back. Trent kicked off the glass and swung down through the open window below. It was dark and very cluttered. Red tarps and construction tape fluttered in the breeze. It seemed as though Trent was alone, but as he searched for a place to set up, a distant flash of yellow light caught his attention. At the opposite end of the building, Trent could see two men walking around with flashlights.

He assumed they must be part of the Russian police force guarding the exposed building against looters. As they came in his direction, Trent quietly stepped over to the open elevator shaft. He ducked under the safety tape and reached out to the steel cable in the center of the shaft. He slid down to the fifty-second floor and jumped in. Trent glanced around and saw that this time, he was alone. It seemed that no police occupied this floor and that gave Trent the freedom to set up wherever he wanted.

His eyes traveled east to the direction of his target. Beside the wall to his left was a covered scaffold next to a foldable table with several metal pipes on top of it. Trent walked over to the table and slid the barrel of his rifle inside a pipe on the far right. He pulled up a five-gallon bucket to sit on and draped some of the scaffolding's red tarps over himself and his scope. Trent sighted in on the distant rooftop of the Pylon Weapons Laboratory where the party would be held. Now all he had to do was wait.

It was 12:38 and by 1:44 AM, the private after-party had begun. The guests filed in one by one. Trent examined their faces as he searched for his target. He lined up the crosshairs in between their eyes and the scope's computer automatically searched for matches.

Men and women draped in elegant apparel quickly enveloped the now well-lit and decorated rooftop.

After a short moment, Trent saw him. His face matched the scans on his scope, and the photo Trent had memorized on the flight out here. Trent grinned as he sighted in on his face. *Sure hate to spoil such a nice-looking party.*

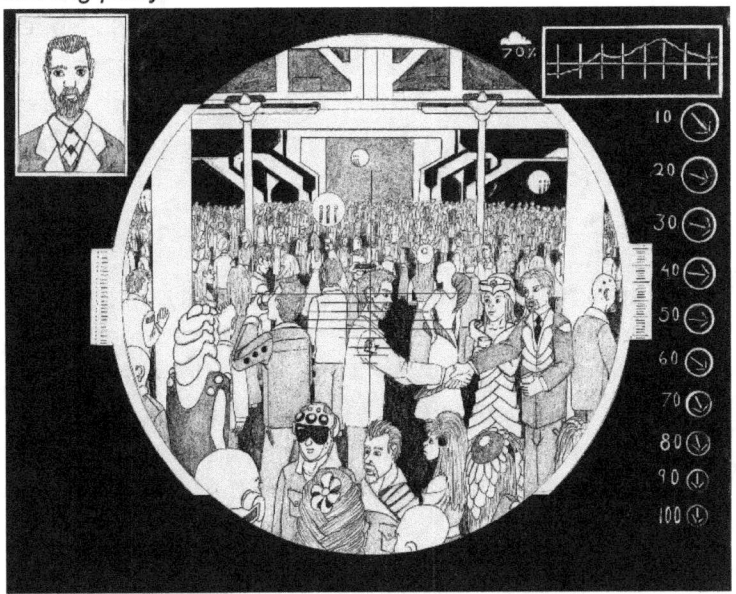

As Trent exhaled, he slowly squeezed down on the trigger, but before any round could exit the barrel, Trent's view was suddenly blocked by an obstruction he was not expecting. A party blimp had drifted in view of his target.

Trent's finger jumped off the trigger as he saw hundreds of people dancing on top of the upper half of the blimp. Shaped like an expensive yacht with a massive stage and a glass pool in the center. It hovered between the buildings with three air turbines on each side of an inflated underbelly. It moved slowly, and Trent had to wait for it to eventually get out of the way.

A scratching noise drew Trent's eyes off his scope and into the eyes of a rat crawling across the pipes toward his face. Suddenly, it stood still as a light beamed on it from the right. Trent froze as the footsteps of the two police officers approached him. They stepped closer, keeping their lights on the rat. Trent was well-hidden underneath the red tarp and his barrel was concealed inside the metal pipe. As the police approached, the rat stood on its hind legs sniffing in their direction. The officers spoke in Russian and the computer on Trent's scope listened in, translating the words for him at the bottom of the screen.

There he is. Same place as yesterday. It read.

The two police leaned forward and began feeding the little rodent some crackers. Trent softly breathed out his mouth as the policemen were no more than two feet away. He still didn't have the shot; the blimp was moving slowly. Trent feared the police would nudge the pipe and offset his alignment on the building. It was difficult for him to keep his heart rate down, but as the blimp finally disappeared from his view, Trent had to search through the crowds again and regain sight of his target.

Once Trent spotted him, he quickly aimed at his chest and for one short instant, Trent's world fell still. He slowly exhaled and waited for his heart to stop beating before he squeezed the trigger. The bolt was released, and the pin ignited the round blowing it out the barrel and racing above the many buildings below. Upon impact, the man's neck and shoulders were instantly obliterated like a watermelon in the path of a semi-truck. The party guests stood in shock as they were showered with the illuminated scarlet blood.

The round's shockwave blew the tarp off Trent's head, and the piercing noise scared the life out of the two officers along with the small rat. Trent immediately stood up. Unclipping his taser, he aimed at the two men, firing into center mass. They dropped to the floor, surprised looks still adorning their faces as they twitched on the ground. The rat jumped over their bodies and scurried into the distance.

For a moment, Trent thought he was in the clear, but this thought was proven false by the immense light now shining on him by the headlights of the party blimp. It lit up the entire floor, and the hundreds of passengers on board stared and mumbled amongst themselves as to who the strange man was. Seeing this, Trent knew if he didn't leave now, he would most likely be welcomed to this city by the screeching voice of a speeding bullet aimed right at his head.

He dropped the taser, darting toward the closest stairwell and radioing his pilot to start the engines. The headlights of the blimp shut off again as Trent raced up to the 53rd floor. Peering through the empty windows he saw the blimp turn and drift away. He continued up the stairs since this was the only way up due to the elevator being under construction on the first floor. If he could just attach himself to his 1080 rig, it could quickly zip him back up to the roof. As he rounded the corner to the 57th floor, he stumbled as the entire building shook. Trent's gaze shot out the nearby open window to his left and took note of something he hadn't planned for. Nine enemy tanks were aiming their main cannons at the support beams and firing

261

to bring down the building. They had come from a nearby parking garage. It looks like the enemy was expecting someone to make an attempt on the target's life tonight. Trent radioed his pilot.

"Take off now!"

The first floor collapsed. The tanks backed away, and Trent felt the whole building shift. His pilot took off. Cracks formed in the ceiling and floor as the windows shattered, and dust filled the streets. Trent had no time left. He skipped steps as he rushed up to the 58th floor. The cable was now in view, but it was at the other side of the room.

As Trent ran, the building began to collapse on the center floors due to the previous damage from the gas explosion three days ago. This caused the top half of the building to lean forward. The tilted floor fell beneath Trent's feet, and he landed on his back, sliding toward the open windows. He pulled out his suppressed pistol and shot out the new replacement glass beside the opening so he would have more room to fall through. Debris from the falling building tumbled behind him as he fired.

He reached the edge of the window and threw his gun, grabbing the carabiner and hooking it to his belt. Trent dropped out of the window and the leaning upper half of the building above him (where his rope was attached) sent him swinging over the streets below and toward the next building across from him. The rooftop smashed into the adjacent building causing a shockwave that shattered all the glass down the building Trent was swinging toward. Grabbing his knife, Trent sliced his rope. He fell forward, dropping two floors and crashing through the shattered glass. He landed on his side and tumbled into a metal office desk, but still, he wasn't safe.

The upper half of the collapsed building was bringing this second building down with it. Trent saw the party blimp hovering outside the window at the opposite end of the room. He got up and began limping as he ran, cracks formed beneath his feet, and a thick cloud of gray dust raced behind him. He ignored his limp, running faster, jumping over desks, and finally reaching the cracking windows. He smashed through, diving out toward the center of the blimp. He dropped one story as all the windows to that floor exploded behind him.

Dust engulfed the aircraft as Trent fell into the open pool in the center. The crowds of people on board ducked as the six rotating intake fans sucked in the debris and spit out fire from the exhaust. They malfunctioned and began shutting off. Holes formed in the inflated underbelly of the blimp as metal, glass and concrete blew out and punctured it. Trent swam to the surface, and the citizens aboard began to panic as the blimp slowly drifted downward. A large river ran through the center of the city and the pilot of the blimp steered toward it. The aircraft struggled to stay in the air. Trent climbed out of the pool and the people on board cleared away from him.

"You need to pick me up!" Trent said into his radio.

"You're still alive! Where are you?" the pilot responded.

"I'm in the burning blimp about to crash into the river; come get me now!" Trent yelled.

The blimp dropped to about 35 feet above the water, the two right intake engines failed causing the aircraft to lean. The pilot of the blimp switched the remaining right engine on full, keeping it leaning but still afloat. This caused all the passengers to slide down onto the railing, piling up like marbles. The water from the pool drained out over the people, and Trent fell back inside, standing on the inner glass wall of the pool.

Trent's pilot arrived and hovered close to the pile of screaming people. Climbing out of the pool Trent slid across the floor. He landed softly on the people and crawled over them onto the railing. Eyeing in on the black skids of the Super Hawk Trent shot out his arms as he jumped for them. He grabbed hold and his pilot hit the engines to full as Trent's legs dangled down below. He was finally able to climb aboard and turned to watch the blimp slowly drift down and splash into the river as they flew away.

Chapter 26- The Crimson Pillar

February 21st 12:36 PM

"Skymont Air Force Base, Abner speaking... Who? He's where?"

Abner hung up the phone and yelled into the intercom on his desk.

"Jim and Dirk, report to my office immediately!"

Dirk and I heard the announcement and ran to his office. We entered through his door, and Abner stood up from behind his desk.

"Congratulations, I have a mission for both of you."

"What kind of mission sir?" Dirk asked.

"Rescue mission," he replied, barely looking at us as he shuffled through folders strewn across the desktop.

"For who?" I asked.

"Isaac Richards, Wes' son."

"What?"

"Where is he?" Dirk asked.

"Saudi Arabia," Abner said abruptly as he found the folder he was searching for. He scribbled some coordinates on the inside and handed it to Dirk.

"He's trapped behind enemy lines and apparently, he has a recording of some secret information regarding the enemy. I need you two to go in and secure his safety. Whatever recording he has might just be the kind of leverage we need to end this war before it gets any worse."

"When do we go?" I asked.

"Now," he expressed swiftly.

Dirk and I turned to leave but before we could Abner stopped us.

"Wait! Before you go, you'll need these. Your new patches just came in and they need a positive debut so you two get the honor of sporting them on your suits."

Abner then pulled out two rainbow flag patches. Dirk glanced at me as he took his, but as Abner reached out to me, I remained still.

"Sir, I can't wear that. It goes against my beliefs as a Christian."

Abner glared at me as though I had spoken a different language.

"Isaac is waiting on you, Mr. Phillips," he stated sternly.

I looked away and exhaled as I took the patch and walked out of the room with Dirk. He and I quickly suited up and boarded one of Skymont's largest and fastest jets. We were to fly to Isaac's location and join up with a small American strike force already on route to his position. This was going to be a long flight, and once onboard and in the air, I made sure no one was watching before I pulled out the patch and cut it in half with my knife.

Dirk did the same and to pass the time, I listened to some music on my recorder. As I sat there, I thought to myself, what was Isaac doing in Saudi Arabia? And what information could he have that's so important? I guess it's a good thing Wes left before anyone knew about his kid. It's never good to be distracted before a mission. It's why I listen to music. It helps get my mind off things like that stupid patch Abner wants us to wear.

Time seemed to go by slowly. We flew through the night and into the next morning. Eventually, the jet slowed as we approached Isaac's coordinates. Already, about one mile away from the drop zone, gunfire and small explosions could be seen from our windows. That wasn't good. It meant that the enemy was already in combat with the American troops. Our jet circled closer, and Dirk pointed out a window.

"There's Isaac's plane."

It was crashed in the sand at the center of the small firefight.

"Do you think he's still in it?" I asked.

Dirk turned to me, "Let's hope so."

My heart began to race as I eyed it. Isaac is one kid I had to save. I couldn't afford any mistakes on this mission; the life of my best friend's son is at stake. We grabbed our parachutes and quickly strapped them on over our suits. The pilot steered lower and opened the back door. The sun shone across our visors as the door lowered. A tremendous gust of wind from the vacuum flapped around the straps on our suits. The green light above our exit lit up, and Dirk and I ran out the back door diving into the battlefield.

We fell face first, drifting toward the U.S. strike force. The desert floor quickly approached, but it was hard to judge depth from the uneven sand below. At an altitude of two thousand feet, Dirk and I fell below critical altitude, and we deployed our chutes. Our feet swung down below us as the chutes jerked us back. The battleground below was approximately one hundred feet away and approaching fast. We drifted behind the American troops as the enemy soldiers opened fire on us. Bullets smacked against our suits and filled our chutes with holes.

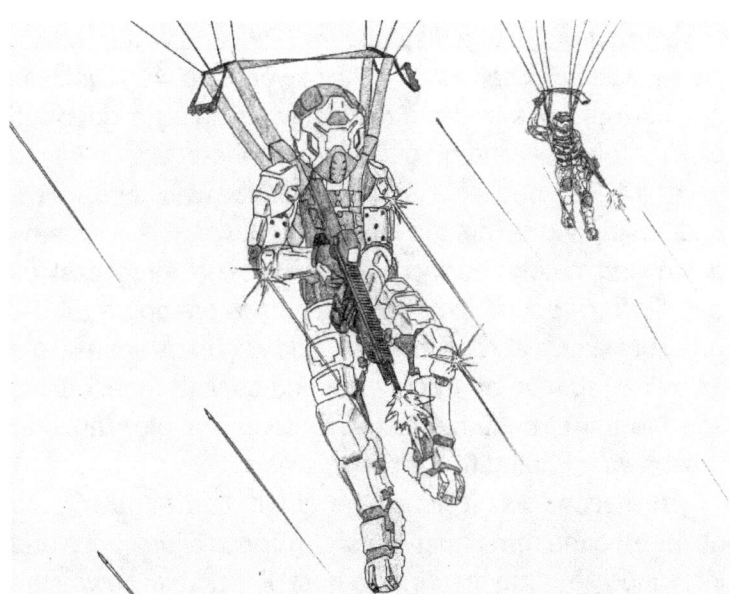

We briefly returned fire before Dirk and I simultaneously hit the cord, detaching the parachutes, and dropped twenty feet down. Our boots hit the sand throwing dust around us. Dirk and I grabbed our smart rifles and ran toward the American troops. Two soldiers came rushing over to us.

"What's the situation?" Dirk asked. Small explosions came up over the peak of the dune in front of us.

"It's not good, we've been pinned down all morning."

"What are we up against?" I asked.

"There's about twenty of them," he answered quickly.

"And we only have five men left." another soldier added.

"We'll manage," Dirk said as he and I proceeded to the top of the dune.

The men lying prone at the top watched as we walked past. Immediately, a glowing hailstorm of bullets rained toward us from over a distant dune. Dirk and I returned fire as we walked. Their small-caliber weapons were useless against our suits and at first, we were doing a good job picking them off one by one. The American troops joined in, and it seemed as though the battle was ours, but a sudden and unexpected blast from over the hill came down and detonated in between us. The force cast us apart from each other like a rope snapping under pressure. I skid across the sand and sat up as I came to a stop. Taking hold of my gun, I aimed back at them only to see the barrel bent in a forty-five-degree angle - another reason why I hated these cheap smart rifles.

A second blast from the dune came down and obliterated the remaining American troops. Torn limbs and intestines flew into the air as a gust of wind blew away the thick cloud of misty blood. The enemy soldiers were firing some kind of rocket launcher. I caught sight of them, seeing the few remaining split off into three groups of two. The couple closest to me aimed their guns in my direction and began firing away. Sand and dust kicked up around me as I reached to my hip and unclipped my handgun. I got to my feet and fired two precise shots into their faces. They dropped to the ground, but the second couple was closer to Dirk, and they quickly grabbed hold of him. Seeing this, I began sprinting to his aid.

The men pinned Dirk to the bottom of the dune and the soldier closest to his head attempted to pry off Dirk's helmet. He tugged and pulled at the straps but couldn't figure out how to undo them. Dirk grabbed the man's face and dug his thumbs into his eyes. The soldier screamed and grabbed Dirk's wrists, trying to make him stop, but Dirk didn't let up. He drove his thumbs deeper and popped the retinas as he held the man's head close to his chest.

Blood poured down his forearms. Dirk let go and the soldier stood up screaming in pain as he ran into the distance.

Dirk leaned forward and smashed his armored fist into the second man's nose. He let go of Dirk's legs and fell backward. Dirk stood up and unclipped his sidearm, firing three shots into the soldier's head, dislodging his face into three sections held together by skin. He then aimed at the first soldier running blindly into the desert. Dirk stretched out his arm and fired one round into the back of the man's head.

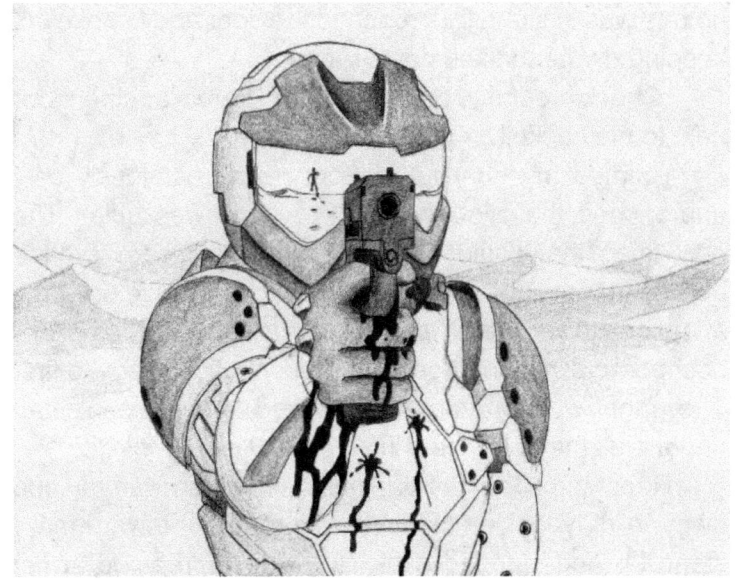

I caught up to Dirk just as he did this.

"Come on, Jim. Isaac can't wait on you all day."

I smiled, happy to see that he was okay. The two of us caught sight of the remaining two soldiers as they sprinted toward Isaac's plane. I watched them, seeing the soldier on the left was larger and appeared to be much stronger than the other. I'll have to be careful around him.

Dirk and I raced after them, firing occasional pistol shots as we ran. Our bullets smashed into the tail section of the plane over the open back door. The two soldiers jumped aboard, but just before the smaller man could move out of view, one of Dirk's rounds struck him in the back of the neck, dropping him to the floor, dead. Dirk's pistol clicked empty, and he took a quick second to reload as I reached the door to the plane. I jumped inside and aimed my .45 up toward the cockpit, but to my surprise, no one was in sight. Dirk reached the door and I spoke up, keeping my head fixed down range.

"Check around to the other side. There's another door next to the cockpit."

I aimed my gun out in front of me cautiously as I approached the pilot chairs. Everything was quiet. The only thing that could be heard was the steady breeze picking up outside. Then a faint scratching noise drew my attention to a metal panel underneath the co-pilot's dashboard. Kneeling beside it I held my gun ready to fire. The panel wasn't attached; it looked like someone had undone all the bolts. Yanking it open, I aimed inside.

Reaching out of the darkness a hand shoved my gun away. A dirty-looking kid came crawling out toward me. I stood up and stepped back as the kid screamed at my helmet. His face was half-covered in dirt and blood, his skin was badly bruised, and his hair was thick and scraggly. I hadn't seen Isaac in a long time, but even now I could recognize his face, but he didn't recognize me. I remember visiting him at one of his birthday parties and Wes telling me how when Isaac was only four years old his favorite thing in the world was a little toy airplane he got for Christmas. But look at him now, trapped inside one, acting like a wild animal. I grabbed his shoulders and forced him onto the ground.

"Isaac! ISAAC! Hey! It's okay. I'm here to help. I'm one of the good guys."

Isaac's eyes widened. "GETAWAY!"

Isaac struggled to get out from under my grip. I unclipped my helmet and set it aside grabbing Isaac's face pulling it toward mine.

"Isaac, it's me! Jim Phillips. You know me. Your father's name is Wesley Richards. I went to your fourteenth birthday. You got a leather jacket, a new phone and some razors. I know you love to fly and cut your own hair."

I took note of his scruffy appearance.

"You sure have a lot to cut now. You know me... I'm your friend."

He squinted his eyes and tilted his head as I let go of him.

"I remember you. You're my dad's friend? D- did you come to save me?" Isaac asked.

"Yes, Isaac, I'm going to get you out of here."

Isaac teared up as my words filled his ears. Then he reached up and handed me something. It was a small black box with a digital screen on the top.

"What's this?" I asked.

"The flight recorder. It has something on it that may be important."

I stuffed it into my vest pocket and put his arm over me, helping him to his feet. We faced the open door I had entered through and began walking toward it. Suddenly, a black metal disk shot out from the back of the plane and latched itself onto my chest plate. My head shot down and my eyes flung open as I was pulled forward, dropping Isaac to the floor. An arm reached out from behind a tarp hanging down from the back of the plane. I came to a sudden stop as if sucked into the grasp of a tightening hand wrapping around my neck. A large man stepped out from behind the tarp and stared into my eyes.

"You're in my way, boy."

"No, not him," Isaac said.

I reached down to my knife, but before I could unsheathe it, I was thrown out the door of the plane landing in the sand on my back. The disk detached from my chest plate and flew back onto the man's glove. He showed his back to me and walked toward Isaac. I got up and jumped back inside checking left toward the man but the second I did; my head shot down as something small rolled toward me. A grenade! My eyes widened, and I covered my exposed face as it detonated, but instead of an aggressive explosion, a thick, red jelly-like foam sprang up to the ceiling and sealed in place, blocking my way to Isaac. I ran up to the now solid obstruction and pounded my fist on it.

"ISAAC!" I yelled, but there was no answer.

At that moment, Dirk reached the second hatch at the front of the plane to the right of the cockpit. He slid it open and was met with a boot to the chest as the large man kicked him down to the sand. The man jumped out and rushed toward him. I could hear the two of them scuffling outside, and I jumped out the door to my left. Running around to the front end of the plane I saw Isaac jump out the door from the cockpit. I was relieved to see he was okay, but still there was the matter of his attacker. Isaac was holding my helmet; I took it from him.

"Jim, that man's insane. You have to kill him."

"Who is he?" I asked.

"His name is Anton Von Janko. He's been trying to kill me."

"I won't let him," I assured as I strapped on my helmet and bolted toward him.

Anton turned away from Dirk and sent the Keylex disk flying at me. I smacked it into the sand before it could contact my suit. Anton charged at me, raising his right hand into a fist as I got closer. The second before our bodies collided, I dropped to my knees and sunk my fist into his stomach. Spit blew out his mouth as his torso fell over top my shoulders. This seemed to only anger him further as Anton then wrapped his arms around from my back and grabbed the fabric covering my stomach. The next thing I knew, I was being lifted up with my face toward the ground and my legs reaching up to the sky. Anton was about to snap my neck into the hot desert sand, but to my relief Dirk smashed his shoulder into Anton's back, knocking us all to the ground.

Suddenly, a loud horn rang in the distance, I looked up from the sand and witnessed something unexpected crawling over the distant horizon. Four monstrous half-tracked vehicles with a head shaped similar to a sperm whale approached us. Anton saw them and jumped to his feet, quickly sprinting toward a large dune. Dirk and I stood up and watched as he retreated.

"That can't be good," I stated, and in an instant, Isaac's plane was obliterated by a small missile launched by one of the strange vehicles. The three of us hit the floor as fire and debris blew over our heads and tumbled across the sand. I helped Isaac up and we began sprinting for cover as more missiles rained down around us. Dirk and I kept Isaac between us, so the small chunks of shrapnel were less likely to hit him. We climbed up the closest dune and slid down over the peak.

"What's the plan?" Isaac yelled as more missiles flew over our heads and detonated in the desert beyond.

"I'm working on it!" I yelled back and shifted to Dirk, seeing that he was pressing buttons on his radio.

"What are you doing?" I yelled.

"I'm calling in an airstrike!" he said.

"By what?"

"The Crimson Pillar."

I squinted at his answer. "You can't call for that it's never been used before. Abner won't approve it."

Dirk turned to me.

"He will for us. If we stay here any longer, we will die! Look at Isaac!"

I glanced back to Isaac's squinting eyes as he held up his arms to cover his head. Seeing how terrified he was, I turned back to Dirk.

"I'm making this call." he declared and dialed it in.

The airstrike he was asking for was the United States' most destructive non-nuclear weapon. Dirk entered the coordinates of the enemy vehicles as tanks and hundreds of infantry men began forming around them.

To my surprise Dirk's call got the green light, and the launch codes were sent up to a satellite known as the Crimson Pillar. Three of them orbited Earth giving America full coverage of the planet with the closest one aiming toward Saudi Arabia.

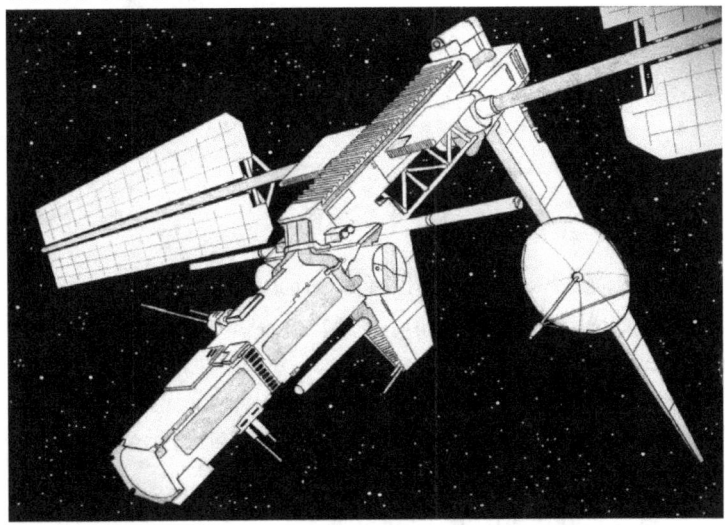

A rectangular panel detached, releasing seven, fifteen-foot-long red missiles that hurtled toward the coordinates Dirk had sent in. Upon breaching the atmosphere, the missiles released a chemical that reacted with the air igniting into red and blue flames. The missiles spun like a bullet causing the trail of fire to twirl around in a whirlwind. The three of us watched in awe as seven tornadoes of blazing fire shot down from space and detonated in a hurricane of fire and debris. The hundreds of soldiers were instantly vaporized as the tanks and four massive vehicles melted into glowing puddles of molten liquid.

Seeing them destroyed, Isaac stood up in the open as he threw out his arms and yelled at the top of his lungs.

"YESSSSS!"

We watched as the flames whorled around before us. I had never seen anything like this. After the initial blast, the only thing remaining was a steadily dying fire surrounded by a large field of green glass created by the intense flames. I stood up and patted Isaac on the shoulder.

"Are you ready to go home."

He faced me with the biggest smile and hugged me.

"Thank you."

Anton watched the flames from a distance and then turned away, slipping quietly into the desert as he pulled out a phone and made a call of his own.

Soon after, Dirk and I flipped on our suit trackers and awaited assistance. It didn't take long and soon we found ourselves on our flight home. In the seat next to me, Isaac laid his head back finding rest in what I assumed was a long time. I looked at him, relieved that he was alright, but also sad for the men we lost to get him back.

How many would have to die before we stopped these people? I turned away, gazing out the window hoping the view would take my mind off things. Just then I noticed a small black plane flying at an incredible speed in the opposite direction as us. It was oddly shaped, looking like a stingray without a tail and I, unfortunately, didn't think too much of it at the time.

Chapter 27- Dr. Krull

February 20th 6AM

Katrina sat patiently on the coast of Africa letting her boots soke in the water as the incoming tides crashed against them. The red African sun rose behind her shining through her brown hair as it fluttered in the wind. The crashing waves soothed her troubled mind, especially after the night she just had. Far off over the horizon Katrina could see the flashing light from her chopper coming into view. It was still a long way off, but the thought of seeing Trent once she returned to base brought a smile to her face.

Then the sight of something odd erased the joy on her lips. She stared intensely at the flashing strobe as it curved sharply and dove into the ocean. Katrina stood up with her helmet in hand watching as her ride home crashed into the water. Pulling out her radio she hurried to call for help but before any number could be dialed, Katrina was struck on the back of her head. She fell face down unconscious and unaware that at that moment she had just been stolen by the enemy.

February 22nd

A large steel door slowly lifted open to reveal a dark room ahead. Men took Katrina's arms and dragged her inside. They dropped her on the cold floor. One man stood to the left flipping a switch and pressed a button causing the room to shake before calming and gradually going downward. It took about two minutes for the elevator to come to a stop. Hydraulic steam drained from the doors above and slowly slid open. Two more men entered the room and took hold of Katrina.

They sat her on a wheeled aluminum cart and pushed her past large copper coils suspended like two donuts held face to face. Heading down the hall they proceeded left into the next room, filled with metal hoses running up and down the walls. One man came in and placed a plastic cover over her mouth and nose.

Afterward, he made his exit from the room and sealed the doors, flipping on the hoses. About two dozen jets of water cleaned Katrina and her suit. White steam filled the space and the skin on her face turned red from the high water pressure. The men shut it off and re-entered to take off her mask. They loaded her back on the cart. Katrina was slowly waking up. Bright lights from the ceiling shone in her eyes and the men strapped her down onto the cart with thick leather straps.

With a blurry mind, her eyes wandered around, unaware as to what was happening. The men took her down a second hall and into a small room. For a moment, Katrina thought she was back at Skymont Air Force Base, but that thought was far from the truth. A solitary metal table stood alone in the center of the room. A large, thick one-way window faced it from the right wall.

The men lifted her up and onto the table, strapping her down and pricking her forehead with a needle. It was the only exposed area on her body. Blood drained out and the men collected it in a small glass vile. Then they injected her with something and left the room, shutting the door behind them. It was quiet. Katrina was all alone and as she passed in and out of consciousness, she felt the muscles in her body tingle as if she were being stabbed by thousands of needles.

After about twenty minutes, Katrina's skin was totally pale. Her lips were purple and her whole body was shaking. She squinted at the intense lights beaming down above her face. Seconds later, ten men in lab coats came in and gathered around her. One man, much older than the rest, stood to her right shoulder. He leaned his head over hers, blocking the light from her face. Katrina opened her eyes and stared up at him. He was Chinese and looked to be about fifty.

"Good morning, I am Dr. Krull. Welcome to Dalara station."

"What is this place? Who are you?" Katrina mumbled.

"Who we are is not important. This place and who you are, is," he said.

"I'm not saying anything," Katrina stated.

Dr. Krull chuckled. "That's fine. Any secrets you may hold carry no importance to us. But since you brought it up, I might as well ask about your suit. What is it made of? And how do we get it off."

At that, Katrina knew where this was leading.

"You're just going to kill me."

Dr. Krull smiled. "If we wanted to kill you, we would have just thrown you into a tub of acid and dissolved you out of your armor. Especially after what you destroyed. But we're not in that business. We're here to save you."

"What do you mean?" she asked.

"When you wake up, you'll understand."

The doctor nodded over to the man next to him and whispered,

"Prepare the transmitter."

He turned back to Katrina.

"Like all things, you and the destruction of your nation are inevitable. Once it's all over, you'll realize this was all done to help you, even now when you didn't even know you needed it. Take note, my students, that is the kindness of Morgan," the doctor proclaimed to the other scientists in the room. Katrina listened in as he continued.

"You must understand, the thing that binds us, the thing that traps us all, is about to be overthrown."

"What?" Katrina asked, frustrated with his riddles.

"What I mean, little girl, is that I have held the heart of this Earth in my hands, and do you know what I felt... it was beautiful," he said.

"You're crazy," Katrina asserted.

"It's quite the opposite actually. I knew a man once; he was like you. Very foolish, so I... altered him. His body was no longer of human origin. He was made from something only found deep within the core. Something that very few people have been around and lived to talk about. His body became something more. More than I ever thought possible. But I didn't know how to sustain

283

him, and he died, in such a way that baffled even me. I watched him vanish before my eyes. It was quite the conundrum."

The doctor peered away in wonder and glanced at the man next to him.

"Professor, you and your students may proceed."

Dr. Krull left the room, and the remaining men began trying to unstrap Katrina's suit. The team unclipped the armored sections but didn't take them off her body because each section was connected to the wires that sent electrical currents to the explosive agent under the Fragmight layer. They didn't want to cut them because Dr. Krull had ordered them not to damage the suit in any way. One man next to Katrina injected a second chemical into her neck. Katrina began to feel sleepy. It was only a matter of time until they figured it out, but time was all she needed. Since her suit was emitting her location back to base Katrina was at ease knowing Trent was on his way.

She gazed around at the scientists inspecting her from all directions, examining every inch of her suit, measuring, and taking pictures. Eventually, one man took notice of the small circular latch on her left shoulder. He flipped it open revealing the keyhole. The Hell switch. After taking a quick picture, he alerted Dr. Krull and the fellow men in the room, addressing it as a possible way to unlock her suit.

The doctor stared intently through the glass with a smirk, believing this was in fact the way to open it. Katrina's heart dropped to her stomach at the thought of them turning the key. All she had to do was speak up and tell how to really open the suit. Unwinding the spring bolts required a code which needed to be entered into a screen on her left arm. Glancing down at it she just barely managed to twist her wrist and hide it from their view. *Not yet.*

The man standing beside her noticed a key under the latch on her shoulder. He picked it up and looked to Dr. Krull for his order to proceed. The doctor took note of them and nodded. The key was inserted into the hole just as thoughts of Trent flashed across her mind.

"Please watch over him." she whispered.

Dr. Krull said something in Chinese to the man with the key but still, Katrina remained silent. *I'm sorry Trent.* She closed her eyes as if preparing to fall asleep, seeing in her mind a memory of him on their wedding day. A tear dripped down her cheek splashing onto the cold table just as the key was turned. In that instant, there was silence, a brief moment of total peace. Then booming into existence, a sudden clap of scarlet fire vaporized everything in the room, killing everyone inside and eviscerating Katrina along with her suit.

Dr. Krull jolted back in shock as the reinforced walls in front of him bloated outward from the blast. The thick glass cracked and was painted with the blood of all who were once living inside. The toxic fumes from the burnt chemical agent filled the room and the doctors began venting it out. As they did this Dr. Krull scrambled over to the digital monitors trying to understand what went wrong. Then as a picture came into view he fell still as something he couldn't have imagined appeared before him.

The whole room went quiet. Dr. Krull looked back through the glass and watched speechless as suddenly before his very eyes stood a young man who was not there before. He was trembling silently in the center of the scorched room. From out of thin air, he appeared just as the flames went out. Gray hair covered his head. There was blood and scars across his entire body. He was missing his right eye as well as the lower half of his left leg. This man looked up at the doctor locking eyes with him for a moment, and then without warning, he vanished. The room was silent, and Dr. Krull remained speechless. The beeping monitors to his right drew his eye where he examined the temperature recorded from the detonation.

"Change of plan." Dr. Krull said with widened eyes.

"As of this moment, the science team's number one priority is to find the remaining Hellbenders."

Chapter 28- Broken Soldiers

Dirk and I arrived with Isaac back at base later that afternoon. Our plane landed, and we stepped onto the tarmac. Isaac was still smiling at the thought of finally being home and safe from the enemy. Adam was there standing alone, waiting to greet us.

"Adam, this is Isaac Richards, Wes's son."

Adam shook his hand. "Good to meet you."

He sounded strange, and his tone was off. His eyes turned to me.

"Something's happened."

Before Adam told us anything, we sent Isaac to the infirmary and walked up to our barracks. Zack and Peter were there. Both of them were sitting in silence.

"What's going on?" Dirk asked.

Adam faced the two of us.

"The morning after Katrina completed her mission, she activated her tracker. After Abner sent her exfil, it was shot down before it could reach her, and she was taken. A rescue team was sent out to retrieve her but was also shot down. Two days later, all they saw on the monitors was the blip from her suit moving across the sky toward Saudi Arabia at an incredible speed."

I thought back to that oddly shaped black jet I'd seen fly past us.

"It finally stopped at an abandoned city in the middle of the desert, at which point Abner organized a much larger rescue team, but moments before they took off, Katrina's vitals and tracker shut down. And the only way for that to happen is if her suit were to detonate. Which means... she's gone."

I took a step back as if I were just punched in the chest.

"What?" I asked in disbelief.

Falling backward onto the couch, I was unable to hold back the tears as they blurred my vision. How are we ever going to tell Trent?

Hours later, Wes and Trent arrived at base from their missions. Wes came first. We delivered the bad news, and he, like the rest of us, was devastated. I told him about his son, and he went immediately to Isaac's side. Trent arrived soon after, he stepped down onto the tarmac and general Abner was there to meet him. The general hadn't stood by on the tarmac to greet someone since Oddball was taken out, so Trent instantly knew something was up.

"Trent, you and I need to talk."

Trent nodded and couldn't help but think he had done something wrong during his mission. Abner took him up to his office and together they sat face to face. The General peered into Trent's eyes and was silent as he searched for the right words.

"Trent, there's no easy way to say this so I'm just going to come out and say it. Something's happened to Katrina."

"What do you mean?" he asked.

"We have reason to believe that after Katrina's mission was completed, she was captured and… then killed."

Trent was silent for a moment.

"That's not even funny. Where is she?"

"I'm sorry, Trent, but this is not a joke... she didn't make it back."

Trent stared intensely into the general's eyes. Seconds later he began to breathe heavily as he slowly realized it was true. Abner stood up.

"I'll give you a moment."

Trent sat alone, motionless and silent as the thought of never seeing Katrina again took hold of him.

Wes stepped inside the infirmary and asked for the number to Isaac's room. He stopped when he reached his door. This would be the first time the two of them would be face to face since Isaac's 14th birthday. Wes rehearsed the many things he had neglected to say over the years, but as he opened the door and met eyes with his son, he was speechless. Isaac laid under the white covers of his bed, hooked up to an IV, and wiped clean from head to toe. His face was heavily marked with stitches and white bandages from his many beatings. Wes noticed Isaac's heart rate increase as he walked into the room. A tear dropped from Wes's eye as he looked into Isaac's gaze. From only a single glance he knew Isaac still hated him.

"Why are you here?" Isaac asked.

Wes took a deep breath and stepped closer.

"I heard you were in some trouble."

"I heard you were in prison and then became some big-shot soldier. Why did they let you out?"

"Because I'm innocent." Wes confessed plainly.

"No, you're not. You killed Mom," Isaac stated.

"No. She chose to do that herself and not a day has gone by that I haven't missed her. Not a day has gone by that I haven't missed you."

Isaac frowned. "Prove it."

"Prove what?" Wes asked.

"That you're innocent."

Wes shook his head. "Son, I wouldn't be here if I was guilty."

"Don't call me your son!" Isaac demanded. "You're not a man! You're not a soldier and you're not my dad. You haven't been for five years."

Wes's eyes filled with rage. "You're my son and I'm your-"

"Shut up! How long ago was it when you were freed from jail?"

"Isaac, that's not important," Wes uttered.

"HOW LONG!" Isaac yelled.

"Three years."

"So, for three years you never once called or came to see me."

"I couldn't," Wes said. "The only way they would take my case is if I agreed to do a job for the military. And after I was done, they wiped my identity clean. I no longer existed to the public, especially not to my family. If I contacted you or anyone, they would be monitoring our calls and guards showing up at your house to make sure I wasn't committing treason. I was forced to be a stranger to keep the people who wanted me dead from going after you."

"Am I supposed to say thank you?" Isaac questioned. "I needed my dad, but it sounds like you were off pretending to play hero. And if all this is true then maybe your right and I don't really need you in my life."

"Isaac, you can't live all by yourself."

"I've had to do it alone so far, because you left. You don't have the right to tell me what I can't do... so just leave. I don't ever want to see you again."

Wes closed his eyes and turned away, leaving his son and heading down to the barracks.

That night, Abner entered the audio room at base. He sat down next to a young cadet.

"Okay, play it." he said.

The cadet flipped on the flight recorder from Isaac's plane and plugged it into a machine to magnify the sound. The enemy broadcast played out, and Abner wrote down the names as it ended.

"Dr. Krull... Hector, and the Kronos. Well, let's find out who these people are."

Abner and the cadet spun around and slid themselves into a desk where a computer sat facing them. Abner logged onto a program called the L.O.F.T. (Library of Foreign Terrorists) and typed in the names, but only one came up with a file.

"Dr. Shen Krull, a Chinese physicist, born in 2057. Has a sister in the city of New Otoma working as a prostitute apparently. Parents died in 2092 and the doctor was arrested for illegal human experimentation. He went to jail in 2080 but escaped and is now unaccounted for." Abner leaned back in his chair.

"So why was he broken out? What does the enemy need him for and who are these other names?" Abner glanced at the cadet who shrugged his shoulders.

"Let's see what Isaac knows."

Abner came to visit Isaac and sat down beside his bed.

"How are you feeling?"

"Good enough," Isaac said.

"Did you know you're being awarded the Purple Heart? That's pretty impressive for a nineteen-year-old." Isaac just stared back at him with a blank face.

"Isaac, I listened to the recording from your plane, and I need you to tell me if you know what any of it means."

"Sir, all I could make out is that there is something big coming, and I have no idea what it is. But I do remember one more name that wasn't on the recording. Morgan. A man named Anton Von Janko mentioned him. Do you know him?"

"Morgan what? What's the last name?"

Isaac shook his head. "I don't know."

Abner said nothing and looked away saying, "Neither do I."

Chapter 29- Call to Action

March 10th 2099

Two days later, news had spread that a Hellbender had died. Some people mourned, others laughed and cheered. They didn't know how she died, but they hoped it was slow. The videos made to mock her were beyond evil. Some said she was the first of us to be deployed into Hell as if that thought was supposed to be comforting. But Katrina's death only reenforced the juvenile superstition that Hellbenders don't go to Heaven. But despite all this no one's words hurt me more than Trent's. The first thing he said to me after coming back to base was, Katrina had waited on me to say goodbye before her mission. But because I had prioritized speaking with Joi over her, I was the sole thing that made Katrina lose focus before she left. She died thinking I didn't have time for her, just like my parents did. And for that, I hated myself.

Today was Katrina's funeral. There was no body, so her coffin was filled with flowers and pictures of times when things were happier. It was buried at a secret location out in the woods, hidden from view of the world. I glanced around at the people. There were no smiles, there were no laughs, only tears. No more so than Trent who sobbed bitterly in view of everyone present as the coffin was lowered into the ground out of his sight forever. The ceremony was short, and we all headed back to base wondering how things could ever be the same.

Back in our barracks I sat beside Katrina's parents. They had lost both of their children. First their son, Ben, now Katrina. All that was left was Trent, their son-in-law.

They told us many stories of Katrina and Ben playing together as children.

"Now they will be together again." Katrina's dad said.

"I never said goodbye." I uttered as tears streamed down my face. Trent shook his head and Katrina's mother's eyes fell upon me.

"Don't punish yourself. Whatever mistakes you've made don't compare to what I've done to her."

I turned to her as Katrina's dad reached over, placing his arm around her. Trent and I looked into her eyes as she spoke through tears.

"On the day I found out I was pregnant with her; I told my husband I wanted an abortion because my first pregnancy was so hard. He convinced me to keep her, but seven months in I couldn't take it anymore and I went behind his back to have one anyway. It was only by God's grace, the poisons failed, and Katrina was born early. She was so small and had trouble breathing, but the moment I first set eyes on her, I had never been more in love with anyone in my entire life. I hated myself for trying to do what I did, I was scared and scared people make wrong decisions. These people may have taken her away, but they weren't the first to try. Because I was."

Days went by and voices were spoken low if they were spoken at all, especially from Trent who didn't really talk anymore. Dirk came back to our lunch table, but even then, conversation around us was rare. As we sat together Peter received a message on his phone from another man asking for a hook up. The man said it would cheer him up. Peter blocked his number. Then Dirk mentioned the pilot who flew us back from Isaac's rescue told Abner I hadn't worn the pride flag on my suit that day. So naturally Abner was furious with me, but I couldn't care less. I just missed my friend. I glanced over at Trent who now sat by himself at one of the longer tables in the middle of the cafeteria. He had been wearing the necklace Katrina gave him the last time they were together. His head was hung low over his food, and his plate was soggy from the pain dripping from his eyes.

That night, Trent sat out on the ledge where he and Katrina had first kissed. He stared off into the distant mountains as nothing but hate filled his heart.

"Why? Why her? She was the one person who was convincing me to believe the most. Was taking her away supposed to make me believe more? Of all the people it could have been she should have been last? She loved you more than she loved me so where were You when she was taken? WHERE WERE YOU!"

Tears poured out from his eyes as he whispered.

"Take me too. I know You're listening and if You ever loved me then give me this one thing. Don't make me do it without You."

Trent stared up into the stars but saw nothing. He stared for hours searching for a sign or hint at direction, but finally, as his tears dried, he declared,

"Fine."

Isaac spoke little to his father who he had not seen since their last visit. Isaac, finding it unbearable to sit in bed all day, finally got up and hobbled over to the bathroom. He stood at the sink and gazed at his appearance in the mirror. It was as if a stranger was gazing back at him. His head lowered, unable to look anymore, and there beside his hand were a pair of surgical scissors. Upon seeing them he took hold before gazing back into his reflection. Isaac raised the scissors in hand and began to trim his hair.

Later on, Wes approached me in the hall and stopped me in my tracks.

"Jim, Trent's about to make a huge mistake!"

"What are you talking about?"

"I overheard him talking to Adam saying tonight they're planning to steal a plane and fly to Saudi Arabia to take revenge on the people responsible for Katrina's death."

"Good," I said.

"What?"

"Wes, Trent hates me. This could be my only chance to make things up to him."

"You're joking? Do you know what will happen if you all get caught?"

"Yes, and I don't care. This is the right thing to do."

"Remember what you said to me after you stopped me from killing Oddball. This is the same thing." I thought for a moment, recalling that day.

"No, I'm going to be there to do the same for Trent." Wes shook his head.

"I can't go with you. I'm already in too much trouble for failing my mission in China. I had to call in for help after I was washed seven miles down the river. Abner had to send in a whole team of soldiers to retrieve me so that I didn't end up dead, too. Jim, if they ask me where you three went, I can't lie to them."

I looked at him quietly as I considered the risks.

"I understand. Be here for your son, he needs you the most."

Running past Wes, I made my way down to my barracks and pushed open the door. Trent and Adam were inside packing their bags alone.

"Stop!" I yelled.

Trent unclipped his pistol and stared into my eyes. "You can't stop me."

"I know. I'm not here to stop you. I came to help." Adam glanced at Trent then back to me.

"You'll need this." He threw me a black tactical vest.

"We're leaving tonight."

Chapter 30- The Hands of Revenge

March 16th

At 3 AM, Adam snuck over to my bed and woke me up.

"It's time," he whispered. Trent was already standing by the door ready to leave. He must have been too angry to sleep as a look of fury was clear on his face. I sat up and quietly grabbed my pack from under my bed. We had to leave our suits behind. Not only could they be tracked from here at base but strapping them on would be too loud and would most likely wake someone up.

The three of us couldn't risk waking Dirk, he didn't know about our mission and if he did, he would try and stop us. We threw on our packs and snuck out the door. Bringing our smart rifles wasn't an option either. Just like our suits, we knew they could be tracked and shut off by Abner from base, so we took old-fashioned mechanical ones instead.

Once we get out of the building, flying out of base would be relatively straightforward, but before we got to that point, we would have to make it past the woman at the front desk. She sat facing away from us as we came out of the dark hallway behind her. She was one of the few people at base awake at this time of night, making this the riskiest part of our departure. We held our boots as we walked in socks to the window at the far end of the room. Adam unlocked the hinges and slid them open. He climbed up and stepped through, Trent followed and once I was out, I shut the window behind me.

We slipped on our boots and ran across the tarmac. The bright moon lit our way toward a small hanger. Once at the door, Trent reached in his pack, pulling out a pair of bolt cutters. We cut the locks and slid open the massive door, but suddenly I noticed something in the distance. It was a man running toward us from across the tarmac.

"Stop, stop," I whispered.

We stood in silence as the man got closer, once again Trent unclipped his pistol, but then we recognized who had come. It was Zack. We met him halfway and noticed the silver trails of tears reflecting in the moonlight on his cheeks.

"I'm coming, too," he told Trent before glancing at Adam. "I'm a better pilot anyway."

Adam and I nodded, happy Zack was with us, though I don't think Trent cared. He just turned and walked back toward the plane. It was a twin exhaust Night Rider, similar to an Osprey but much faster. We filled its gas tank and climbed aboard.

Zack took the throttle and Trent sat in the passenger seat. Adam and I sat strapped in the back. This was it, the second Zack flips on those engines I knew someone would wake up and notice what's going on, but the thing was, we would be long gone before they could send anyone after us. The engines sparked to life, Zack pulled out of the hangar, and within seconds, we were gone.

The door to the barracks swung open, the lights flipped on, and Wes and Dirk jumped out of their beds as General Abner stepped in.

"Where are they?"

Dirk took note of the room and saw that he and Wes were the only ones in their beds, he snapped at Wes.

"What have they done?"

Wes looked down at the clock; it was 4:30 AM. He faced back at Abner.

"Wherever they are and whatever they have decided to do, it is beyond any of our control now."

Rage enveloped Abner's face. He stepped closer to Wes about to say something. Just then a man came into the room.

"Sir. We need you now!"

Abner snapped around at him. "It can wait!"

"No! Now sir! All our satellites were just shot down. We have no signal from the Crimson Pillar."

Abner tilted his head and stared at him blankly before slowly widening his worried eyes.

March 17th

An orange glow overtook the morning sky as we approached Saudi Arabia.

"How do you think he's feeling?" Adam asked as he stared at Trent in the co-pilot's seat.

"I can't imagine," I admitted.

"When Trent told me his plan to come out here, I was hesitant at first. But then I thought, what if it were Amy? If she was the one who I'd lost, I don't know what I would do." said Adam.

"I feel the same way about Joi," I added. Adam scratched his head.

"Jim, about Joi. You should probably know that... well, what I mean is-"

Zack's voice came over the radio. "We're here, get ready."

A distant city became visible as we approached the coordinates of Katrina's last position. The city was named Lolsouladad. It was abandoned, and the buildings were in ruins after being left to the elements for years. Some streets were completely covered in sand. Dust blew off the rooftops as we flew over them.

"Trent, I don't think we're going to find anyone here," Zack stated.

"They're here," Trent said. "They all are."

Zack shrugged in doubt and examined the city floor for an LZ. A courtyard was nearby. Zack banked in its direction. He hovered over it and steadily descended. Zack opened the back door, and Adam and I held up our rifles as we went around the aircraft and met up with Zack and Trent.

"I'll wait here and keep the engines running in case you need a quick exit," Zack said.

"We'll stay on comms," Adam assured.

We proceeded into a nearby alley. Adam took the lead and came out on the other side gazing up at a partly collapsed highway supported by large cement columns. More of the city was viewable now as a second grounded highway lay before us. Across it was a vast multitude of small buildings. Scanning over it all, it was clear this was going to take a while.

We searched for hours around the ruins for anything that might suggest the enemy's presence, but nothing came to view. I was beginning to think this was a wasted trip until Adam blew out my comms.

"Meet me at the end of the highway! I've got something!"

Immediately, I sprinted down the road rushing toward his position. As I came to the end, Adam ran out of an alleyway.

"I found them," he whispered softly. "Two armed men are guarding a door to a large building."

"Show me," I said.

Adam led me down the alley, stopping before the end as he quickly stuck his head around the corner and back. He nodded and I slowly peeked around at them. Two armed soldiers in black armored vests stood facing away from the door.

"How should we do this?" I asked.

"I think we could sneak around this next building and come up from behind, then..."

As I was still speaking Trent showed up and walked past us, now in full view of the two men. He raised his pistol and with only two shots he dropped them both. Adam and I ran out to help but saw that Trent didn't need any. We walked up to the door the men were guarding, and Trent pushed a button on the side. Steam shot from the roof as the door lowered.

We stepped inside, and Trent pressed a second button on the wall. The whole room shook as it began to descend. Orange lights flashed across our faces. I noticed the muscles in Trent's cheeks flexing. The anger he carried must have been unbearable. Soon, the elevator came to a stop and two vacuum-sealed glass doors opened below a green light. We all stepped in, not even aiming our guns because the room was clearly abandoned and appeared to be stripped clean in a hurry.

There was a door at the far end of the room and as we walked toward it, I noticed a ripped piece of paper lying on the floor. I reached down picking it up only to see math equations well beyond my understanding. It looked like some kind of quantum physics. There was a diagram depicting a black sphere with two wire coils on either side of it.

Hoping to make sense of it later, I stuffed it into my pocket and continued to the door. Adam pushed it open, and we filed in, aiming down one end of a hallway. I turned around and saw that the hall continued off in the opposite direction as well.

Trent proceeded down the right side. Adam followed behind, but I went left to cover more ground. I came upon a small room located at the end of the hall. It had at least two dozen metal nozzles aiming toward the ground. I glanced right, down a second hall, and noticed a closed door at the end. Bright lights shone through a small rectangular window on the door. I raised my rifle and cautiously approached it. The glass was foggy, and I couldn't see through.

As I reached the door, I gently turned the lever. It was unlocked. I swung it open and aimed around the room expecting to find the enemy, but what I found instead was far worse. This room was empty for all but one thing. At the center was a smaller room with four steel walls bloated outward like a pumpkin. The thick glass of the window on the wall was mostly covered in blood from the inside. I inspected the monitors to my left and saw still images of Katrina before the detonation. This was it; this was where it happened. This was the exact spot where she died. I dropped my gun and fell to my knees as tears came to my eyes.

Never in my life had I seen a sight more traumatizing than the remains of one of my best friends still smeared on the walls. My head dropped as I wiped my eyes dry. Standing up I walked up to the glass. I put my hand on it and peered inside. Even now after seeing what's left, I couldn't believe she was really gone. Suddenly a tremendous blast from outside shook the room around me. It almost sounded like muffled trumpets. What in the world was that?

Something may have happened to Adam and Trent. I snapped back to the door and ran out of the room, darting left, I sprinted down the hallway, coming face to face with my two friends. I smiled, relieved to see they were okay.

"What did you do?" Adam yelled.

"Nothing. What are you talking about?" I asked.

"What was that sound?"

"I don't know," I said. Trent stepped into the elevator.

"Come on, there's no one down here."

The two of us followed, and Adam activated the elevator, the room once again shook as it ascended. Halfway up, a second, louder blast rattled the elevator, almost bringing it to a stop and causing me to worry that we might not make it all the way up. If we did, what would be waiting for us at the top? The room came to a halt as we reached the surface. Steam shot from the hydraulics and the heavy metal door lowered to the ground. Adam and I stepped out and saw a group of armed soldiers standing around two Humvees. Walking toward us were two Chinese men wearing tactical vests.

"It's fine, there's still time to get…" one of the men said before falling silent as he saw us. I glimpsed his name tag and read, 'Dr. Krull,' printed on it. He seemed surprised to see us and for a moment, all was quiet as we stared at each other.

"How can you be here?" Dr. Krull asked as he eyed me.

Trent pushed me aside and flipped to full auto as he unloaded a sudden barrage of glowing lead at the crowd of armed men. They shot back and as Adam and I fired our guns, I was clipped in the shoulder by one of the oncoming rounds. I dropped down to one knee, still firing away.

The enemy troops scattered. Dr. Krull fell to the ground and scrambled behind one of the Humvees. The second Humvee drove off into an alley. Adam and I chased after the retreating men as Dr. Krull ran into a second alley evading Trent's fire. Dr. Krull was dressed differently from the other men and to Trent that was an indication of his importance.

He dropped his now empty gun and charged after the doctor, quickly gaining on him. As Dr. Krull reached the end of the alley he ran behind a ten-foot-tall steel gate. He spun around and swung it closed, slamming it into place and locking the latch just as Trent rammed his shoulder into the bars, reaching his arm through toward the Dr. Trent grabbed hold of his right shoulder, tearing off a sliver of his own shirt as he jerked out of Trent's grip.

"Come back!"

"Enough!" the doctor yelled. "Who are you?"

Trent continued reaching through the bars at him.

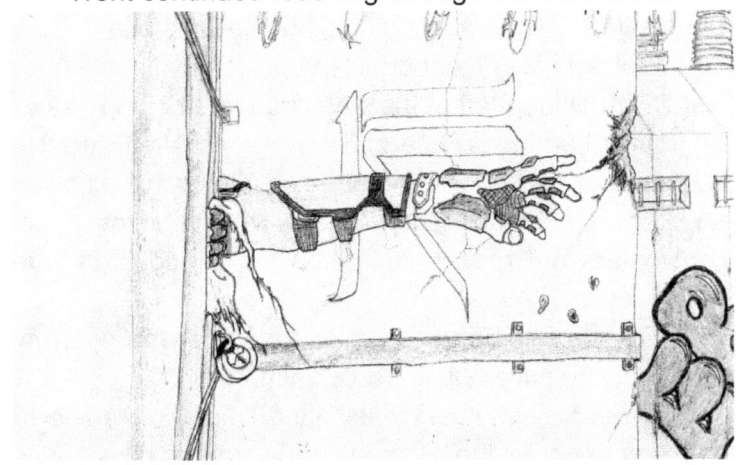

A third trumpet-like blast far louder than thunder erupted from the sky and shook the ground.

"Where are they?" Trent demanded.

"Who!" the Dr asked.

"The ones who killed her." The Dr. grinned.

"Ah. You're here for revenge, aren't you?" he questioned.

"You did it. Didn't you?" Trent presumed as his gaze pierced into the Dr's eyes.

Dr. Krull shrugged. "Unfortunate yes. Especially after my men had their turn on her. They probably loved her more then you ever did, but I know one day you'll thank me."

Trent's eyes widened as rage and a fiery lust for vengeance overtook him.

"I'LL KILL YOU!"

Trent shook the steel bars as he screamed.

"I WON'T STOP UNTIL YOUR ALL DEAD! YOU MOST OF ALL!"

Forcing his face in the thin gap between the bars, Trent's gaping eyes saw nothing but the Dr's face.

"I will kill you." Trent promised.

Dr. Krull laughed as he watched tears begin to swell up from a burning source of Trent's unsatisfied fury. He had come so close to his revenge only to be inches away and know that he had failed. Dr. Krull stepped closer, just centimeters out of Trent's reach. He glared back into Trent's eyes.

"Try." he said before stepping back and walking away as a Humvee pulled up in front of him.

It was at this moment that I found Trent. I looked down into the alley as the Humvee drove away. Trent was kneeling down with his back against the wall. I ran up to him as a fourth blast erupted above us. Tears spilled out of his eyes as I tried to pick him up.

"Leave me," he demanded.

"We have to go!" I yelled.

Just as I pulled him to his feet, he turned, forcing me against the wall. Reaching down, he unclipped my knife and screamed into my face as he pressed the blade firmly on the skin of my neck. It began cutting me, and he held it there for a moment. All was quiet. The steady breeze cooled the sweat on our faces as I stared into his eyes.

"Put it down," I said cautiously.

With jagged breaths, he glared at me and slowly lowered the blade as Adam ran into the alley.

"Zack moved the plane. We have to go now!" Trent gave me my knife and began walking toward Adam.

Taking a moment to catch my breath I followed behind them. Soon we began running down the center of the cracked highway. A fifth blast rang our ears as we turned onto the sand leaving the outskirts of the city as a sixth and then seventh blast stopped us in our tracks. The ground shook like an earthquake. I peered out into the distance and saw Zack waiting.

We ran faster, and faster when suddenly the ground beneath us shook violently as something large crashed into the earth. Falling to our faces we glanced back as a massive tidal wave of sand and dirt rained down on top of us. It swept over our heads blocking out the sun and throwing us to the ground. I couldn't breathe and the weight of the sand pressed down onto me.

The soil was loose. Reaching above my head I felt the wind on my fingertips. I pushed away the sand until my head breached the surface where I sucked in the fresh air. Wiping the sand from my eyes I looked at the ground before me. It was dark as if the sun had suddenly vanished. It wasn't the sun; there was something else beside me. Something large and I was in its shadow.

At that moment, as I turned my head and gazed up, my eyes fell upon an object. It was enormous, black, and spherical. It had crashed down from somewhere above and buried us under the expelled mass of its crater. The sun peeked up over the side, piercing my gaze, and all I could think was, what on this good earth am I staring at?

To be continued…